I0760888

Planet Stories Collection: 10 by Ray Bradbury

The

PLANET stories

Collection:

10 by Ray Bradbury

Part of the

2021

Planet Stories Collection: 10 by Ray Bradbury

"Jonah of the Jove Run" was first published in *Planet Stories*, Spring 1948.
"Zero Hour" was first published in *Planet Stories*, Fall 1947.
"Rocket Summer" was first published in *Planet Stories*, Spring 1947.
"Lorelei of the Red Mist" was first published in *Planet Stories*, Summer 1946.
"The Creatures That Time Forgot" was first published in *Planet Stories*, Fall 1946.
"Asleep in Armageddon" was first published in *Planet Stories*, Winter 1948.
"Defense Mech" was first published in *Planet Stories*, Spring 1946.
"Lazarus Come Forth" was first published in *Planet Stories*, Winter 1944.
"Morgue Ship" was first published in *Planet Stories*, Summer 1944.
"The Monster Maker" was first published in *Planet Stories*, Spring 1944.

First Edition – Published in the United States – Bullard, Texas

ISBN: 978-1-954929-00-5

1 2 3 4 5 6 7 8 9 10 IS 17 18 19 20 21

"The magic is only in what books say, how they stitched the patches of the universe together into one garment for us."

—Ray Bradbury, *Fahrenheit 451*

Table of Contents

Jonah of the Jove-Run 1

Zero Hour 27

Rocket Summer 47

Lorelei of the Red Mist 70

The Creatures That Time Forgot 175

Asleep in Armageddon 248

Defense Mech 273

Lazarus Come Forth 296

Morgue Ship 317

The Monster Maker 336

Jonah of the Jove-Run

They hated this little beat-up old guy. Even if his crazy cosmic brain could track a meteor clear across the Galaxy, why did he have to smash the super-sensitive detectors?

*****

Nibley stood in the changing shadows and sounds of Marsport, watching the great supply ship TERRA being entered and left by a number of officials and mechanics. Something had happened. Something was wrong. There were a lot of hard faces and not much talk. There was a bit of swearing and everybody looked up at the night sky of Mars, waiting.

But nobody came to Nibley for his opinion or his help. He stood there, a very old man, with a slack-gummed face and eyes like the little bubbly stalks of crayfish looking up at you from a clear creek. He stood there fully neglected. He stood there and talked to himself.

"They don't want me, or need me," he said. "Machines are better, nowadays. Why should they want an old man like me with a taste for Martian liquor? They shouldn't! A machine isn't old and foolish, and doesn't get drunk!"

Way out over the dead sea bottoms, Nibley sensed something moving. Part of himself was suddenly awake and sensitive. His small sharp eyes moved in his withered face. Something inside of his small skull reacted and he shivered. He *knew*. He knew that what these men were watching and waiting for would never come.

Nibley edged up to one of the astrogators from the TERRA. He touched him on the shoulder. "Say," he said. "I'm busy," said the astrogator. "I know," said Nibley, "but if you're waiting for that small repair rocket to come through with the extra auxiliary asteroid computator on it, you're wasting your time."

"Like hell," said the astrogator, glaring at the old man. "That repair rocket's got to come through, and quick; we need it. It'll get here."

"No, it won't," said Nibley, sadly, and shook his head and closed his eyes. "It just crashed, a second ago, out on the dead sea bottom. I—*felt*—it crash. I sensed it going down. It'll never come through."

"Go away, old man," said the astrogator. "I don't want to hear that kind of talk. It'll come through. Sure, sure, it has to come through." The astrogator turned away and looked at the sky, smoking a cigarette.

"I know it as a fact," said Nibley, but the young astrogator wouldn't listen. He didn't want to hear the truth. The truth was not a pleasant thing. Nibley went on, to himself. "I know it for a fact, just like I was always able to know the course of meteors with my mind, or the orbits or parabolas of asteroids. I tell you—"

The men stood around waiting and smoking. They didn't know yet about the crash out there. Nibley felt a great sorrow rise in himself for them. That ship meant a great deal to them and now it had crashed. Perhaps their lives had crashed with it.

A loud speaker on the outer area of the landing tarmac opened out with a voice: "Attention, crew of the Terra. The repair ship just radioed in a report that it has been fired upon from somewhere over the dead seas. It crashed a minute ago."

The report was so sudden and quiet and matter-of-fact that the standing smoking men did not for a moment understand it.

Then, each in his own way, they reacted to it. Some of them ran for the radio building to verify the report. Others sat down and put their hands over their faces. Still more of them stood staring at the sky as if staring might put the repair ship back together again and get it here safe and intact. Instinctively, at last, all of them looked up at the sky.

Jupiter was there, with its coterie of moons, bright and far away. Part of their lives lived on Jupiter. Most of them had children and wives there and certain duties to perform to insure the longevity of said children and wives. Now, with the speaking of a few words over a loudspeaker, the distance to Jupiter was suddenly an immense impossibility.

The captain of the Rocket Terra walked across the field slowly. He stopped several times to try and light a cigarette, but the night wind blew it out. He stood in the rocket shadow and looked up at Jupiter and swore quietly, again and again and finally threw down his cigarette and heeled it with his shoe.

Nibley walked up and stood beside the captain.

"Captain Kroll...."

Kroll turned. "Oh, hello, Grandpa—"

"Tough luck."

"Yeah. Yeah. I guess that's what you'd call it. Tough luck."

"You're going to take off anyway, Captain?"

"Sure," said Kroll quietly, looking at the sky. "Sure."

"How's the protective computator on board your ship?"

"Not so hot. Bad, in fact. It might conk out before we get half way through the asteroids."

"That's not good," said Nibley.

"It's lousy. I feel sick. I need a drink. I wish I was dead. I wish we'd never started this damned business of being damned pioneers. My family's up there!" He jerked his hand half way to Jupiter, violently. He settled down and tried to light another cigarette. No go. He threw it down after the other.

"Can't get through the asteroids without an asteroid computator to protect you, without that old radar set-up, captain," said Nibley, blinking wetly. He shuffled his small feet around in the red dust.

"We had an auxiliary computator on that repair ship coming from Earth," said Kroll, standing there. "And it had to crash."

"The Martians shoot it down, you think?"

"Sure. They don't like us going up to Jupiter. They got claims there, too. They'd like to see our colony die out. Best way to kill a colony is starve the colony. Starve the people. That means my family and lots of families. Then when you starve out the families the Martians can step in and take over, damn their filthy souls!"

*****

Kroll fell silent Nibley shifted around. He walked around in front of Kroll so Kroll would see him. "Captain?"

Kroll didn't even look at him.

Nibley said, "Maybe I can help."

"You?"

"You heard about me, captain! You heard about me."

"What about you?"

"You can't wait a month for another auxiliary computator to come through from Earth. You got to push off tonight, to Jupiter, to get to your family and the colony and all that, captain, sure!" Nibley was hasty, he sort of fidgeted around, his voice high, and excited. "An' if your only computator conks out in the middle of the asteroids, well, you know what that means. Bang! No more ship! No more you. No more colony on Jupiter! Now, you know about me, my ability, you know, you heard."

Kroll was cool and quiet and far away. "I heard about you, old man. I heard lots. They say you got a funny brain and do things machines can't do. I don't know. I don't like the idea."

"But you got to like the idea, captain. I'm the only one can help you now!"

"I don't trust you. I heard about your drinking that time and wrecking that ship. I remember that."

"But I'm not drinking now. See. Smell my breath, go ahead! You see?"

Kroll stood there. He looked at the ship and he looked at the sky and then at Nibley. Finally he sighed. "Old man, I'm leaving right now. I might just as well take you along as leave you. You might do some good. What can I lose?"

"Not a damned thing, Captain, and you won't be sorry," cried Nibley.

"Step lively, then!"

They went to the Rocket, Kroll running, Nibley hobbling along after.

Trembling excitedly, Nibley stumbled into the Rocket. Everything had a hot mist over it. First time on a rocket in—ten years, by god. Good. Good to be aboard again. He smelled it. It smelled fine. It felt fine. Oh, it was very fine indeed. First time since that trouble he got into off the planet Venus ... he brushed that thought away. That was over and past.

He followed Kroll up through the ship to a small room in the prow.

Men ran up and down the rungs. Men who had families out there on Jupiter and were willing to go through the asteroids with a faulty radar set-up to reach those families and bring them the necessary cargo of machinery and food they needed to go on.

Out of a warm mist, old Nibley heard himself being introduced to a third man in the small room.

"Douglas, this is Nibley, our auxiliary computating machine."

"A poor time for joking, Captain."

"It's no joke," cried Nibley. "Here I am."

Douglas eyed Nibley with a very cold and exact eye. "No," he said. "No. I can't use him. I'm computant-mechanic."

"And I'm captain," said Kroll.

Douglas looked at Kroll. "We'll shove through to Jupiter with just our leaky set of radar-computators; that's the way it'll have to be. If we're wrecked halfway, well, we're wrecked. But I'll be damned if I go along with a decrepit son-of-a-witch-doctor!"

Nibley's eyes watered. He sucked in on himself. There was a pain round his heart and he was suddenly chilled.

Kroll started to speak, but a gong rattled and banged and a voice shouted, "Stations! Gunners up! Hammocks! Takeoff!"

"*Takeoff!*"

"Stay here!" Kroll snapped it at the old man. He leaped away and down the rungs of the ladder, leaving Nibley alone in the broad shadow of the bitter-eyed Douglas. Douglas looked him up and down in surly contempt. "So you know arcs, parabolas and orbits as good as my machines, do you?"

Nibley nodded, angry now that Kroll was gone:

"Machines," shrilled Nibley. "Can't do everything! They ain't got no intuition. Can't understand sabotage and hatreds and arguments. Or people. Machines're too damn slow!"

Douglas lidded his eyes. "You—*you're* faster?"

"I'm faster," said Nibley.

Douglas flicked his cigarette toward a wall-disposal slot.

"Predict that orbit!"

Nibley's eyes jerked. "Gonna miss it!"

The cigarette lay smouldering on the deck.

Douglas scowled at the cigarette.

Nibley made wheezy laughter. He minced to his shock-hammock, zipped into it. "Not bad, not bad, eh?"

The ship rumbled.

Angrily, Douglas snatched up the cigarette, carried it to his own hammock, rolled in, zipped the zipper, then, deliberately, he flicked the cigarette once more. It flew.

"Another miss," predicted Nibley.

Douglas was still glaring at the floored cigarette when the Rocket burst gravity and shot up into space toward the asteroids.

*****

Mars dwindled into the sun. Asteroids swept silently down the star-tracks, all metal, all invisible, shifting and shifting to harry the Rocket—

Nibley sprawled by the great thick visiport feeling the computators giving him competition under the floor in the level below, predicting meteors and correcting the Terra's course accordingly.

Douglas stood behind Nibley, stiff and quiet. Since he was computant-mechanic, Nibley was his charge. He was to protect Nibley from harm. Kroll had said so. Douglas didn't like it at all.

Nibley was feeling fine. It was like the old days. It was good. He laughed. He waved at nothing outside the port. "Hi, there!" he called. "Meteor," he explained in an aside to Douglas. "You see it?"

"Lives at stake and you sit there playing."

"Nope. Not playin'. Just warmin' up. I can see 'em beatin' like hell all up and down the line, son. God's truth."

"Kroll's a damned fool," said Douglas. "Sure, you had a few lucky breaks in the old days before they built a good computator. A few lucky breaks and you lived off them. Your day's done."

"I'm *still* good."

"How about the time you swilled a quart of rot-gut and almost killed a cargo of civilian tourists? I heard about that. All I have to say is one word and your ears'd twitch. Whiskey."

At the word, saliva ran alarmingly in Nibley's mouth. He swallowed guiltily. Douglas, snorting, turned and started from the room. Nibley grabbed a monkey-wrench on impulse, heaved it. The wrench hit the wall and fell down. Nibley wheezed, "Wrench got an orbit like everything. Fair bit of computation I did. One point over and I'd have flanked that crumb!"

There was silence now, as he hobbled back and sat wearily to stare into the stars. He felt all of the ship's men around him. Vague warm electrical stirrings of fear, hope, dismay, exhaustion. All their orbits coming into a parallel trajectory now. All living in the same path with him. And the asteroids smashed down with an increasing swiftness. In a very few hours the main body of missiles would be encountered.

Now, as he stared into space he felt a dark orbit coming into conjunction with his own. It was an unpleasant orbit. One that touched him with fear. It drew closer. It was dark. It was very close now.

A moment later a tall man in a black uniform climbed the rungs from below and stood looking at Nibley.

"I'm Bruno," he said. He was a nervous fellow, and kept looking around, looking around, at the walls, the deck, at Nibley. "I'm food specialist on board. How come you're up here? Come down to mess later. Join me in a game of Martian chess."

Nibley said, "I'd beat the hell out of you. Wouldn't pay. It's against orders for me to be down below, anyways."

"How come?"

"Never you never mind. Got things to do up here. I *notice* things. I'm chartin' a special course in a special way. Even Captain Kroll don't know *every* reason why I'm makin' this trip. Got my own personal reasons. I see 'em comin' and goin', and I got their orbits picked neat and dandy. Meteors, planets *and* men. Why, let me tell you—"

Bruno tensed somewhat forward. His face was a little too interested. Nibley didn't like the feel of the man. He was off-trajectory. He—smelled—funny. He *felt* funny.

Nibley shut up. "Nice day," he said.

"Go ahead," said Bruno. "You were saying?"

Douglas stepped up the rungs. Bruno cut it short, saluted Douglas, and left.

Douglas watched him go, coldly. "What'd Bruno want?" he asked of the old man. "Captain's orders, you're to see *nobody*."

Nibley's wrinkles made a smile. "Watch that guy Bruno. I got his orbit fixed all round and arced. I see him goin' now, and I see him reachin' aphelion and I see him comin' back."

Douglas pulled his lip. "You think Bruno might be working for the Martian industrial *clique*? If I thought he had anything to do with stopping us from getting to the Jovian colony—"

"He'll be back," said Nibley. "Just before we reach the *heavy* Asteroid Belt. Wait and see."

The ship swerved. The computators had just dodged a meteor. Douglas smiled. That griped Nibley. The machines were stealing his feathers. Nibley paused and closed his eyes.

"Here come two more meteors! I beat the machine this time!"

They waited. The ship swerved, twice.

"Damn it," said Douglas.

*****

Two hours passed. "It got lonely upstairs," said Nibley apologetically.

Captain Kroll glanced nervously up from the mess-table where he and twelve other men sat. Williams, Simpson, Haines, Bruno, McClure, Leiber, and the rest. All were eating, but not hungry. They all looked a little sick. The ship was swerving again and again, steadily, steadily, back and forth. In a short interval the Heavy Belt would be touched. Then there would be real sickness.

"Okay," said Kroll to Nibley. "You can eat with us, this once. And only this once, remember that."

Nibley ate like a starved weasel. Bruno looked over at him again and again and finally asked, "How about that chess game?"

"Nope. I always win. Don't want to brag but I was the best outfielder playing baseball when I was at school. Never struck out at bat, neither. Damn good."

Bruno cut a piece of meat. "What's your business now, Gramps?"

"Findin' out where things is goin'," evaded Nibley.

Kroll snapped his gaze at Nibley. The old man hurried on, "Why, I know where the whole blamed universe is headin'." Everybody looked up from their eating. "But you wouldn't believe me if I told you," laughed the old man.

Somebody whistled. Others chuckled. Kroll relaxed. Bruno scowled. Nibley continued, "It's a feelin'. You can't describe stars to a blind man, or God to anybody. Why, hell's bells, lads, if I wanted I could write a formula on paper and if you worked it out in your mind you'd drop dead of symbol poison."

Again laughter. A bit of wine was poured all around as a bracer for the hours ahead. Nibley eyed the forbidden stuff and got up. "Well, I got to go." "Have some wine," said Bruno. "No, thanks," said Nibley. "Go ahead, have some," said Bruno. "I don't like it," said Nibley, wetting his lips. "That's a laugh," said Bruno, eyeing him. "I got to go upstairs. Nice to have ate with you boys. See you later, after we get through the Swarms—"

Faces became wooden at the mention of the approaching Belt. Fingers tightened against the table edge. Nibley spidered back up the rungs to his little room alone.

An hour later, Nibley was drunk as a chromium-plated pirate.

He kept it a secret. He hid the wine-bottle in his shock-hammock, groggily. Stroke of luck. Oh yes, oh yes, a stroke, a stroke of luck, yes, yes, yes, finding that lovely fine wonderful wine in the storage cabinet near the visiport. Why, yes! And since he'd been thirsty for so long, so long, so long. Well? Gurgle, gurgle!

Nibley was drunk.

He swayed before the visiport, drunkenly deciding the trajectories of a thousand invisible nothings. Then he began to argue with himself, drowsily, as he always argued when wine-webs were being spun through his skull by red, drowsy spiders. His heart beat dully. His little sharp eyes flickered with sudden flights of anger.

"You're some liar, Mr. Nibley," he told himself. "You point at meteors, but who's to prove you right or wrong, right or wrong, eh? You sit up here and wait and wait and wait. Those machines down below spoil it. You never have a chance to prove your ability! No! The captain won't use you! He won't need you! None of those men believe in you. Think you're a liar. Laugh at you. Yes, laugh. Yes, they call you an old, old liar!"

Nibley's thin nostrils quivered. His thin wrinkled face was crimsoned and wild. He staggered to his feet, got hold of his favorite monkey-wrench and waved it slowly back and forth.

*****

For a moment his heart almost stopped in him. In panic he clutched at his chest, pushing, pulling, pumping at his heart to keep it running. The wine. The excitement. He dropped the wrench. "No, not yet!" he looked down at his chest, wildly tearing at it. "Not just yet, oh please!" he cried. "Not until I *show* them!"

His heart went on beating, drunkenly, slowly.

He bent, retrieved the wrench and laughed numbly. "I'll show 'em," he cried, weaving across the deck. "Show them how good I am. Eliminate competition! I'll run the ship myself!"

He climbed slowly down the rungs to destroy the machines.

It made a lot of noise.

Nibley heard a shout. "Get him!" His hand went down again, again. There was a scream of whistles, a jarring of flung metal, a minor explosion. His hand went down again, the wrench in it. He felt himself cursing and pounding away. Something shattered. Men ran toward him. *This* was the computator! He hit upon it once more. Yes! Then he was caught up like an empty sack, smashed in the face by someone's fist, thrown to the deck. "Cut acceleration!" a voice cried far away. The ship slowed. Somebody kicked Nibley in the face. Blackness. Dark. Around and around down into darkness....

When he opened his eyes again people were talking:

"We're turning back."

"The hell we are. Kroll says we'll go on, anyway."

"That's suicide! We can't hit that Asteroid Belt without radar."

Nibley looked up from the floor. Kroll was there, over him, looking down at the old man. "I might have known," he said, over and over again. He wavered in Nibley's sobering vision.

The ship hung motionless, silent. Through the ports, Nibley saw they were based on the sunward side of a large planetoid, waiting, shielded from most of the asteroid particles.

"I'm sorry," said Nibley.

"He's sorry." Kroll swore. "The very man we bring along as relief computator sabotages our machine! Hell!"

Bruno was in the room. Nibley saw Bruno's eyes dilate at Kroll's exclamation. Bruno knew now.

Nibley tried to get up. "We'll get through the Swarm, anyway. I'll take you through. That's why I broke that blasted contraption. I don't like competition. I can clear a path through them asteroids big enough to lug Luna through on Track Five!"

"Who gave you the wine?"

"I found it, I just found it, that's all."

The crew hated him with their eyes. He felt their hatred like so many meteors coming in and striking at him. They hated his shriveled, wrinkled old man guts. They stood around and waited for Kroll to let them kick him apart with their boots.

Kroll walked around the old man in a circle. "You think I'd chance you getting us through the Belt!" He snorted. "What if we got half through and you got potted again!" He stopped, with his back to Nibley. He was thinking. He kept looking over his shoulder at the old man. "I can't trust you." He looked out the port at the stars, at where Jupiter shone in space. "And yet—" He looked at the men. "Do you want to turn back?"

Nobody moved. They didn't have to answer. They didn't want to go back. They wanted to go ahead.

"We'll keep on going, then," said Kroll.

Bruno spoke. "We crew-members should have some say. I say go back. We can't make it. We're just wasting our lives."

Kroll glanced at him, coolly. "You seem to be alone." He went back to the port. He rocked on his heels. "It was no accident Nibley got that wine. Somebody planted it, knowing Nibley's weakness. Somebody who was paid off by the Martian Industrials to keep this ship from going through. This was a clever set-up. The machines were smashed in such a way as to throw suspicion directly on an innocent, well, almost innocent, party. Nibley was just a tool. I'd like to know who handled that tool—"

Nibley got up, the wrench in his gnarled hand. "I'll tell you who planted that wine. I been thinking and now—"

Darkness. A short-circuit. Feet running on the metal deck. A shout. A thread of fire across the darkness. Then a whistling as something flew, hit. Someone grunted.

The lights came on again. Nibley was at the light control.

On the floor, gun in hand, eyes beginning to numb, lay Bruno. He lifted the gun, fired it. The bullet hit Nibley in the stomach.

Nibley grabbed at the pain. Kroll kicked at Bruno's head. Bruno's head snapped back. He lay quietly.

The blood pulsed out between Nibley's fingers. He watched it with interest, grinning with pain. "I knew his orbit," he whispered, sitting down cross-legged on the deck. "When the lights went out I chose my own orbit back to the light switch. I knew where Bruno'd be in the dark. Havin' a wrench handy I let fly, choosin' my arc, naturally. Guess he's got a hard skull, though...."

*****

They carried Nibley to a bunk. Douglas stood over him, dimly, growing older every second. Nibley squinted up. All the men tightened in upon it. Nibley felt their dismay, their dread, their worry, their nervous anger.

Finally, Kroll exhaled. "Turn the ship around," he said. "Go back to Mars."

The crew stood with their limp hands at their sides. They were tired. They didn't want to live any more. They just stood with their feet on the deck. Then, one by one, they began to walk away like so many cold, dead men.

"Hold on," cried Nibley, weakening. "I ain't through yet. I got two orbits to fix. I got one to lay out for this ship to Jupiter. And I got to finish out my own separate secret personal orbit. You ain't turnin' back nowhere!"

Kroll grimaced. "Might as well realize it, Grandpa. It takes seven hours to get through the Swarms, and you haven't another *two* hours in you."

The old man laughed. "Think I don't know that? Hell! Who's supposed to know all these things, me or you?"

"You, Pop."

"Well, then, dammit—bring me a bulger!"

"Now, look—"

"You heard me, by God—a bulger!"

"Why?"

"You ever hear of a thing called triangulation? Well, maybe I won't live long enough to go with you, but, by all the sizes and shapes of behemoths—this ship is jumpin' through to Jupiter!"

Kroll looked at him. There was a breathing silence, a heart beating silence in the ship. Kroll sucked in his breath, hesitated, then smiled a grey smile.

"You heard him, Douglas. Get him a bulger."

"And get a stretcher! And tote this ninety pounds of bone out on the biggest asteroid around here! Got that?"

"You heard him, Haines! A stretcher! Stand by for maneuvering!" Kroll sat down by the old man. "What's it all about, Pop? You're—sober?"

"Clear as a bell!"

"What're you going to do?"

"Redeem myself of my sins, by George! Now get your ugly face away so I can think! And tell them bucks to hurry!"

Kroll bellowed and men rushed. They brought a space-suit, inserted the ninety pounds of shrill and wheeze and weakness into it—the doctor had finished with his probings and fixings—buckled, zipped and welded him into it. All the while they worked, Nibley talked.

"Remember when I was a kid. Stood up to that there plate poundin' out baseballs North, South and six ways from Sundays." He chuckled. "Used to hit 'em, and predict which window in what house they'd break!" Wheezy laughter. "One day I said to my Dad, 'Hey, Dad, a meteor just fell on Simpson's Garage over in Jonesville.' 'Jonesville is six miles from here', said my father, shakin' his finger at me. 'You quit your lyin', Nibley boy, or I'll trot you to the woodshed!'"

"Save your strength," said Kroll.

"That's all right," said Nibley. "You know the funny thing was always that I lied like hell and everybody said I lied like hell, but come to find out, later, I wasn't lyin' at all, it was the truth. I just *sensed* things."

The ship maneuvered down on a windless, empty planetoid. Nibley was carried on a stretcher out onto alien rock.

"Lay me down right here. Prop up my head so I can see Jupiter and the whole damned Asteroid Belt. Be sure my headphones are tuned neat. There. Now, give me a piece of paper."

Nibley scribbled a long weak snake of writing on paper, folded it. "When Bruno comes to, give him this. Maybe he'll believe me when he reads it. Personal. Don't pry into it yourself."

The old man sank back, feeling pain drilling through his stomach, and a kind of sad happiness. Somebody was singing somewhere, he didn't know where. Maybe it was only the stars moving on the sky.

"Well," he said, clearly. "Guess this is it, children. Now get the hell aboard, leave me alone to think. This is going to be the biggest, hardest, damnedest job of computatin' I ever latched onto! There'll be orbits and cross orbits, big balls of fire and little bitty specules, and, by God, I'll chart 'em all! I'll chart a hundred thousand of the damned monsters and their offspring, you just wait and see! Get aboard! I'll tell you what to do from there on."

Douglas looked doubtful.

Nibley caught the look. "What ever happens," he cried. "Will be worth it, won't it? It's better than turnin' back to Mars, ain't it? Well, *ain't* it?"

"It's better," said Douglas. They shook hands.

"Now all of you, get!"

*****

Nibley watched the ship fire away and his eyes saw it and the Asteroid Swarm and that brilliant point of light that was massive Jupiter. He could almost feel the hunger and want and waiting up there in that star flame.

He looked out into space and his eyes widened and space came in, opened out like a flower, and already, natural as water flowing, Nibley's mind, tired as it was, began to shiver out calculations. He started talking.

"Captain? Take the ship straight out now. You hear?"

"*Fine*," answered the captain.

"Look at your dials."

"*Looking*."

"If number seven reads 132:87, okay. Keep 'er there. If she varies a point, counteract it on Dial Twenty to 56.90. Keep her hard over for seventy thousand miles, all that is clear so far. Then, after that, a sharp veer in number two direction, over a thousand miles. There's a big sweep of meteors coming in on that other path for you to dodge. Let me see, let me see—" He figured. "Keep your speed at a constant of one hundred thousand miles. At that rate—check your clocks and watches—in exactly an hour you'll hit the second part of the Big Belt. Then switch to a course roughly five thousand miles over to number 3 direction, veer again five minutes on the dot later and—"

"*Can you see all those asteroids, Nibley. Are you sure?*"

"Sure. Lots of 'em. Every single one going every which way! Keep straight ahead until two hours from now, after that last direction of mine—then slide off at an angle toward Jupiter, slow down to ninety thousand for ten minutes, then up to a hundred ten thousand for fifteen minutes. After that, one hundred fifty thousand all the way!"

Flame poured out of the rocket jets. It moved swiftly away, growing small and distant.

"Give me a read on dial 67!"

"*Four.*"

"Make it six! And set your automatic pilot to 61 and 14 and 35. Now—everything's okay. Keep your chronometer reading this way—seven, nine, twelve. There'll be a few tight scrapes, but you'll hit Jupiter square on in 24 hours, if you jump your speed to 700,000 six hours from now and hold it that way."

"*Square on it is, Mr. Nibley.*"

Nibley just lay there a moment. His voice was easy and not so high and shrill any more. "And on the way back to Mars, later, don't try to find me. I'm going out in the dark on this metal rock. Nothing but dark for me. Back to perihelion and sun for you. Know—know where *I'm* going?"

"*Where?*"

"Centaurus!" Nibley laughed. "So help me God I am. No lie!"

He watched the ship going out, then, and he felt the compact, collected trajectories of all the men in it. It was a good feeling to know that he was the guiding theme. Like in the old days....

Douglas' voice broke in again.

"*Hey, Pop. Pop, you still there?*"

A little silence. Nibley felt blood pulsing down inside his suit. "Yep," he said.

"*We just gave Bruno your little note to read. Whatever it was, when he finished reading it, he went insane.*"

Nibley said, quiet-like. "Burn that there paper. Don't let anybody else read it."

A pause. "*It's burnt. What was it?*"

"Don't be inquisitive," snapped the old man. "Maybe I proved to Bruno that he didn't really exist. To hell with it!"

The rocket reached its constant speed. Douglas radioed back: "*All's well. Sweet calculating, Pop. I'll tell the Rocket Officials back at Marsport. They'll be glad to know about you. Sweet, sweet calculating. Thanks. How goes it? I said—how goes it? Hey, Pop! Pop?*"

Nibley raised a trembling hand and waved it at nothing. The ship was gone. He couldn't even see the jet-wash now, he could only feel that hard metal movement out there among the stars, going on and on through a course he had set for it. He couldn't speak. There was just emotion in him. He had finally, by God, heard a compliment from a mechanic of radar-computators!

He waved his hand at nothing. He watched nothing moving on and on into the crossed orbits of other invisible nothings. The silence was now complete.

He put his hand down. Now he had only to chart that one last personal orbit. The one he had wanted to finish only in space and not grounded back on Mars.

It didn't take lightning calculation to set it out for certain.

Life and death were the parabolic ends to his trajectory. The long life, first swinging in from darkness, arcing to the inevitable perihelion, and now moving back out, out and away—

Into the soft, encompassing dark.

"By God," he thought weakly, quietly. "Right up to the last, my reputation's good. Never fluked a calculation yet, and I never will...."

He didn't.

Zero Hour

Oh, it was to be so jolly! What a game! Such excitement they hadn't known in years. The children catapulted this way and that across the green lawns, shouting at each other, holding hands, flying in circles, climbing trees, laughing.... Overhead, the rockets flew and beetle-cars
whispered by on the streets, but the children played on. Such fun, such tremulous joy, such tumbling and hearty screaming.

Mink ran into the house, all dirt and sweat. For her seven years she was loud and strong and definite. Her mother, Mrs. Morris, hardly saw her as she yanked out drawers and rattled pans and tools into a large sack.

"Heavens, Mink, what's going on?"

"The most exciting game ever!" gasped Mink, pink-faced.

"Stop and get your breath," said the mother.

"No, I'm all right," gasped Mink. "Okay I take these things, Mom?"

"But don't dent them," said Mrs. Morris.

"Thank you, thank you!" cried Mink and boom! she was gone, like a rocket.

Mrs. Morris surveyed the fleeing tot. "What's the name of the game?"

"Invasion!" said Mink. The door slammed.

In every yard on the street children brought out knives and forks and pokers and old stove pipes and can-openers.

It was an interesting fact that this fury and bustle occurred only among the younger children. The older ones, those ten years and more disdained the affair and marched scornfully off on hikes or played a more dignified version of hide-and-seek on their own.

Meanwhile, parents came and went in chromium beetles. Repair men came to repair the vacuum elevators in houses, to fix fluttering television sets or hammer upon stubborn food-delivery tubes. The adult civilization passed and repassed the busy youngsters, jealous of the fierce energy of the wild tots, tolerantly amused at their flourishings, longing to join in themselves.

"This and this and *this*," said Mink, instructing the others with their assorted spoons and wrenches. "Do that, and bring *that* over here. No! *Here*, ninnie! Right. Now, get back while I fix this—" Tongue in teeth, face wrinkled in thought. "Like that. See?"

"Yayyyy!" shouted the kids.

Twelve-year-old Joseph Connors ran up.

"Go away," said Mink straight at him.

"I wanna play," said Joseph.

"Can't!" said Mink.

"Why not?"

"You'd just make fun of us."

"Honest, I wouldn't."

"No. We know *you*. Go away or we'll kick you."

Another twelve-year-old boy whirred by on little motor-skates. "Aye, Joe! Come on! Let them sissies play!"

Joseph showed reluctance and a certain wistfulness. "I *want* to play," he said.

"You're old," said Mink, firmly.

"Not *that* old," said Joe sensibly.

"You'd only laugh and spoil the Invasion."

The boy on the motor-skates made a rude lip noise. "Come on, Joe! Them and their fairies! Nuts!"

Joseph walked off slowly. He kept looking back, all down the block.

Mink was already busy again. She made a kind of apparatus with her gathered equipment. She had appointed another little girl with a pad and pencil to take down notes in painful slow scribbles. Their voices
rose and fell in the warm sunlight.

All around them the city hummed. The streets were lined with good green and peaceful trees. Only the wind made a conflict across the city, across the country, across the continent. In a thousand other cities there were trees and children and avenues, businessmen in their quiet offices taping their voices, or watching televisors. Rockets hovered like darning needles in the blue sky. There was the universal, quiet conceit and easiness of men accustomed to peace, quite certain there would never be trouble again. Arm in arm, men all over earth were a united front. The perfect weapons were held in equal trust by all nations. A situation of incredibly beautiful balance had been brought about. There were no traitors among men, no unhappy ones, no disgruntled ones; therefore the world was based upon a stable ground. Sunlight illumined half the world and the trees drowsed in a tide of warm air.

Mink's mother, from her upstairs window, gazed down.

The children.

She looked upon them and shook her head. Well, they'd eat well, sleep well, and be in school on Monday. Bless their vigorous little bodies. She listened.

Mink talked earnestly to someone near the rose-bush—though there was no one there.

These odd children. And the little girl, what was her name? Anna? Anna took notes on a pad. First, Mink asked the rose-bush a question, then called the answer to Anna.

"Triangle," said Mink.

"What's a tri," said Anna with difficulty, "angle?"

"Never mind," said Mink.

"How you spell it?" asked Anna.

"T-R-I-" spelled Mink, slowly, then snapped, "Oh, spell it yourself!" She went on to other words. "Beam," she said.

"I haven't got tri," said Anna, "angle down yet!"

"Well, hurry, hurry!" cried Mink.

Mink's mother leaned out the upstairs window. "A-N-G-L-E," she spelled down at Anna.

"Oh, thanks, Mrs. Morris," said Anna.

"Certainly," said Mink's mother and withdrew, laughing, to dust the hall with an electro-duster-magnet.

The voices wavered on the shimmery air. "Beam," said Anna. Fading.

"Four-nine-seven-A-and-B-and-X," said Mink, far away, seriously. "And a fork and a string and a—hex-hex-agony...hexagon*al*!"

*****

At lunch, Mink gulped milk at one toss and was at the door. Her mother slapped the table.

"You sit right back down," commanded Mrs. Morris. "Hot soup in a minute." She poked a red button on the kitchen butler and ten seconds later something landed with a bump in the rubber receiver. Mrs. Morris opened it, took out a can with a pair of aluminum holders, unsealed it
with a flick and poured hot soup into a bowl.

During all this, Mink fidgeted. "Hurry, Mom! This is a matter of life and death! Aw—!"

"I was the same way at your age. Always life and death. I know."

Mink banged away at the soup.

"Slow down," said Mom.

"Can't," said Mink. "Drill's waiting for me."

"Who's Drill? What a peculiar name," said Mom.

"You don't know him," said Mink.

"A new boy in the neighborhood?" asked Mom.

"He's new all right," said Mink. She started on her second bowl.

"Which one is Drill?" asked Mom.

"He's around," said Mink, evasively. "You'll make fun. Everybody pokes fun. Gee, darn."

"Is Drill shy?"

"Yes. No. In a way. Gosh, Mom, I got to run if we want to have the Invasion!"

"Who's invading what?"

"Martians invading Earth—well, not exactly Martians. They're—I don't know. From up." She pointed with her spoon.

"And *inside*," said Mom, touching Mink's feverish brow.

Mink rebelled. "You're laughing! You'll kill Drill and *every*body."

"I didn't mean to," said Mom. "Drill's a Martian?"

"No. He's—well—maybe from Jupiter or Saturn or Venus. Anyway, he's had a hard time."

"I imagine." Mrs. Morris hid her mouth behind her hand.

"They couldn't figure a way to attack earth."

"We're impregnable," said Mom, in mock-seriousness.

"That's the word Drill used! Impreg—That was the word, Mom."

"My, my. Drill's a brilliant little boy. Two-bit words."

"They couldn't figure a way to attack, Mom. Drill says—he says in order to make a good fight you got to have a new way of surprising people. That way you win. And he says also you got to have help from your enemy."

"A fifth column," said Mom.

"Yeah. That's what Drill said. And they couldn't figure a way to surprise Earth or get help."

"No wonder. We're pretty darn strong," laughed Mom, cleaning up. Mink sat there, staring at the table, seeing what she was talking about.

"Until, one day," whispered Mink, melodramatically, "they thought of children!"

"*Well*!" said Mrs. Morris brightly.

"And they thought of how grown-ups are so busy they never look under rose-bushes or on lawns!"

"Only for snails and fungus."

"And then there's something about dim-dims."

"Dim-dims?"

"Dimens-shuns."

"Dimensions?"

"Four of 'em! And there's something about kids under nine and imagination. It's real funny to hear Drill talk."

Mrs. Morris was tired. "Well, it must be funny. You're keeping Drill waiting now. It's getting late in the day and, if you want to have your Invasion before your supper bath, you'd better jump."

"Do I have to take a bath?" growled Mink.

"You do. Why is it children hate water? No matter what age you live in children hate water behind the ears!"

"Drill says I won't have to take baths," said Mink.

"Oh, he does, does he?"

"He told all the kids that. No more baths. And we can stay up till ten o'clock and go to two televisor shows on Saturday 'stead of one!"

"Well, Mr. Drill better mind his p's and q's. I'll call up his mother and—"

Mink went to the door. "We're having trouble with guys like Pete Britz and Dale Jerrick. They're growing up. They make fun. They're worse than parents. They just won't believe in Drill. They're so snooty, cause they're growing up. You'd think they'd know better. They were little
only a coupla years ago. I hate them worst. We'll kill them *first*."

"Your father and I, last?"

"Drill says you're dangerous. Know why? Cause you don't believe in Martians! They're going to let *us* run the world. Well, not just us, but the kids over in the next block, too. I might be queen." She opened the door. "Mom?"

"Yes?"

"What's—lodge...ick?"

"Logic? Why, dear, logic is knowing what things are true and not true."

"He *mentioned* that," said Mink. "And what's im—pres—sion—able?" It took her a minute to say it.

"Why, it means—" Her mother looked at the floor, laughing gently. "It means—to be a child, dear."

"Thanks for lunch!" Mink ran out, then stuck her head back in. "Mom, I'll be sure you won't be hurt, much, really!"

"Well, thanks," said Mom.

Slam went the door.

*****

At four o'clock the audio-visor buzzed. Mrs. Morris flipped the tab. "Hello, Helen!" she said, in welcome.

"Hello, Mary. How are things in New York?"

"Fine, how are things in Scranton? You look tired."

"So do you. The children. Underfoot," said Helen.

Mrs. Morris sighed, "My Mink, too. The super Invasion."

Helen laughed. "Are your kids playing that game, too?"

"Lord, yes. Tomorrow it'll be geometrical jacks and motorized hopscotch. Were we this bad when we were kids in '48?"

"Worse. Japs and Nazis. Don't know how my parents put up with me. Tomboy."

"Parents learn to shut their ears."

A silence.

"What's wrong, Mary?" asked Helen.

Mrs. Morris' eyes were half-closed; her tongue slid slowly,
thoughtfully over her lower lip. "Eh," She jerked. "Oh, nothing. Just thought about *that*. Shutting ears and such. Never mind. Where were we?"

"My boy Tim's got a crush on some guy named—*Drill*, think it was."

"Must be a new password. Mink likes him, too."

"Didn't know it got as far as New York. Word of mouth, I imagine. Looks like a scrap drive. I talked to Josephine and she said her kids—that's in Boston—are wild on this new game. It's sweeping the country."

At this moment, Mink trotted into the kitchen to gulp a glass of water. Mrs. Morris turned. "How're things going?"

"Almost finished," said Mink.

"Swell," said Mrs. Morris. "What's *that*?"

"A yo-yo," said Mink. "Watch."

She flung the yo-yo down its string. Reaching the end it—

It vanished.

"See?" said Mink. "Ope!" Dibbling her finger she made the yo-yo reappear and zip up the string.

"Do that again," said her mother.

"Can't. Zero hour's five o'clock! 'Bye."

Mink exited, zipping her yo-yo.

On the audio-visor, Helen laughed. "Tim brought one of those yo-yo's in this morning, but when I got curious he said he wouldn't show it to me, and when I tried to work it, finally, it wouldn't work."

"You're not *impressionable*," said Mrs. Morris.

"What?"

"Never mind. Something I thought of. Can I help you, Helen?"

"I wanted to get that black-and-white cake recipe—"

*****

The hour drowsed by. The day waned. The sun lowered in the peaceful
blue sky. Shadows lengthened on the green lawns. The laughter and excitement continued. One little girl ran away, crying.

Mrs. Morris came out the front door.

"Mink, was that Peggy Ann crying?"

Mink was bent over in the yard, near the rose-bush. "Yeah. She's a scarebaby. We won't let her play, now. She's getting too old to play. I guess she grew up all of a sudden."

"Is that why she cried? Nonsense. Give me a civil answer, young lady, or inside you come!"

Mink whirled in consternation, mixed with irritation. "I can't quit now. It's almost time. I'll be good. I'm sorry."

"Did you hit Peggy Ann?"

"No, honest. You ask her. It was something—well, she's just a scaredy-pants."

The ring of children drew in around Mink where she scowled at her work with spoons and a kind of square shaped arrangement of hammers and pipes. "There and there," murmured Mink.

"What's wrong?" said Mrs. Morris.

"Drill's stuck. Half way. If we could only get him all the way through, it'll be easier. Then all the others could come through after him."

"Can I help?"

"No'm, thanks. I'll fix it."

"All right. I'll call you for your bath in half an hour. I'm tired of watching you."

She went in and sat in the electric-relaxing chair, sipping a little beer from a half-empty glass. The chair massaged her back. Children, children. Children and love and hate, side by side. Sometimes children loved you, hated you, all in half a second. Strange children, did they ever forget or forgive the whippings and the harsh, strict words of command? She wondered. How can you ever forget or forgive those over and above you, those tall and silly dictators?

Time passed. A curious, waiting silence came upon the street, deepening.

Five o'clock. A clock sang softly somewhere in the house, in a quiet, musical voice, "Five o'clock...five o'clock. Time's a wasting. Five o'clock," and purred away into silence.

Zero hour.

Mrs. Morris chuckled in her throat. Zero hour.

A beetle-car hummed into the driveway. Mr. Morris. Mrs. Morris smiled. Mr. Morris got out of the beetle, locked it and called hello to Mink at her work. Mink ignored him. He laughed and stood for a moment watching the children in their business. Then he walked up the front steps.

"Hello, darling."

"Hello, Henry."

She strained forward on the edge of the chair, listening. The children were silent. Too silent.

He emptied his pipe, refilled it. "Swell day. Makes you glad to be alive."

Buzz.

"What's that?" asked Henry.

"I don't know." She got up, suddenly, her eyes widening. She was going to say something. She stopped it. Ridiculous. Her nerves jumped. "Those children haven't anything dangerous out there, have they?" she said.

"Nothing but pipes and hammers. Why?"

"Nothing electrical?"

"Heck, no," said Henry. "I looked."

She walked to the kitchen. The buzzing continued. "Just the same you'd better go tell them to quit. It's after five. Tell them—" Her eyes widened and narrowed. "Tell them to put off their Invasion until tomorrow." She laughed, nervously.

The buzzing grew louder.

"What are they up to? I'd better go look, all right."

The explosion!

*****

The house shook with dull sound. There were other explosions in other yards on other streets.

Involuntarily, Mrs. Morris screamed. "Up this way!" she cried, senselessly, knowing no sense, no reason. Perhaps she saw something from the corners of her eyes, perhaps she smelled a new odor or heard a new noise. There was no time to argue with Henry to convince him. Let him think her insane. Yes, insane! Shrieking, she ran upstairs. He ran after her to see what she was up to. "In the attic!" she screamed. "That's where it is!" It was only a poor excuse to get him in the attic in time—oh God, in time!

Another explosion outside. The children screamed with delight, as if at Were a great fireworks display.

"It's not in the attic!" cried Henry. "It's outside!"

"No, no!" Wheezing, gasping, she fumbled at the attic door. "I'll show you. Hurry! I'll show you!"

They tumbled into the attic. She slammed the door, locked it, took the key, threw it into a far, cluttered corner.

She was babbling wild stuff now. It came out of her. All the
subconscious suspicion and fear that had gathered secretly all afternoon and fermented like a wine in her. All the little revelations and knowledges and sense that had bothered her all day and which she had logically and carefully and sensibly rejected and censored. Now it exploded in her and shook her to bits.

"There, there," she said, sobbing against the door. "We're safe until tonight. Maybe we can sneak out, maybe we can escape!"

Henry blew up, too, but for another reason. "Are you crazy? Why'd you throw that key away! Damn it, honey!"

"Yes, yes, I'm crazy, if it helps, but stay here with me!"

"I don't know how in hell I *can* get out!"

"Quiet. They'll hear us. Oh, God, they'll find us soon enough—"

Below them, Mink's voice. The husband stopped. There was a great universal humming and sizzling, a screaming and giggling. Downstairs, the audio-televisor buzzed and buzzed insistently, alarmingly, violently. ‘Is that Helen calling?’ thought Mrs. Morris. ‘And is she calling about what I *think* she's calling about?’

Footsteps came into the house. Heavy footsteps.

"Who's coming in my house?" demanded Henry, angrily. "Who's tramping around down there?"

Heavy feet. Twenty, thirty, forty, fifty of them. Fifty persons crowding into the house. The humming. The giggling of the children. "This way!" cried Mink, below.

"Who's downstairs?" roared Henry. "Who's there!"

"Hush, oh, nonononono!" said his wife, weakly, holding him. "Please, be quiet. They might go away."

"Mom?" called Mink, "Dad?" A pause. "Where are you?"

Heavy footsteps, heavy, heavy, *very* HEAVY footsteps came up the stairs. Mink leading them.

"Mom?" A hesitation. "Dad?" A waiting, a silence.

Humming. Footsteps toward the attic. Mink's first.

They trembled together in silence in the attic, Mr. and Mrs. Morris. For some reason the electric humming, the queer cold light suddenly visible under the door crack, the strange odor and the alien sound of eagerness in Mink's voice, finally got through to Henry Morris, too. He stood, shivering, in the dark silence, his wife beside him.

"Mom! Dad!"

Footsteps. A little humming sound. The attic lock melted. The door opened. Mink peered inside, tall blue shadows behind her.

"Peek-a-boo," said Mink.

Rocket Summer

The first great rocket flight into space, bearing intrepid pioneers to the Moon. The world's ecstasy flared into red mob-hate when President Stanley canceled the flight. How did he get that way?

*****

The crowd gathered to make a curious noise this cold grey morning before the scheduled Birth. They arrived in gleaming scarlet tumble-bugs and yellow plastic beetles, yawning and singing and ready. The Birth was a big thing for them.

He stood alone up in his high office tower window, watching them with a sad impatience in his grey eyes. His name was William Stanley, president of the company that owned this building and all those other work-hangars down on the tarmac, and all that landing field stretching two miles off into the Jersey mists. William Stanley was thinking about the Birth.

The Birth of *what*? Stanley's large, finely sculptured head felt heavier, older. Science, with a scalpel of intense flame would slash wide the skulls of engineers, chemists, mechanics in a titanic Caesarian, and out would come the Rocket!

"Yezzir! Yezzir!" he heard the far-off, faint and raucous declarations of the vendors and hawkers.

"Buy ya Rocket Toys! Buy ya Rocket Games! Rocket Pictures! Rocket soap! Rocket teethers for the tiny-tot! Rocket, Rocket, Rocket! *Hey!*"

Shutting the open glassite frame before him, his thin lips drew tight. Morning after morning America sent her pilgrims to this shrine. They peered in over the translucent restraint barrier as if the Rocket were a caged beast.

He saw one small girl drop her Rocket toy. It shattered, and was folded under by the moving crowd's feet.

"Mr. Stanley?"

"Uh? Oh, Captain Greenwald. Sorry. Forgot you were here." Stanley measured his slow, thoughtful steps to his clean-topped desk. "Captain," he sighed wearily, "you're looking at the unhappiest man alive." He looked at Greenwald across the desk. "That Rocket is the gift of a too-generous science to a civilization of adult-children who've fiddled with dynamite ever since Nobel invented it. They—"

He got no further. The office door burst inward. A tall, work-grimed man strode swiftly in—all oil, all heat, all sunburnt, wrinkled leather skin. Rocket flame burnt in his dark, glaring eyes. He stopped short at Stanley's desk, breathing heavily, leaning against it.

Stanley noticed the wrench in the man's fist. "Hello, Simpson."

Simpson swore bitterly. "What's all this guff about you stopping the Rocket tomorrow?" he demanded.

Stanley nodded. "This isn't a good time for it to go up."

Simpson snorted. "This isn't a good time," he mimicked. Then he swore again. "By George, it's like telling a woman her baby's been still-born!"

"I know it's hard to understand—"

"Hard, *hell*!" shouted the man. "I'm Head Mechanic! I've worked two years! The others have worked, too! And the Rocket'll travel tomorrow or we'll know why!"

Stanley crushed out his cigar, inside his fist. The room swayed imperceptibly in his vision. Sometimes, one wanted to use a gun—he shook away the thought. He kept his tongue.

Simpson raged on. "Mr. Stanley, you have until three this afternoon to change your mind. We'll pull strings and you'll be out of your job by the week-end! If not—" and he said the next words very slowly, "how would your wife look with her head bashed in, *Mister* Stanley?"

"You can't threaten me!"

The door slammed in Stanley's face. Simpson was gone.

*****

Captain Greenwald put out a manicured hand. On one slender finger shone a diamond ring. His wrist was circled by an expensive watch. His shiny brown eyes were invisibly cupped by contact lenses. Greenwald was past fifty inside; outside he seemed barely thirty. "I advise you to forget it, Stanley. Man's waited a million years for tomorrow."

Stanley's hand shook, lighting a cigarette. "Look here, Captain, where *are* you going?"

"To the stars, of course."

Stanley snapped out the alcohol match. "In the name of heaven, stop the melodrama and inferior semantics. What kind of thing is this you're handing the people? What'll it do to races, morals, men and women?"

Greenwald laughed. "I'm only interested in reaching the Moon. Then I'll come back to earth, and retire, happily, and die."

Stanley stood there, tall and very grey. "Does the effect of the introduction of the crossbow to English and French history interest you?"

"Can't say I know much about it."

"Do you recall what gunpowder's invention did to civilization?"

"That's irrelevant!"

"You must admit if there'd been some subjective planning with the auto and airplane, millions of lives would've been saved, and many wars prevented. An ethical code should've been written for all such inventions and strictly observed, or else the invention forfeited."

Greenwald shook his head, grinning. "I'll let you handle that half of it. I'll do the traveling. I'm willing to abide by any such rules, if you'll draw them up and enforce them. All I want is to reach the Moon first. I've got to get downstairs now. We're still loading the ship, you know, in spite of your decree. We expect to get around you somehow. I'm sympathetic, of course, to your beliefs. I'll do anything you say except ground the Rocket. I won't get violent, but I can't vouch for Simpson. He's a tough man, with strong notions."

They walked from the office to the dropper. Compression slid them down to ground level, where they stepped out, Stanley still re-emphasizing his beliefs. "—for centuries science has given humanity play-toys, ships, machines, guns, cars, and now a Rocket, all with supreme disregard for man's needs."

"Science," announced Greenwald as they emerged onto the tarmac, "has produced, via private enterprise, greater amounts of goods than ever in history! Why, consider the medical developments!"

"Yes," said Stanley doggedly, "we cure man's cancer and preserve his greed in a special serum. They used to say 'Starve a cold, stuff a fever.' Today's fever is materialism. All the things science has produced only touch the *Body*. When Science invents something to touch the Mind, I'll give it its due. No.

"You cloak your voyage with romantic terminology. Outward to the stars! you cry! Words! What's the *fact*? Why, *why* this rocket? Greater production? We have *that*! Adventure? Poor excuse to uproot Earth. Exploration? It *could* wait a few years. Lebensraum? Hardly. *Why*, then, Captain?"

"Eh?" murmured Greenwald distractedly. "Ah. Here's the Rocket, now."

They walked in the incredible Rocket shadow. Stanley looked at the crowd beyond the barrier. "*Look* at them. Their sex still a mixture of Victorian voodoo and clabbered Freud. With education needing reorientation, with wars threatening, with religion and philosophy confused, you want to jump off into space!"

Stanley shook his head. "Oh, I don't doubt your sincerity, Captain. I just say your timing's poor. If we give them a Rocket toy to play with, do you honestly think they'll solve war, education, unity, thought? Why, they'd propel themselves away from it so quickly your head'd swim! Wars would be fought between worlds. But if we want more wars, let's have them *here*, where we can get at their sources, before we leap to the asteroids seeking our lost pride of race.

"What little unity we *do* have would be broken by countries and individuals clamoring and cut-throating for planets and satellites!"

Pausing, Stanley saw the mechanics standing in the Rocket shadow, hating him. Outside the barrier, the crowd recognized him; their murmur grew to a roar of disapproval.

Greenwald indicated them. "They're wondering why you waited so long before deciding to stop the Rocket."

"Tell them I thought there'd be laws controlling it. Tell them the corporations played along, smiling and bobbing to me, until the Rocket was completed. Then they threw off their false faces and withdrew the legislation only this morning. Tell them that, Captain. And tell them the legislation I planned would've meant a slow, intelligent Rocket expansion over an era of three centuries. Then ask them if they think any business man could wait even five *minutes*."

Captain Greenwald scowled. "All I want to do is prove it can be done. After I come back down, if I can help in any way to control the Rocket, I'm your man, Stanley. After I *prove* it's possible, I don't care what in hell happens...."

Stanley slid into his 'copter, waved morosely at the captain. The crowd shouted, waved its fists at him over the barrier. He sat watching their distorted, sullen faces. They detested him. The Rocket balloon man, the Rocket soap man, the tourists detested him.

What was more, when his son Tommy found out, Tommy would hate him, too.

*****

He took his time, heading home. He let the green hills slide under. He set the automatic pilot and sank back into the sponge-softness, suspended in a humming, blissful dream. Music played. Cigarettes and whiskey were in reach if he desired them. Soft music. He could lapse back into the dreaming tide, dissolve worry, smoke, drink, chortle luxuriously, sleep, forget, pull a shell of synthetic, hypnotizing objects in about himself.

And wake ten years from today with his wife disintegrating swiftly in his arms. And one day see his son's skull shattered against a plastic wall.

And his own heart whirled and burst by some vast atom power of a starship passing Earth far out in space!

He dumped the whiskey over the side, followed it with the cigarettes. Finally, he clicked off the soft music.

There was his home. His eyes kindled. It lay out upon a green meadow, far from the villages and towns, salt-white and surrounded by tapered sycamores. As he watched, lowering his 'copter, he saw the blonde streak across the lawn; that was his daughter, Alyce. Somewhere else on the premises his son gamboled. Neither of them feared the dark.

Angrily, Stanley poured on full speed. The landscape jerked and vanished behind him. He wanted to be alone. He couldn't face them, yet. Speed was the answer. Wind whistled, roared, rushed by the hurtling 'copter. He rammed it on. Color rose in his cheeks.

There was music in the garden as he parked his 'copter in the fine blue plastic garage. Oh, beautiful garage, he thought, you contribute to my peacefulness. Oh, wonderful garage, in moments of torment, I think of you, and I am glad I own you.

Like hell.

In the kitchen, Althea was whipping food with mechanisms. Her mother sat with one withered ear to the latest audio drama. They glanced up, pleased.

"Darling, so early!" she cried, kissing him. "How's the Rocket?" piped mother-in-law. "My, I bet you're proud!"

Stanley said nothing.

"Just imagine." The old woman's eyes glowed like little bulbs. "Soon we'll breakfast in New York and supper on Mars!"

Stanley watched her for a long moment, then turned hopefully to Althea. "What do *you* think?"

She sensed a trap. "Well, it would be different, wouldn't it, vacationing our summers on Venus, winters on Mars—wouldn't it?"

"Oh, good Lord," he groaned. He shut his eyes and pounded the table, softly. "Good Lord."

"*Now*, what's wrong. What did *I* say?" demanded Althea, bewildered.

He told them about his order preventing the flight.

Althea stared at him. Mother reached and snapped off the audio. "*What* did you say, young man?"

He repeated it.

Into the waiting silence came a distant "psssheeew!" rushing in from the dining room, flinging the kitchen door wide, his son ran in, waving a bright red Rocket in one grimy fist. "Psssheeew! I'm a Rocket! Gangway! Hi, Dad!" He swung the ship in a quick arc. "Gonna be a pilot when I'm sixteen! Hey." He stopped. "What's everybody standing around for?" He looked at Grandma. "Grammy?" He looked at his mother. "Mom?" And finally at his father. "Dad...?" His hands sank slowly. He read the look in his father's eyes. "Oh, gosh."

*****

By three o'clock that afternoon, he had showered and dressed in clean clothes. The house was very silent. Althea came and sat down in the living room and looked at him with hurt, stricken eyes.

He thought of quoting a few figures at her. Five million people killed in auto accidents since the year 1920. Fifty thousand people killed every year, *now*, in 'copters and jet-planes. But it wasn't in the figures, it was in a feeling he had to make her *feel*. Maybe he could illustrate it to her. He picked up the hand-audio, dialed a number. "Hello, Smitty?"

The voice on the other end said, clearly, "Oh, Mr. Stanley?"

"Smitty, you're a good average man, a pleasant neighbor, a fine farmer. I'd like your opinion. Smitty, if you knew a war was coming, would you help prevent it?"

Althea was watching and listening.

Smitty said, "Hell, yes. Sure."

"Thanks, Smitty. One more thing. What's your opinion of the Rocket?"

"Greatest thing in history. Say, I heard you were going to—"

Stanley did not want to get involved. He hurriedly excused himself and hung up. He looked directly at his wife. "Did you notice the separation of means from end? Smitty thinks two things. He thinks he can prevent war; that's one. He thinks the Rocket is a great thing; that's number two. But they don't match, unfortunately.

"The Rocket isn't a means to happiness the way it'll be used. It's the wrong means. And with a wrong means you invariably wind up with a wrong end. A criminal seeks wealth. Does he get it? Temporarily. In the end, he suffers. All because he took the wrong *means*." Stanley held his hands out, uselessly. "How can I make you understand."

Tears were in her eyes. "I understand *nothing*, and don't need to understand! Your job, they'll take it away from you and fly the Rocket anyway!"

"I'll work on the legislation again, then!"

"And perhaps be killed? No, please, Will."

Killed. He looked at his watch. Exactly three.

He answered the audio when it buzzed. "Stanley talking."

"Stanley, this is Cross, at Cal-Tech."

"Cross! Good Lord, it's good to hear you!"

"I just heard the new-flash," said Cross. He had the same clipped, exact voice he'd had years ago, Stanley realized. "You're really on the spot this time, aren't you, Will? That's why I called. I like your ideas on machinery. I've always thought of machines, myself, as nothing but extensions of man's frustrations and emotions, his losses and compensations in life. We agree. But you're wrong this time, Will. You made a mistake today."

"Now, don't *you* start on me! You're my last friend," retorted Stanley tiredly. "What else could I do—destroy the rocket?"

"That would be negative. No good. Give them something positive. Tell them to go ahead," advised Cross, pleasantly enough. "Warn them, like a kindly father, of the consequences. Then, when their fingers are burnt—"

"Humanity might go down the drain," finished Stanley abruptly.

"Not if you play your cards right, control the variables. There must be some way around them without getting yourself mangled. I'm ready to help when you have a plan. Think it over."

"I still think blowing the damn thing up would be—"

"They'd build a bigger one. And they'd persecute you and your family the rest of your life," explained Cross logically. "You and I may know that science hasn't contributed one whit to man's *mental* progress, but Mr. Everyman likes his babies diapered in disposable tissues and likes to travel from Siberia to Johnstown like an infuriated bullet. You can't stop them, you can only divert them a bit."

Stanley grasped the hand-audio, tightly. He listened.

*****

A great roar of 'copters sounded out in the afternoon sky, directly overhead. The house shook. Althea sprang up lithely and ran to look out. "I can't talk any more, Cross. I'll call you back. *They're* outside, waiting for me, now...."

Cross' voice faded like a dream. "Remember what I tell you. Let them go ahead."

Stanley walked to the door, opened it, stepped half through.

A radio voice boomed out of the bright blue sky.

"STANLEY!" it shouted. It was Simpson's voice. "STANLEY! COME OUT AND TALK! COME OUT AND TELL US, STANLEY! STANLEY!"

Althea would not stay in. She walked with him out onto the moist green lawn, in the open.

The heavens were flooded with 'copters whirling. The sun shook in its place. 'Copters hung everywhere, like huge hummingbirds, swiveling, whirring. Five hundred of them, at least, shadowing the lawns and shaking the house-tops.

"OH, *THERE* YOUR ARE, STANLEY!"

Stanley shaded his eyes. His lips drew away from his teeth in a grimace, as he stared upward, tense and afraid.

"IT'S AFTER THREE O'CLOCK, STANLEY!" came the dull boom of words.

In this moment, with the spiraling 'copters suspended over his lawn, over his wife and children and house, over himself and his beliefs, Stanley swallowed, stepped back, put his hands down and let the idea grow within him. Yes, he would give them their rocket. He would give it to them. You cannot fight the children, he thought. They must have their green apples. If you refuse them, they will find a way around you. Go along with their illogical tide and make logic of it. Let the children eat their full of green apples, many, many green apples to swell their vast stomach into sickness. Yes. A slow smile touched the corners of his mouth, vanished. The plan was complete.

The voice from the sky fell on him like an iron fist! "STANLEY! WHAT IS YOUR WORD NOW? HOW WILL YOU SPEAK NOW? WITH A THOUSAND POUNDS OF NITROGLYCERINE OVER YOUR HOME, HOW WILL YOU TALK?"

The 'copters sank, malignantly. Thunder swept the lawn. Althea's brilliant amber skirt flared in the wash of it.

"WILL THE ROCKET FLY, STANLEY?"

From the corners of his aching, straining eyes, Stanley saw his son poised in the window, watching him.

"RAISE YOUR RIGHT HAND AND WAVE IT," thundered the sky-voice. "IF THE ANSWER IS YES!"

Stanley made them wait for it. He wetted his lips with a slow tongue, then, gradually, very casually, he raised his right hand, palm up, and waved it to the thundering sky.

A torrent of exultation poured in a Niagara from the heavens. Five hundred audios blasted, cheered, exulted! The trees ripped and tore in the cyclone of energy and explosion! The noise continued as Stanley turned, took Althea's elbow, and steered her blindly back to the door.

*****

The little black-jet-plane dropped out of the midnight stars. Moments later, Cross was getting out of it, crossing the dark lawn, grasping Stanley's hand warmly. "Made good time, eh?"

Inside, they downed their glasses of brandy first, then got to business. Stanley outlined his plan, his contacts, his psychology. He was pleased and excited to see an extraordinary smile of approval come to Cross's pink, round face. "Excellent! Now you're talking!" cried Cross.

"I like your plan, Stanley. It places the blame right back on the people. They won't be able to persecute you."

Stanley refilled the glasses. "I'll see to it you're on the Rocket tomorrow. Greenwald—he's the captain—will co-operate, I'm certain, when the trip is over. It's up to you and Greenwald then."

They raised their glasses. "And when it's all over," observed Cross slowly. "We'll have the long, hard struggle to revise our educational system. To begin to apply the scientific method to man's thinking, instead of just to his machines. And when we've built a logical subjective world, then it'll be safe to make machines of all and any kinds. Here's to our plan, may it be completed." They drank.

The next day two million people spread over the rolling hills, through the tiny Jersey towns, sitting atop bugs and plastic beetles. An excitement pervaded the day. The sky was a blue vacuum, the 'copters grounded by law. The Rocket lay gleaming and monstrous and silent.

At noon, the crew ambled across the tarmac, Captain Greenwald leading. Cross walked among them. The huge metal doors slammed, and with a blast of Gargantuan flame, the Rocket heaved upward and vanished.

People cheered and laughed and cried.

Stanley watched his son and daughter and mother-in-law do likewise. He was deeply pleased to see that Althea did not join them. Hand in hand they watched the sky dazzlement fade. The first Rocket to the moon was gone. The world was drunkenly happy in its delirium.

Two weeks passed slowly. Astronomers were unable to keep an eye on the Rocket. It was so small and unaccountable in the void between earth and lunar surface.

Stanley slept little in the passing of the fourteen days. He was constantly attacked by fears and confusions of thought. He dreamed of the Rocket going up. He had seen men month on month walking in the metal shadow of their wonderful Rocket, patting it with their greasy, calloused hands, loving it with their quick, appreciative eyes.

If for one moment you let yourself think of it, you loved it, too, for even though it symbolized wars and destruction, you had to admire its balance and slenderness of structure. With it, you could rub away the fog cosmetic of Venus, re-delineate its prehistorically shy face. And there was Mars, too. Man had been imprisoned a million years. Why not freedom now, at last?

Then he labeled all these fantasies by their correct name, ESCAPE, and settled back, to wait the return of the Rocket.

*****

"The moon Rocket is returning! It will land this morning at nine o'clock!" Everybody's audio was blatting.

Like a yellow seed, the Rocket dropped down the sky, to sprout roots of flame on which to cushion itself. It fried the tarmac and a vast deluge of warm air rushed across the country for miles. People sweltered amidst a sudden rocket summer.

In his tower room, William Stanley watched, solemn and wordless.

The Rocket shimmered. Across the cooling tarmac, the crowd rioted, bursting through the barrier, sweeping the police aside in elation.

The tide halted and boiled and changed form, layer upon layer. A vast hush came upon it.

Now the round air-lock door of the Rocket jetted out air in a compressed sigh.

The thick door, sandwiched into the ship-hull, took two minutes to come outward and pull aside on its oiled hingework. The crowd pressed closer, flesh to flesh, eyes widened. The door was now open completely. A great cheer went up. The crew of the Moon Rocket stood in the air-lock. The cheer faded, almost instantly.

The crew of the Rocket were not exactly standing. They were hunched over.

The captain stepped forward. Well, he didn't exactly *step*. He sort of dragged his feet and shambled. He made a speech.

But all it sounded like, coming from his twisted, swollen lips, was, "Uns—rrrr—oh—god—disss—ease—unh—rrr—nnn—"

He held out his grey-green fingers, raw, bleeding, for all to see. He lifted his face. Those red things, were they actually eyes? That depression, that fallen socket, had it been a nose? And where were the teeth in that gagging, hissing mouth? His hair was thin and grey and infected. He stank.

The hypnotic silence was shattered. The first line of people turned and clawed at the second line. The second turned instinctively to claw the third, and so on. The television cameras caught it all.

Screams, yelling, shouting. Many fell and were trampled, crushed under. The captain and his crew came out, gesturing, calling them to come back. But who would heed their rotting movements? The ridiculous souvenir seekers trampled each other, ripping the clothes from one another's backs!

A souvenir? A scab of crawling flesh, a drop of yellow fluid from their gaping wounds? Souvenirs for earth, buy them right here, get them while they last! We mail anywhere in the United States!

The characters in order of appearance: The Captain, the astrogator, held sagging between two astronomers, who were followed by sixteen mathematicians, technicians, chemists, biologists, radio men, geographers and machinists. Shamble forth, gentlemen, and bring the brave new future with you!

The balloon vendor, in flight, jettisoned his entire stock. Rubber rockets floated wildly, crazily bobbling, bouncing the river of rioting heads until they were devoured, exploded and crumpled underfoot.

Sirens sounded. Police beetles rushed to the field exits. Ten minutes later the tarmac was empty. No sign of captain or crew. A few shreds of their fetid clothing were found, partially disintegrated. An audio-report five minutes later stated simply, "The captain and crew were destroyed on orders of the health bureau! An epidemic was feared—"

The sounds of riot faded. The door to Stanley's office opened, someone entered and stood behind him, and closed the door.

*****

Stanley did not turn from the window for a moment. "Fifty people injured, five of them critically. I'm sorry for that. But it was a small price for the world's security." He turned, slowly.

A horrible creature stood, diseased and swollen, before him. A captain's uniform, filthy and torn, hung tattered from the disgusting flesh. The creature opened its bleeding mouth.

"How was it?" asked the creature, muffledly.

"Fine," said Stanley. "Did you reach the moon?"

"Yes," replied the creature. "Captain Greenwald sends his regards to you. He says he knows we can do it again and again, any time we want, now, and that's all he wanted to know. He wishes you luck and tells you to go ahead. We landed the rocket on the way back from the moon, first of all, up at Fairbanks, Alaska, outside the settlement, naturally, during the night. Things worked as you planned them. We changed crews there. There was a minor fight. Simpson and the original crew, including Captain Greenwald, are still up there, under psycho-hypnosis. They'll live out their lives happily, unaware, with new names. They won't remember anything. We took off from Fairbanks again this morning with the new crew and our act all rehearsed, I think we did all right."

"Where's the substitute crew now?" inquired Stanley.

"Downstairs," said the creature. "Getting psychoed themselves. Getting mental blocs inserted, so they'll forget they ever fooled the world today. Then we'll send them back to their regular jobs. Can I use your shower?"

Stanley pressed a button, a panel slid aside. "Go ahead."

The creature pulled its face around the edges until it shed off into its hands, a green-grey pallid mask of plastic rubber. The sweating pink face of Cross appeared. He wriggled his fingers next, until the green-gray, chemically bleeding horror gloves sucked off. He tossed these into a wall-incinerator. "The day of the Rocket is over," he said, quietly.

"They'll be putting your bill up before the World Legislature tomorrow, or I miss my guess. Carefulness, thought and intellect will now get a start. Humanity is saved from itself."

Stanley watched Cross walk into the shower-cube, peel, and switch on the spray.

He turned to the window again. Two billion people were thinking tonight. He knew what they were thinking. Outside, he heard the explosion as the health department blew up the great Rocket.

That was all. The sound of water on the shower-tiles was a good clean sound.

Lorelei of the Red Mist

Writing with Leigh Brackett

He died—and then awakened in a new body. He found himself on a world of bizarre loveliness, a powerful, rich man. He took pleasure in his turn of good luck ... until he discovered that his new body was hated by all on this strange planet, that his soul was owned by Rann, devil-goddess of Falga, who was using him for her own gain.

*****

The Company dicks were good. They were plenty good. Hugh Starke began to think maybe this time he wasn't going to get away with it.

His small stringy body hunched over the control bank, nursing the last ounce of power out of the Kallman. The hot night sky of Venus fled past the ports in tattered veils of indigo. Starke wasn't sure where he was any more. Venus was a frontier planet, and still mostly a big X, except to the Venusians—who weren't sending out any maps. He did know that he was getting dangerously close to the Mountains of White Cloud. The backbone of the planet, towering far into the stratosphere, magnetic trap, with God knew what beyond. Maybe even God wasn't sure.

But it looked like over the mountains or out. Death under the guns of the Terro-Venus Mines,

Incorporated, Special Police, or back to the Luna cell blocks for life as an habitual felon.

Starke decided he would go over.

Whatever happened, he'd pulled off the biggest lone-wolf caper in history. The T-V Mines payroll ship, for close to a million credits. He cuddled the metal strongbox between his feet and grinned. It would be a long time before anybody equaled that.

His mass indicators began to jitter. Vaguely, a dim purple shadow in the sky ahead, the Mountains of White Cloud stood like a wall against him. Starke checked the positions of the pursuing ships. There was no way through them. He said flatly, "All right, damn you," and sent the Kallman angling up into the thick blue sky.

He had no very clear memories after that. Crazy magnetic vagaries, always a hazard on Venus, made his instruments useless. He flew by the seat of his pants and he got over, and the T-V men didn't. He was free, with a million credits in his kick.

Far below in the virgin darkness he saw a sullen crimson smear on the night, as though someone had rubbed it with a bloody thumb. The Kallman dipped toward it. The control bank flickered with blue flame, the jet timers blew, and then there was just the screaming of air against the falling hull.

Hugh Starke sat still and waited....

He knew, before he opened his eyes, that he was dying. He didn't feel any pain, he didn't feel anything, but he knew just the same. Part of him was cut loose. He was still there, but not attached any more.

He raised his eyelids. There was a ceiling. It was a long way off. It was black stone veined with smoky reds and ambers. He had never seen it before.

His head was tilted toward the right. He let his gaze move down that way. There were dim tapestries, more of the black stone, and three tall archways giving onto a balcony. Beyond the balcony was a sky veiled and clouded with red mist. Under the mist, spreading away from a murky line of cliffs, was an ocean. It wasn't water and it didn't have any waves on it, but there was nothing else to call it. It burned, deep down inside itself, breathing up the red fog. Little angry bursts of flame coiled up under the flat surface, sending circles of sparks flaring out like ripples from a dropped stone.

He closed his eyes and frowned and moved his head restively. There was the texture of fur against his skin. Through the cracks of his eyelids he saw that he lay on a high bed piled with silks and soft tanned pelts. His body was covered. He was rather glad he couldn't see it. It didn't matter because he wouldn't be using it any more anyway, and it hadn't been such a hell of a body to begin with. But he was used to it, and he didn't want to see it now, the way he knew it would have to look.

He looked along over the foot of the bed, and he saw the woman.

She sat watching him from a massive carved chair softened with a single huge white pelt like a drift of snow. She smiled, and let him look. A pulse began to beat under his jaw, very feebly.

She was tall and sleek and insolently curved. She wore a sort of tabard of pale grey spider-silk, held to her body by a jeweled girdle, but it was just a nice piece of ornamentation. Her face was narrow, finely cut, secret, faintly amused. Her lips, her eyes, and her flowing silken hair were all the same pale cool shade of aquamarine.

Her skin was white, with no hint of rose. Her shoulders, her forearms, the long flat curve of her thighs, the pale-green tips of her breasts, were dusted with tiny particles that glistened like powdered diamond. She sparkled softly like a fairy thing against the snowy fur, a creature of foam and moonlight and clear shallow water. Her eyes never left his, and they were not human, but he knew that they would have done things to him if he had had any feeling below the neck.

*****

He started to speak. He had no strength to move his tongue. The woman leaned forward, and as though her movement were a signal four men rose from the tapestried shadows by the wall. They were like her. Their eyes were pale and strange like hers.

She said, in liquid High Venusian, "You're dying, in this body. But *you* will not die. You will sleep now, and wake in a strange body, in a strange place. Don't be afraid. My mind will be with yours, I'll guide you, don't be afraid. I can't explain now, there isn't time, but don't be afraid."

He drew back his thin lips baring his teeth in what might have been a smile. If it was, it was wolfish and bitter, like his face.

The woman's eyes began to pour coolness into his skull. They were like two little rivers running through the channels of his own eyes, spreading in silver-green quiet across the tortured surface of his brain. His brain relaxed. It lay floating on the water, and then the twin streams became one broad flowing stream, and his mind, or ego, the thing that was intimately himself, vanished along it.

It took him a long, long time to regain consciousness. He felt as though he'd been shaken until pieces of him were scattered all over inside. Also, he had an instinctive premonition that the minute he woke up he would be sorry he had. He took it easy, putting himself together.

He remembered his name, Hugh Starke. He remembered the mining asteroid where he was born. He remembered the Luna cell blocks where he had once come near dying. There wasn't much to choose between them. He remembered his face decorating half the bulletin boards between

Mercury and The Belt. He remembered hearing about himself over the telecasts, stuff to frighten babies with, and he thought of himself committing his first crime—a stunted scrawny kid of eighteen swinging a spanner on a grown man who was trying to steal his food.

The rest of it came fast, then. The T-V Mines job, the getaway that didn't get, the Mountains of White Cloud. The crash....

The woman.

That did it. His brain leaped shatteringly. Light, feeling, a naked sense of reality swept over him. He lay perfectly still with his eyes shut, and his mind clawed at the picture of the shining woman with sea-green hair and the sound of her voice saying, *You will not die, you will wake in a strange body, don't be afraid....*

He was afraid. His skin pricked and ran cold with it. His stomach knotted with it. His skin, his stomach, and yet somehow they didn't feel just right, like a new coat that hasn't shaped to you....

He opened his eyes, a cautious crack.

He saw a body sprawled on its side in dirty straw. The body belonged to him, because he could feel the straw pricking it, and the itch of little things that crawled and ate and crawled again.

It was a powerful body, rangy and flat-muscled, much bigger than his old one. It had obviously not been starved the first twenty-some years of its life. It was stark naked. Weather and violence had written history on it, wealed white marks on leathery bronze, but nothing seemed to be missing. There was black hair on its chest and thighs and forearms, and its hands were lean and sinewy for killing.

It was a human body. That was something. There were so many other things it might have been that his racial snobbery wouldn't call human. Like the nameless shimmering creature who smiled with strange pale lips.

Starke shut his eyes again.

He lay, the intangible self that was Hugh Starke, bellied down in the darkness of the alien shell, quiet, indrawn, waiting. Panic crept up on its soft black paws. It walked around the crouching ego and sniffed and patted and nuzzled, whining, and then struck with its raking claws. After a while it went away, empty.

The lips that were now Starke's lips twitched in a thin, cruel smile. He had done six months once in the Luna solitary crypts. If a man could do that, and come out sane and on his two feet, he could stand anything. Even this.

It came to him then, rather deflatingly, that the woman and her four companions had probably softened the shock by hypnotic suggestion. His subconscious understood and accepted the change.

It was only his conscious mind that was superficially scared to death.

Hugh Starke cursed the woman with great thoroughness, in seven languages and some odd dialects. He became healthily enraged that any dame should play around with him like that. Then he thought, What the hell, I'm alive. And it looks like I got the best of the trade-in!

He opened his eyes again, secretly, on his new world.

*****

He lay at one end of a square stone hall, good sized, with two straight lines of pillars cut from some dark Venusian wood. There were long crude benches and tables. Fires had been burning on round brick hearths spaced between the pillars. They were embers now. The smoke climbed up, tarnishing the gold and bronze of shields hung on the walls and pediments, dulling the blades of longswords, the spears, the tapestries and hides and trophies.

It was very quiet in the hall. Somewhere outside of it there was fighting going on. Heavy, vicious fighting. The noise of it didn't touch the silence, except to make it deeper.

There were two men besides Starke in the hall.

They were close to him, on a low dais. One of them sat in a carved high seat, not moving, his big scarred hands flat on the table in front of him. The other crouched on the floor by his feet. His head was bent forward so that his mop of lint-white hair hid his face and the harp between his thighs. He was a little man, a swamp-edger from his albino coloring. Starke looked back at the man in the chair.

The man spoke harshly. "Why doesn't she send word?"

The harp gave out a sudden bitter chord. That was all.

Starke hardly noticed. His whole attention was drawn to the speaker. His heart began to pound. His muscles coiled and lay ready. There was a bitter taste in his mouth. He recognized it. It was hate.

He had never seen the man before, but his hands twitched with the urge to kill.

He was big, nearly seven feet, and muscled like a draft horse. But his body, naked above a gold-bossed leather kilt, was lithe and quick as a greyhound in spite of its weight. His face was square, strong-boned, weathered, and still young. It was a face that had laughed a lot once, and liked wine and pretty girls. It had forgotten those things now, except maybe the wine. It was drawn and cruel with pain, a look as of something in a cage. Starke had seen that look before, in the Luna blocks. There was a thick white scar across the man's forehead. Under it his blue eyes were sunken and dark behind half-closed lids. The man was blind.

Outside, in the distance, men screamed and died.

Starke had been increasingly aware of a soreness and stricture around his neck. He raised a hand, careful not to rustle the straw. His fingers found a long tangled beard, felt under it, and touched a band of metal.

Starke's new body wore a collar, like a vicious dog.

There was a chain attached to the collar. Starke couldn't find any fastening. The business had been welded on for keeps. His body didn't seem to have liked it much. The neck was galled and chafed.

The blood began to crawl up hot into Starke's head. He'd worn chains before. He didn't like them. Especially around the neck.

A door opened suddenly at the far end of the hall. Fog and red daylight spilled in across the black stone floor. A man came in. He was big, half naked, blond, and bloody. His long blade trailed harshly on the flags. His chest was laid open to the bone and he held the wound together with his free hand.

"Word from Beudag," he said. "They've driven us back into the city, but so far we're holding the Gate."

No one spoke. The little man nodded his white head. The man with the slashed chest turned and went out again, closing the door.

A peculiar change came over Starke at the mention of the name Beudag. He had never heard it before, but it hung in his mind like a spear point, barbed with strange emotion. He couldn't identify the feeling, but it brushed the blind man aside. The hot simple hatred cooled. Starke relaxed in a sort of icy quiet, deceptively calm as a sleeping cobra. He didn't question this. He waited, for Beudag.

The blind man struck his hands down suddenly on the table and stood up. "Romna," he said, "give me my sword."

The little man looked at him. He had milk-blue eyes and a face like a friendly bulldog. He said, "Don't be a fool, Faolan."

Faolan said softly, "Damn you. Give me my sword."

Men were dying outside the hall, and not dying silently. Faolan's skin was greasy with sweat. He made a sudden, darting grab toward Romna.

Romna dodged him. There were tears in his pale eyes. He said brutally, "You'd only be in the way. Sit down."

"I can find the point," Faolan said, "to fall on it."

Romna's voice went up to a harsh scream. "Shut up. Shut up and sit down."

Faolan caught the edge of the table and bent over it. He shivered and closed his eyes, and the tears ran out hot under the lids. The bard turned away, and his harp cried out like a woman.

Faolan drew a long sighing breath. He straightened slowly, came round the carved high seat, and walked steadily toward Starke.

"You're very quiet, Conan," he said. "What's the matter? You ought to be happy, Conan. You ought to laugh and rattle your chain. You're going to get what you wanted. Are you sad because you haven't a mind any more, to understand that with?"

He stopped and felt with one sandaled foot across the straw until he touched Starke's thigh. Starke lay motionless.

"Conan," said the blind man gently, pressing Starke's belly with his foot. "Conan the dog, the betrayer, the butcher, the knife in the back. Remember what you did at Falga, Conan? No, you don't remember now. I've been a little rough with you, and you don't remember any more. But I remember, Conan. As long as I live in darkness, I'll remember."

*****

Romna stroked the harp strings and they wept, savage tears for strong men dead of treachery. Low music, distant but not soft. Faolan began to tremble, a shallow animal twitching of the muscles. The flesh of his face was drawn, iron shaping under the hammer. Quite suddenly he went down on his knees. His hands struck Starke's shoulders, slid inward to the throat, and locked there.

Outside, the sound of fighting had died away.

Starke moved, very quickly. As though he had seen it and knew it was there, his hand swept out and gathered in the slack of the heavy chain and swung it.

It started out to be a killing blow. Starke wanted with all his heart to beat Faolan's brains out. But at the last second he pulled it, slapping the big man with exquisite judgment across the back of the head. Faolan grunted and fell sideways, and by that time Romna had come up. He had dropped his harp and drawn a knife. His eyes were startled.

Starke sprang up. He backed off, swinging the slack of the chain warningly. His new body moved magnificently. Outside everything was fine, but inside his psycho-neural setup had exploded into civil war. He was furious with himself for not having killed Faolan. He was furious with himself for losing control enough to want to kill a man without reason. He hated Faolan. He did not hate Faolan because he didn't know him well enough. Starke's trained, calculating, unemotional brain was at grips with a tidal wave of baseless emotion.

He hadn't realized it was baseless until his mental monitor, conditioned through years of bitter control, had stopped him from killing. Now he remembered the woman's voice saying, *My mind will be with yours, I'll guide you....*

Catspaw, huh? Just a hired hand, paid off with a new body in return for two lives. Yeah, two. This Beudag, whoever he was. Starke knew now what that cold alien emotion had been leading up to.

"Hold it," said Starke hoarsely. "Hold everything. *Catspaw! You green-eyed she-devil! You picked the wrong guy this time.*"

Just for a fleeting instant he saw her again, leaning forward with her hair like running water across the soft foam-sparkle of her shoulders. Her sea-pale eyes were full of mocking laughter, and a direct, provocative admiration. Starke heard her quite plainly:

"You may not have any choice, Hugh Starke. They know Conan, even if you don't. Besides, it's of no great importance. The end will be the same for them—it's just a matter of time. You can save your new body or not, as you wish." She smiled. "I'd like it if you did. It's a good body. I knew it, before Conan's mind broke and left it empty."

A sudden thought came to Starke. "My box, the million credits."

"Come and get them." She was gone. Starke's mind was clear, with no alien will tramping around in it. Faolan crouched on the floor, holding his head. He said:

"Who spoke?"

Romna the bard stood staring. His lips moved, but no sound came out.

Starke said, "I spoke. Me, Hugh Starke. I'm not Conan, and I never heard of Falga, and I'll brain the first guy that comes near me."

Faolan stayed motionless, his face blank, his breath sobbing in his throat. Romna began to curse, very softly, not as though he were thinking about it. Starke watched them.

Down the hall the doors burst open. The heavy reddish mist coiled in with the daylight across the flags, and with them a press of bodies hot from battle, bringing a smell of blood.

Starke felt the heart contract in the hairy breast of the body named Conan, watching the single figure that led the pack.

Romna called out, "Beudag!"

She was tall. She was built and muscled like a lioness, and she walked with a flat-hipped arrogance, and her hair was like coiled flame. Her eyes were blue, hot and bright, as Faolan's might have been once. She looked like Faolan. She was dressed like him, in a leather kilt and sandals, her magnificent body bare above the waist. She carried a longsword slung across her back, the hilt standing above the left shoulder. She had been using it. Her skin was smeared with blood and grime. There was a long cut on her thigh and another across her flat belly, and bitter weariness lay on her like a burden in spite of her denial of it.

"We've stopped them, Faolan," she said. "They can't breach the Gate, and we can hold Crom Dhu as long as we have food. And the sea feeds us." She laughed, but there was a hollow sound to it. "Gods, I'm tired!"

She halted then, below the dais. Her flame-blue gaze swept across Faolan, across Romna, and rose to meet Hugh Starke's, and stayed there.

The pulse began to beat under Starke's jaw again, and this time his body was strong, and the pulse was like a drum throbbing.

Romna said, "His mind has come back."

*****

There was a long, hard silence. No one in the hall moved. Then the men back of Beudag, big brawny kilted warriors, began to close in on the dais, talking in low snarling undertones that rose toward a mob howl. Faolan rose up and faced them, and bellowed them to quiet.

"He's mine to take! Let him alone."

Beudag sprang up onto the dais, one beautiful flowing movement. "It isn't possible," she said. "His mind broke under torture. He's been a drooling idiot with barely the sense to feed himself. And now, suddenly, you say he's normal again?"

Starke said, "You know I'm normal. You can see it in my eyes."

"Yes."

He didn't like the way she said that. "Listen, my name is Hugh Starke. I'm an Earthman. This isn't Conan's brain come back. This is a new deal. I got shoved into this body. What it did before I got it I don't know, and I'm not responsible."

Faolan said, "He doesn't remember Falga. He doesn't remember the longships at the bottom of the sea." Faolan laughed.

Romna said quietly, "He didn't kill you, though. He could have, easily. Would Conan have spared you?"

Beudag said, "Yes, if he had a better plan. Conan's mind was like a snake. It crawled in the dark, and you never knew where it was going to strike."

Starke began to tell them how it happened, the chain swinging idly in his hand. While he was talking he saw a face reflected in a polished shield hung on a pillar. Mostly it was just a tangled black mass of hair, mounted on a frame of long, harsh, jutting bone. The mouth was sensuous, with a dark sort of laughter on it. The eyes were yellow. The cruel, brilliant yellow of a killer hawk.

Starke realized with a shock that the face belonged to him.

"A woman with pale green hair," said Beudag softly. "Rann," said Faolan, and Romna's harp made a sound like a high-priest's curse.

"Her people have that power," Romna said. "They can think a man's soul into a spider, and step on it."

"They have many powers. Maybe Rann followed Conan's mind, wherever it went, and told it what to say, and brought it back again."

"Listen," said Starke angrily. "I didn't ask...."

Suddenly, without warning, Romna drew Beudag's sword and threw it at Starke.

Starke dodged it. He looked at Romna with ugly yellow eyes. "That's fine. Chain me up so I can't fight and kill me from a distance." He did not pick up the sword. He'd never used one. The chain felt better, not being too different from a heavy belt or a length of cable, or the other chains he'd swung on occasion.

Romna said, "Is that Conan?"

Faolan snarled, "What happened?"

"Romna threw my sword at Conan. He dodged it, and left it on the ground." Beudag's eyes were narrowed. "Conan could catch a flying sword by the hilt, and he was the best fighter on the Red Sea, barring you, Faolan."

"He's trying to trick us. Rann guides him."

"The hell with Rann!" Starke clashed his chain. "She wants me to kill the both of you, I still don't know why. All right. I could have killed Faolan, easy. But I'm not a killer. I never put down anyone except to save my own neck. So I didn't kill him in spite of

Rann. And I don't want any part of you, or Rann either. All I want is to get the hell out of here!"

Beudag said, "His accent isn't Conan's. And the look in his eyes is different, too." Her voice had an odd note in it. Romna glanced at her. He fingered a few rippling chords on his harp, and said:

"There's one way you could tell for sure."

A sullen flush began to burn on Beudag's cheekbones. Romna slid unobtrusively out of reach. His eyes danced with malicious laughter.

Beudag smiled, the smile of an angry cat, all teeth and no humor. Suddenly she walked toward Starke, her head erect, her hands swinging loose and empty at her sides. Starke tensed warily, but the blood leaped pleasantly in his borrowed veins.

Beudag kissed him.

Starke dropped the chain. He had something better to do with his hands.

After a while he raised his head for breath, and she stepped back, and whispered wonderingly,

"It isn't Conan."

*****

The hall had been cleared. Starke had washed and shaved himself. His new face wasn't bad. Not bad at all. In fact, it was pretty damn good. And it wasn't known around the System. It was a face that could own a million credits and no questions asked. It was a face that could have a lot of fun on a million credits.

All he had to figure out now was a way to save the neck the face was mounted on, and get his million credits back from that beautiful she-devil named Rann.

He was still chained, but the straw had been cleaned up and he wore a leather kilt and a pair of sandals. Faolan sat in his high seat nursing a flagon of wine. Beudag sprawled wearily on a fur rug beside him. Romna sat cross-legged, his eyes veiled sleepily, stroking soft wandering music out of his harp. He looked fey. Starke knew his swamp-edgers. He wasn't surprised.

"This man is telling the truth," Romna said. "But there's another mind touching his. Rann's, I think. Don't trust him."

Faolan growled, "I couldn't trust a god in Conan's body."

Starke said, "What's the setup? All the fighting out there, and this Rann dame trying to plant a killer on the inside. And what happened at Falga? I never heard of this whole damn ocean, let alone a place called Falga."

The bard swept his hand across the strings. "I'll tell you, Hugh Starke. And maybe you won't want to stay in that body any longer."

Starke grinned. He glanced at Beudag. She was watching him with a queer intensity from under lowered lids. Starke's grin changed. He began to sweat. Get rid of this body, hell! It was really a body. His own stringy little carcass had never felt like this.

The bard said, "In the beginning, in the Red Sea, was a race of people having still their fins and scales. They were amphibious, but after a while part of this race wanted to remain entirely on land. There was a quarrel, and a battle, and some of the people left the sea forever. They settled along the shore. They lost their fins and most of their scales. They had great mental powers and they loved ruling. They subjugated the human peoples and kept them almost in slavery. They hated their brothers who still lived in the sea, and their brothers hated them.

"After a time a third people came to the Red Sea. They were rovers from the North. They raided and rieved and wore no man's collar. They made a settlement on Crom Dhu, the Black Rock, and built longships, and took toll of the coastal towns.

"But the slave people didn't want to fight against the rovers. They wanted to fight with them and destroy the sea-folk. The rovers were human, and blood calls to blood. And the rovers like to rule, too, and this is a rich country. Also, the time had come in their tribal development when they were ready to change from nomadic warriors to builders in their own country.

"So the rovers, and the sea-folk, and the slave-people who are caught between the two of them, began their struggle for the land."

The bard's fingers thrummed against the strings so that they beat like angry hearts. Starke saw that Beudag was still watching him, weighing every change of expression on his face. Romna went on:

"There was a woman named Rann, who had green hair and great beauty, and ruled the sea-folk. There was a man called Faolan of the Ships, and his sister Beudag, which means Dagger-in-the-Sheath, and they two ruled the outland rovers. And there was the man called Conan."

The harp crashed out like a sword-blade striking.

"Conan was a great fighter and a great lover. He was next under Faolan of the Ships, and Beudag loved him, and they were plighted. Then Conan was taken prisoner by the sea-folk during a skirmish, and Rann saw him—and Conan saw Rann."

Hugh Starke had a fleeting memory of Rann's face smiling, and her low voice saying, *It's a good body. I knew it, before....*

Beudag's eyes were two stones of blue vitriol under her narrow lids.

"Conan stayed a long time at Falga with Rann of the Red Sea. Then he came back to Crom Dhu, and said that he had escaped, and had discovered a way to take the longships into the harbor of Falga, at the back of Rann's fleet, and from there it would be easy to take the city, and Rann with it. And Conan and Beudag were married."

Starke's yellow hawk eyes slid over Beudag, sprawled like a young lioness in power and beauty. A muscle began to twitch under his cheekbone. Beudag flushed, a slow deep color. Her gaze did not waver.

"So the longships went out from Crom Dhu, across the Red Sea. And Conan led them into a trap at Falga, and more than half of them were sunk. Conan thought his ship was free, that he had Rann and all she'd promised him, but Faolan saw what had happened and went after him. They fought, and Conan laid his sword across Faolan's brow and blinded him; but Conan lost the fight. Beudag brought them home.

"Conan was chained naked in the market place. The people were careful not to kill him. From time to time other things were done to him. After a while his mind broke, and Faolan had him chained here in the hall, where he could hear him babble and play with his chain. It made the darkness easier to bear.

"But since Falga, things have gone badly from Crom Dhu. Too many men were lost, too many ships. Now Rann's people have us bottled up here. They can't break in, we can't break out. And so we stay, until...." The harp cried out a bitter question, and was still.

*****

After a minute or two Starke said slowly, "Yeah, I get it. Stalemate for both of you. And Rann figured if I could kill off the leaders, your people might give up." He began to curse. "What a lousy, dirty, sneaking trick! And who told her she could use me...." He paused. After all, he'd be dead now. After all, a new body, and a cool million credits. Ah, the hell with Rann. He hadn't asked her to do it. And he was nobody's hired killer. Where did she get off, sneaking around his mind, trying to make him do things he didn't even know about? Especially to someone like Beudag.

Still, Rann herself was nobody's crud.

And just where was Hugh Starke supposed to cut in on this deal? Cut was right. Probably with a longsword, right through the belly. Swell spot he was in, and a good three strikes on him already.

He was beginning to wish he'd never seen the T-V Mines payroll ship, because then he might never have seen the Mountains of White Cloud.

He said, because everybody seemed to be waiting for him to say something, "Usually when there's a deadlock like this, somebody calls in a third party. Isn't there somebody you can yell for?"

Faolan shook his rough red head. "The slave people might rise, but they haven't arms and they're not used to fighting. They'd only get massacred, and it wouldn't help us any."

"What about those other—uh—people that live in the sea? And just what is that sea, anyhow? Some radiation from it wrecked my ship and got me into this bloody mess."

Beudag said lazily, "I don't know what it is. The seas our forefathers sailed on were water, but this is different. It will float a ship, if you know how to build the hull—very thin, of a white metal we mine from the foothills. But when you swim in it, it's like being in a cloud of bubbles. It tingles, and the farther down you go in it the stranger it gets, dark and full of fire. I stay down for hours sometimes, hunting the beasts that live there."

Starke said, "For hours? You have diving suits, then."

"What are they?" Starke told her. She shook her head, laughing. "Why weigh yourself down that way? There's no trouble to breathe in this ocean."

"For cripesake," said Starke. "Well I'll be damned. Must be a heavy gas, then, radioactive, surface tension under atmospheric pressure, enough to float a light hull, and high oxygen content without any dangerous mixture. Well, well. Okay, why doesn't somebody go down and see if the sea-people will help? They don't like Rann's branch of the family, you said."

"They don't like us, either," said Faolan. "We stay out of the southern part of the sea. They wreck our ships, sometimes." His bitter mouth twisted in a smile. "Did you want to go to them for help?"

Starke didn't quite like the way Faolan sounded. "It was just a suggestion," he said.

Beudag rose, stretching, wincing as the stiffened wounds pulled her flesh. "Come, on, Faolan. Let's sleep."

He rose and laid his hand on her shoulder. Romna's harpstrings breathed a subtle little mockery of sound. The bard's eyes were veiled and sleepy. Beudag did not look at Starke, called Conan.

Starke said, "What about me?"

"You stay chained," said Faolan. "There's plenty of time to think. As long as we have food—and the sea feeds us."

He followed Beudag, through a curtained entrance to the left. Romna got up, slowly, slinging the harp over one white shoulder. He stood looking steadily into Starke's eyes in the dying light of the fires.

"I don't know," he murmured.

Starke waited, not speaking. His face was without expression.

"Conan we knew. Starke we don't know. Perhaps it would have been better if Conan had come back." He ran his thumb absently over the hilt of the knife in his girdle. "I don't know. Perhaps it would have been better for all of us if I'd cut your throat before Beudag came in."

Starke's mouth twitched. It was not exactly a smile.

"You see," said the bard seriously, "to you, from Outside, none of this is important, except as it touches you. But we live in this little world. We die in it. To us, it's important."

The knife was in his hand now. It leaped up glittering into the dregs of the firelight, and fell, and leaped again.

"You fight for yourself, Hugh Starke. Rann also fights through you. I don't know."

Starke's gaze did not waver.

Romna shrugged and put away the knife. "It is written of the gods," he said, sighing. "I hope they haven't done a bad job of the writing."

He went out. Starke began to shiver slightly. It was completely quiet in the hall. He examined his collar, the rivets, every separate link of the chain, the staple to which it was fixed. Then he sat down on the fur rug provided for him in place of the straw. He put his face in his hands and cursed, steadily, for several minutes, and then struck his fists down hard on the floor. After that he lay down and was quiet. He thought Rann would speak to him. She did not.

The silent black hours that walked across his heart were worse than any he had spent in the Luna crypts.

*****

She came soft-shod, bearing a candle. Beudag, the Dagger-in-the-Sheath. Starke was not sleeping. He rose and stood waiting. She set the candle on the table and came, not quite to him, and stopped. She wore a length of thin white cloth twisted loosely at the waist and dropping to her ankles. Her body rose out of it straight and lovely, touched mystically with shadows in the little wavering light.

"Who are you?" she whispered. "What are you?"

"A man. Not Conan. Maybe not Hugh Starke any more. Just a man."

"I loved the man called Conan, until...." She caught her breath, and moved closer. She put her hand on Starke's arm. The touch went through him like white fire. The warm clean healthy fragrance of her tasted sweet in his throat. Her eyes searched his.

"If Rann has such great powers, couldn't it be that Conan was forced to do what he did? Couldn't it be that Rann took his mind and moulded it her way, perhaps without his knowing it?"

"It could be."

"Conan was hot-tempered and quarrelsome, but he...."

Starke said slowly, "I don't think you could have loved him if he hadn't been straight."

Her hand lay still on his forearm. She stood looking at him, and then her hand began to tremble, and in a moment she was crying, making no noise about it. Starke drew her gently to him. His eyes blazed yellowly in the candlelight.

"Woman's tears," she said impatiently, after a bit. She tried to draw away. "I've been fighting too long, and losing, and I'm tired."

He let her step back, not far. "Do all the women of Crom Dhu fight like men?"

"If they want to. There have always been shield-maidens. And since Falga, I would have had to fight anyway, to keep from thinking." She touched the collar on Starke's neck. "And from seeing."

He thought of Conan in the market square, and Conan shaking his chain and gibbering in Faolan's hall, and Beudag watching it. Starke's fingers tightened. He slid his palms upward along the smooth muscles of her arms, across the straight, broad planes of her shoulders, onto her neck, the proud strength of it pulsing under his hands. Her hair fell loose. He could feel the redness of it burning him.

She whispered, "You don't love me."

"No."

"You're an honest man, Hugh Starke."

"You want me to kiss you."

"Yes."

"You're an honest woman, Beudag."

Her lips were hungry, passionate, touched with the bitterness of tears. After a while Starke blew out the candle....

"I could love you, Beudag."

"Not the way I mean."

"The way you mean. I've never said that to any woman before. But you're not like any woman before. And—I'm a different man."

"Strange—so strange. Conan, and yet not Conan."

"I could love you, Beudag—if I lived."

Harpstrings gave a thrumming sigh in the darkness, the faintest whisper of sound. Beudag started, sighed, and rose from the fur rug. In a minute she had found flint and steel and got the candle lighted. Romna the bard stood in the curtained doorway, watching them.

Presently he said, "You're going to let him go."

Beudag said, "Yes."

Romna nodded. He did not seem surprised. He walked across the dais, laying his harp on the table, and went into another room. He came back almost at once with a hacksaw.

"Bend your neck," he said to Starke.

The metal of the collar was soft. When it was cut through Starke got his fingers under it and bent the ends outward, without trouble. His old body could never have done that. His old body could never have done a lot of things. He figured Rann hadn't cheated him. Not much.

He got up, looking at Beudag. Beudag's head was dropped forward, her face veiled behind shining hair.

"There's only one possible way out of Crom Dhu," she said. There was no emotion in her voice. "There's a passage leading down through the rock to a secret harbor, just large enough to moor a skiff or two. Perhaps, with the night and the fog, you can slip through Rann's blockade. Or you can go aboard one of her ships, for Falga." She picked up the candle. "I'll take you down."

"Wait," Starke said. "What about you?"

She glanced at him, surprised. "I'll stay, of course."

He looked into her eyes. "It's going to be hard to know each other that way."

"You can't stay here, Hugh Starke. The people would tear you to pieces the moment you went into the street. They may even storm the hall, to take you.

Look here." She set the candle down and led him to a narrow window, drawing back the hide that covered it.

Starke saw narrow twisting streets dropping steeply toward the sullen sea. The longships were broken and sunk in the harbor. Out beyond, riding lights flickering in the red fog, were other ships. Rann's ships.

"Over there," said Beudag, "is the mainland. Crom Dhu is connected to it by a tongue of rock. The sea-folk hold the land beyond it, but we can hold the rock bridge as long as we live. We have enough water, enough food from the sea. But there's no soil nor game on Crom Dhu. We'll be naked after a while, without leather or flax, and we'll have scurvy without grain and fruit. We're beaten, unless the gods send us a miracle. And we're beaten because of what was done at Falga. You can see how the people feel."

Starke looked at the dark streets and the silent houses leaning on each other's shoulders, and the mocking lights out in the fog. "Yeah," he said. "I can see."

"Besides, there's Faolan. I don't know whether he believes your story. I don't know whether it would matter."

Starke nodded. "But you won't come with me?"

She turned away sharply and picked up the candle again. "Are you coming, Romna?"

The bard nodded. He slung his harp over his shoulder. Beudag held back the curtain of a small doorway far to the side. Starke went through it and Romna followed, and Beudag went ahead with the candle. No one spoke.

*****

They went along a narrow passage, past store rooms and armories. They paused once while Starke chose a knife, and Romna whispered: "Wait!" He listened intently. Starke and Beudag strained their ears along with him. There was no sound in the sleeping dun. Romna shrugged. "I thought I heard sandals scraping stone," he said. They went on.

The passage lay behind a wooden door. It led downward steeply through the rock, a single narrow way without side galleries or branches. In some places there were winding steps. It ended, finally, in a flat ledge low to the surface of the cove, which was a small cavern closed in with the black rock. Beudag set the candle down.

There were two little skiffs built of some light metal moored to rings in the ledge. Two long sweeps leaned against the cave wall. They were of a different metal, oddly vaned. Beudag laid one across the thwarts of the nearest boat. Then she turned to Starke. Romna hung back in the shadows by the tunnel mouth.

Beudag said quietly, "Goodbye, man without a name."

"It has to be goodbye."

"I'm leader now, in Faolan's place. Besides, these are my people." Her fingers tightened on his wrists. "If you could...." Her eyes held a brief blaze of hope. Then she dropped her head and said, "I keep forgetting you're not one of us. Goodbye."

"Goodbye, Beudag."

Starke put his arms around her. He found her mouth, almost cruelly. Her arms were tight about him, her eyes half closed and dreaming. Starke's hands slip upward, toward her throat, and locked on it.

She bent back, her body like a steel bow. Her eyes got fire in them, looking into Starke's but only for a moment. His fingers pressed expertly on the nerve centers. Beudag's head fell forward limply, and then Romna was on Starke's back and his knife was pricking Starke's throat.

Starke caught his wrist and turned the blade away. Blood ran onto his chest, but the cut was not into the artery. He threw himself backward onto the stone. Romna couldn't get clear in time. The breath went out of him in a rushing gasp. He didn't let go of the knife. Starke rolled over. The little man didn't have a chance with him. He was tough and quick, but Starke's sheer size smothered him. Starke could remember when Romna would not have seemed small to him. He hit the bard's jaw with his fist. Romna's head cracked hard against the stone. He let go of the knife. He seemed to be through fighting. Starke got up. He was sweating, breathing heavily, not because of his exertion. His mouth was glistening and eager, like a dog's. His muscles twitched, his belly was hot and knotted with excitement. His yellow eyes had a strange look.

He went back to Beudag.

She lay on the black rock, on her back. Candlelight ran pale gold across her brown skin, skirting the sharp strong hollows between her breasts and under the arching rim of her rib-case. Starke knelt, across her body, his weight pressed down against her harsh breathing. He stared at her. Sweat stood out on his face. He took her throat between his hands again.

He watched the blood grow dark in her checks. He watched the veins coil on her forehead. He watched the redness blacken in her lips. She fought a little, very vaguely, like someone moving in a dream. Starke breathed hoarsely, animal-like, through an open mouth.

Then, gradually his body became rigid. His hands froze, not releasing pressure, but not adding any. His yellow eyes widened. It was as though he were trying to see Beudag's face and it was hidden in dense clouds.

Back of him, back in the tunnel, was the soft, faint whisper of sandals on uneven rock. Sandals, walking slowly. Starke did not hear. Beudag's face glimmered deep in a heavy mist below him, a blasphemy of a face, distorted, blackened.

Starke's hands began to open.

They opened slowly. Muscles stood like coiled ropes in his arms and shoulders, as though he moved them against heavy weights. His lips peeled back from his teeth. He bent his neck, and sweat dropped from his face and glittered on Beudag's breast.

Starke was now barely touching Beudag's neck. She began to breathe again, painfully.

Starke began to laugh. It was not nice laughter. "Rann," he whispered. "Rann, you she-devil." He half fell away from Beudag and stood up, holding himself against the wall. He was shaking violently. "I wouldn't use your hate for killing, so you tried to use my passion." He cursed her in a flat sibilant whisper. He had never in his profane life really cursed anyone before.

He heard an echo of laughter dancing in his brain.

Starke turned. Faolan of the Ships stood in the tunnel mouth. His head was bent, listening, his blind dark eyes fixed on Starke as though he saw him.

*****

Faolan said softly "I hear you, Starke. I hear the other breathing, but they don't speak."

"They're all right. I didn't mean to do...."

Faolan smiled. He stepped out on the narrow ledge. He knew where he was going, and his smile was not pleasant.

"I heard your steps in the passage beyond my room. I knew Beudag was leading you, and where, and why. I would have been here sooner, but it's a slow way in the dark."

The candle lay in his path. He felt the heat of it close to his leg, and stopped and felt for it, and ground it out. It was dark, then. Very dark, except for a faint smudgy glow from the scrap of ocean that lay along the cave floor.

"It doesn't matter," Faolan said, "as long as I came in time."

Starke shifted his weight warily. "Faolan...."

"I wanted you alone. On this night of all nights I wanted you alone. Beudag fights in my place now, Conan. My manhood needs proving."

Starke strained his eyes in the gloom, measuring the ledge, measuring the place where the skiff was moored. He didn't want to fight Faolan. In Faolan's place he would have felt the same. Starke understood perfectly. He didn't hate Faolan, he didn't want to kill him, and he was afraid of Rann's power over him when his emotions got control. You couldn't keep a determined man from killing you and still be uninvolved emotionally. Starke would be damned if he'd kill anyone to suit Rann.

He moved, silently, trying to slip past Faolan on the outside and get into the skiff. Faolan gave no sign of hearing him. Starke did not breathe. His sandals came down lighter than snowflakes. Faolan did not swerve. He would pass Starke with a foot to spare. They came abreast.

Faolan's hand shot out and caught in Starke's long black hair. The blind man laughed softly and closed in.

Starke swung one from the floor. Do it the quickest way and get clear. But Faolan was fast. He came in so swiftly that Starke's fist jarred harmlessly along his ribs. He was bigger than Starke, and heavier, and the darkness didn't bother him.

Starke bared his teeth. Do it quick, brother, and clear out! Or that green-eyed she-cat.... Faolan's brute bulk weighed him down. Faolan's arm crushed his neck. Faolan's fist was knocking his guts loose. Starke got moving.

He'd fought in a lot of places. He'd learned from stokers and tramps, Martian Low-Canalers, red-eyed Nahali in the running gutters of Lhi. He didn't use his knife. He used his knees and feet and elbows and his hands, fist and flat. It was a good fight.

Faolan was a good fighter, but Starke knew more tricks.

One more, Starke thought. One more and he's out. He drew back for it, and his heel struck Romna, lying on the rock. He staggered, and Faolan caught him with a clean swinging blow. Starke fell backward against the cave wall. His head cracked the rock. Light flooded crimson across his brain and then paled and grew cooler, a wash of clear silver-green like water. He sank under it....

He was tired, desperately tired. His head ached. He wanted to rest, but he could feel that he was sitting up, doing something that had to be done. He opened his eyes.

He sat in the stern of a skiff. The long sweep was laid into its crutch, held like a tiller bar against his body. The blade of the sweep trailed astern in the red sea, and where the metal touched there was a spurt of silver fire and a swirling of brilliant motes. The skiff moved rapidly through the sullen fog, through a mist of blood in the hot Venusian night.

Beudag crouched in the bow, facing Starke. She was bound securely with strips of the white cloth she had worn. Bruises showed dark on her throat. She was watching Starke with the intent, unwinking, perfectly expressionless gaze of a tigress.

Starke looked away, down at himself. There was blood on his kilt, a brown smear of it across his chest. It was not his blood. He drew the knife slowly out of its sheath. The blade was dull and crusted, still a little wet.

Starke looked at Beudag. His lips were stiff, swollen. He moistened them and said hoarsely, "What happened?"

She shook her head, slowly, not speaking. Her eyes did not waver.

A black, cold rage took hold of Starke and shook him. Rann! He rose and went forward, letting the sweep go where it would. He began to untie Beudag's wrists.

A shape swam toward them out of the red mist. A longship with two heavy sweeps bursting fire astern and a slender figurehead shaped like a woman. A woman with hair and eyes of aquamarine. It came alongside the skiff.

A rope ladder snaked down. Men lined the low rail. Slender men with skin that glistened white like powdered snow, and hair the color of distant shallows.

One of them said, "Come aboard, Hugh Starke."

Starke went back to the sweep. It bit into the sea, sending the skiff in a swift arc away from Rann's ship.

Grapnels flew, hooking the skiff at thwart and gunwale. Bows appeared in the hands of the men, wicked curving things with barbed metal shafts on the string. The man said again, politely, "Come aboard."

Hugh Starke finished untying Beudag. He didn't speak. There seemed to be nothing to say. He stood back while she climbed the ladder and then followed. The skiff was cast loose. The longship veered away, gathering speed.

Starke said, "Where are we going?"

The man smiled. "To Falga."

Starke nodded. He went below with Beudag into a cabin with soft couches covered with spider-silk and panels of dark wood beautifully painted, dim fantastic scenes from the past of Rann's people. They sat opposite each other. They still did not speak.

*****

They raised Falga in the opal dawn—a citadel of basalt cliffs rising sheer from the burning sea, with a long arm holding a harbor full of ships. There were green fields inland, and beyond, cloaked in the eternal mists of Venus, the Mountains of White Clouds lifted spaceward. Starke wished that he had never seen the Mountains of White Cloud. Then, looking at his hands, lean and strong on his long thighs, he wasn't so sure. He thought of Rann waiting for him. Anger, excitement, a confused violence of emotion set him pacing nervously.

Beudag sat quietly, withdrawn, waiting.

The longship threaded the crowded moorings and slid into place alongside a stone quay. Men rushed to make fast. They were human men, as Starke judged humans, like Beudag and himself. They had the shimmering silver hair and fair skin of the plateau peoples, the fine-cut faces and straight bodies. They wore leather collars with metal tags and they went naked like beasts, and they were gaunt and bowed with labor. Here and there a man with pale blue-green hair and resplendent harness stood godlike above the swarming masses.

Starke and Beudag went ashore. They might have been prisoners or honored guests, surrounded by their escort from the ship. Streets ran back from the harbor, twisting and climbing crazily up the cliffs. Houses climbed on each others backs. It had begun to rain, the heavy steaming downpour of Venus, and the moist heat brought out the choking stench of people, too many people.

They climbed, ankle deep in water sweeping down the streets that were half stairway. Thin naked children peered out of the houses, out of narrow alleys. Twice they passed through market squares where women with the blank faces of defeat drew back from stalls of coarse food to let the party through.

There was something wrong. After a while Starke realized it was the silence. In all that horde of humanity no one laughed, or sang, or shouted. Even the children never spoke above a whisper. Starke began to feel a little sick. Their eyes had a look in them....

He glanced at Beudag, and away again.

The waterfront streets ended in a sheer basalt face honeycombed with galleries. Starke's party entered them, still climbing. They passed level after level of huge caverns, open to the sea. There was the same crowding, the same stench, the same silence. Eyes glinted in the half-light, bare feet moved furtively on stone. Somewhere a baby cried thinly, and was hushed at once.

They came out on the cliff top, into the clean high air. There was a city here. Broad streets, lined with trees, low rambling villas of the black rock set in walled gardens, drowned in brilliant vines and giant ferns and flowers. Naked men and women worked in the gardens, or hauled carts of rubbish through the alleys, or hurried on errands, slipping furtively across the main streets where they intersected the mews.

The party turned away from the sea, heading toward an ebon palace that sat like a crown above the city. The steaming rain beat on Starke's bare body, and up here you could get the smell of the rain, even through the heavy perfume of the flowers. You could smell Venus in the rain—musky and primitive and savagely alive, a fecund giantess with passion flowers in her outstretched hands.

Starke set his feet down like a panther and his eyes burned a smoky amber.

They entered the palace of Rann....

She received them in the same apartment where Starke had come to after the crash. Through a broad archway he could see the high bed where his old body had lain before the life went out of it. The red sea steamed under the rain outside, the rusty fog coiling languidly through the open arches of the gallery. Rann watched them lazily from a raised couch set massively into the wall. Her long sparkling legs sprawled arrogantly across the black spider-silk draperies. This time her tabard was a pale yellow. Her eyes were still the color of shoal-water, still amused, still secret, still dangerous.

Starke said, "So you made me do it after all."

"And you're angry." She laughed, her teeth showing white and pointed as bone needles. Her gaze held Starke's. There was nothing casual about it. Starke's hawk eyes turned molten yellow, like hot gold, and did not waver.

Beudag stood like a bronze spear, her forearms crossed beneath her bare sharp breasts. Two of Rann's palace guards stood behind her.

Starke began to walk toward Rann.

She watched him come. She let him get close enough to reach out and touch her, and then she said slyly, "It's a good body, isn't it?"

*****

Starke looked at her for a moment. Then he laughed. He threw back his head and roared, and struck the great corded muscles of his belly with his fist. Presently he looked straight into Rann's eyes and said:

"I know you."

She nodded. "We know each other. Sit down, Hugh Starke." She swung her long legs over to make room, half erect now, looking at Beudag. Starke sat down. He did not look at Beudag.

Rann said, "Will your people surrender now?"

Beudag did not move, not even her eyelids. "If Faolan is dead—yes."

"And if he's not?"

Beudag stiffened. Starke did too.

"Then," said Beudag quietly, "they'll wait."

"Until he is?"

"Or until they must surrender."

Rann nodded. To the guards she said, "See that this woman is well fed and well treated."

Beudag and her escort had turned to go when Starke said, "Wait." The guards looked at Rann, who nodded, and glanced quizzically at Starke. Starke said:

"Is Faolan dead?"

Rann hesitated. Then she smiled. "No. You have the most damnably tough mind, Starke. You struck deep, but not deep enough. He may still die, but.... No, he's not dead." She turned to Beudag and said with easy mockery, "You needn't hold anger against Starke. I'm the one who should be angry." Her eyes came back to Starke. They didn't look angry.

Starke said, "There's something else. Conan—the Conan that used to be, before Falga."

"Beudag's Conan."

"Yeah. Why did he betray his people?"

Rann studied him. Her strange pale lips curved, her sharp white teeth glistening wickedly with barbed humor. Then she turned to Beudag. Beudag was still standing like a carved image, but her smooth muscles were ridged with tension, and her eyes were not the eyes of an image.

"Conan or Starke," said Rann, "she's still Beudag, isn't she? All right, I'll tell you. Conan betrayed his people because I put it into his mind to do it. He fought me. He made a good fight of it. But he wasn't quite as tough as you are, Starke."

There was a silence. For the first time since entering the room, Hugh Starke looked at Beudag. After a moment she sighed and lifted her chin and smiled, a deep, faint smile. The guards walked out beside her, but she was more erect and lighter of step than either of them.

"Well," said Rann, when they were gone, "and what about you, Hugh-Starke-Called-Conan."

"Have I any choice?"

"I always keep my bargains."

"Then give me my dough and let me clear the hell out of here."

"Sure that's what you want?"

"That's what I want."

"You could stay a while, you know."

"With you."

Rann lifted her frosty-white shoulders. "I'm not promising half my kingdom, or even part of it. But you might be amused."

"I got no sense of humor."

"Don't you even want to see what happens to Crom Dhu?"

Starke got up. He said savagely, "The hell with Crom Dhu."

"And Beudag."

"And Beudag." He stopped, then fixed Rann with uncompromising yellow eyes. "No. Not Beudag. What are you going to do to her?"

"Nothing."

"Don't give me that."

"I say again, nothing. Whatever is done, her own people will do."

"What do you mean?"

"I mean that little Dagger-in-the-Sheath will be rested, cared for, and fattened, for a few days. Then I shall take her aboard my own ship and join the fleet before Crom Dhu. Beudag will be made quite comfortable at the masthead, where her people can see her plainly. She will stay there until the Rock surrenders. It depends on her own people how long she stays. She'll be given water. Not much, but enough."

Starke stared at her. He stared at her a long time. Then he spat deliberately on the floor and said in a perfectly flat voice: "How soon can I get out of here?"

Rann laughed, a small casual chuckle. "Humans," she said, "are so damned queer. I don't think I'll ever understand them." She reached out and struck a gong that stood in a carved frame beside the couch. The soft deep shimmering note had a sad quality of nostalgia. Rann lay back against the silken cushions and sighed.

"Goodbye, Hugh Starke."

A pause. Then, regretfully:

"Goodbye—Conan!"

*****

They had made good time along the rim of the Red Sea. One of Rann's galleys had taken them to the edge of the Southern Ocean and left them on a narrow shingle beach under the cliffs. From there they had climbed to the rimrock and gone on foot—Hugh-Starke-Called-Conan and four of Rann's arrogant shining men. They were supposed to be guide and escort. They were courteous, and they kept pace uncomplainingly though Starke marched as though the devil were pricking his heels. But they were armed, and Starke was not.

Sometimes, very faintly. Starke was aware of Rann's mind touching his with the velvet delicacy of a cat's paw. Sometimes he started out of his sleep with her image sharp in his mind, her lips touched with the mocking, secret smile. He didn't like that. He didn't like it at all.

But he liked even less the picture that stayed with him waking or sleeping. The picture he wouldn't look at. The picture of a tall woman with hair like loose fire on her neck, walking on light proud feet between her guards.

She'll be given water, Rann said. Not much, but enough.

Starke gripped the solid squareness of the box that held his million credits and set the miles reeling backward from under his sandals.

On the fifth night one of Rann's men spoke quietly across the campfire. "Tomorrow," he said, "we'll reach the pass."

Starke got up and went away by himself, to the edge of the rimrock that fell sheer to the burning sea. He sat down. The red fog wrapped him like a mist of blood. He thought of the blood on Beudag's breast the first time he saw her. He thought of the blood on his knife, crusted and dried. He thought of the blood poured rank and smoking into the gutters of Crom Dhu. The fog has to be red, he thought. Of all the goddam colors in the universe, it has to be red. Red like Beudag's hair.

He held out his hands and looked at them, because he could still feel the silken warmth of that hair against his skin. There was nothing there now but the old white scars of another man's battles.

He set his fists against his temples and wished for his old body back again—the little stunted abortion that had clawed and scratched its way to survival through sheer force of mind. A most damnably tough mind, Rann had said. Yeah. It had had to be tough. But a mind was a mind. It didn't have emotions. It just figured out something coldly and then went ahead and never questioned, and it controlled the body utterly, because the body was only the worthless machinery that carried the mind around. Worthless. Yeah. The few women he'd ever looked at had told him that—and he hadn't even minded much. The old body hadn't given him any trouble.

He was having trouble now.

Starke got up and walked.

Tomorrow we reach the pass.

Tomorrow we go away from the Red Sea. There are nine planets and the whole damn Belt. There are women on all of them. All shapes, colors, and sizes, human, semi-human, and God knows what. With a million credits a guy could buy half of them, and with Conan's body he could buy the rest. What's a woman, anyway? Only a....

Water. She'll be given water. Not much, but enough.

Conan reached out and took hold of a spire of rock, and his muscles stood out like knotted ropes. "Oh God," he whispered, "what's the matter with me?"

"*Love.*"

It wasn't God who answered. It was Rann. He saw her plainly in his mind, heard her voice like a silver bell.

"Conan was a man, Hugh Starke. He was whole, body and heart and brain. He knew how to love, and with him it wasn't women, but one woman—and her name was Beudag. I broke him, but it wasn't easy. I can't break you."

Starke stood for a long, long time. He did not move, except that he trembled. Then he took from his belt the box containing his million credits and threw it out as far as he could over the cliff edge. The red mist swallowed it up. He did not hear it strike the surface of the sea. Perhaps in that sea there was no splashing. He did not wait to find out.

He turned back along the rimrock, toward a place where he remembered a cleft, or chimney, leading down. And the four shining men who wore Rann's harness came silently out of the heavy luminous night and ringed him in. Their sword-points caught sharp red glimmers from the sky.

Starke had nothing on him but a kilt and sandals, and a cloak of tight-woven spider-silk that shed the rain.

"Rann sent you?" he said.

The men nodded.

"To kill me?"

Again they nodded. The blood drained out of Starke's face, leaving it grey and stony under the bronze. His hand went to his throat, over the gold fastening of his cloak.

The four men closed in like dancers.

*****

Starke loosed his cloak and swung it like a whip across their faces. It confused them for a second, for a heartbeat—no more, but long enough. Starke left two of them to tangle their blades in the heavy fabric and leaped aside. A sharp edge slipped and turned along his ribs, and then he had reached in low and caught a man around the ankles, and used the thrashing body for a flail.

The body was strangely light, as though the bones in it were no more than rigid membrane, like a fish.

If he had stayed to fight, they would have finished him in seconds. They were fighting men, and quick. But Starke didn't stay. He gained his moment's grace and used it. They were hard on his heels, their points all but pricking his back as he ran, but he made it. Along the rimrock, out along a narrow tongue that jutted over the sea, and then outward, far outward, into red fog and dim fire that rolled around his plummeting body.

Oh God, he thought, if I guessed wrong and there *is* a beach....

The breath tore out of his lungs. His ears cracked, went dead. He held his arms out beyond his head, the thumbs locked together, his neck braced forward against the terrific upward push. He struck the surface of the sea.

There was no splash.

Dim coiling fire that drifted with infinite laziness around him, caressing his body with slow, tingling sparks. A feeling of lightness, as though his flesh had become one with the drifting fire. A sense of suffocation that had no basis in fact and gave way gradually to a strange exhilaration. There was no shock of impact, no crushing pressure. Merely a cushioning softness, like dropping into a bed of compressed air. Starke felt himself turning end over end, pinwheel fashion, and then that stopped, so that he sank quietly and without haste to the bottom.

Or rather, into the crystalline upper reaches of what seemed to be a forest.

He could see it spreading away along the downward-sloping floor of the ocean, into the vague red shadows of distance. Slender fantastic trunks upholding a maze of delicate shining branches, without leaves or fruit. They were like trees exquisitely molded from ice, transparent, holding the lambent shifting fire of the strange sea. Starke didn't think they were, or ever had been, alive. More like coral, he thought, or some vagary of mineral deposit. Beautiful, though. Like something you'd see in a dream. Beautiful, silent, and somehow deadly.

He couldn't explain that feeling of deadliness. Nothing moved in the red drifts between the trunks. It was nothing about the trees themselves. It was just something he sensed.

He began to move among the upper branches, following the downward drop of the slope.

He found that he could swim quite easily. Or perhaps it was more like flying. The dense gas buoyed him up, almost balancing the weight of his body, so that it was easy to swoop along, catching a crystal branch and using it as a lever to throw himself forward to the next one.

He went deeper and deeper into the heart of the forbidden Southern Ocean. Nothing stirred. The fairy forest stretched limitless ahead. And Starke was afraid.

Rann came into his mind abruptly. Her face, clearly outlined, was full of mockery.

"I'm going to watch you die, Hugh-Starke-Called-Conan. But before you die, I'll show you something. Look."

Her face dimmed, and in its place was Crom Dhu rising bleak into the red fog, the longships broken and sunk in the harbor, and Rann's fleet around it in a shining circle.

One ship in particular. The flagship. The vision in Starke's mind rushed toward it, narrowed down to the masthead platform. To the woman who stood there, naked, erect, her body lashed tight with thin cruel cords.

A woman with red hair blowing in the slow wind, and blue eyes that looked straight ahead like a falcon's, at Crom Dhu.

Beudag.

Rann's laughter ran across the picture and blurred it like a ripple of ice-cold water.

"You'd have done better," she said, "to take the clean steel when I offered it to you."

She was gone, and Starke's mind was as empty and cold as the mind of a corpse. He found that he was standing still, clinging to a branch, his face upturned as though by some blind instinct, his sight blurred.

He had never cried before in all his life, nor prayed.

There was no such thing as time, down there in the smoky shadows of the sea bottom. It might have been minutes or hours later that Hugh Starke discovered he was being hunted.

*****

There were three of them, slipping easily among the shining branches. They were pale golden, almost phosphorescent, about the size of large hounds. Their eyes were huge, jewel-like in their slim sharp faces. They possessed four members that might have been legs and arms, retracted now against their arrowing bodies. Golden membranes spread wing-like from head to flank, and they moved like wings, balancing expertly the thrust of the flat, powerful tails.

They could have closed in on him easily, but they didn't seem to be in any hurry. Starke had sense enough not to wear himself out trying to get away. He kept on going, watching them. He discovered that the crystal branches could be broken, and he selected himself one with a sharp forked tip, shoving it swordwise under his belt. He didn't suppose it would do much good, but it made him feel better.

He wondered why the things didn't jump him and get it over with. They looked hungry enough, the way they were showing him their teeth. But they kept about the same distance away, in a sort of crescent formation, and every so often the ones on the outside would make a tentative dart at him, then fall back as he swerved away. It wasn't like being hunted so much as....

Starke's eyes narrowed. He began suddenly to feel much more afraid than he had before, and he wouldn't have believed that possible.

The things weren't hunting him at all. They were herding him.

There was nothing he could do about it. He tried stopping, and they swooped in and snapped at him, working expertly together so that while he was trying to stab one of them with his clumsy weapon, the others were worrying his heels like sheepdogs at a recalcitrant wether.

Starke, like the wether, bowed to the inevitable and went where he was driven. The golden hounds showed their teeth in animal laughter and sniffed hungrily at the thread of blood he left behind him in the slow red coils of fire.

After a while he heard the music.

It seemed to be some sort of a harp, with a strange quality of vibration in the notes. It wasn't like anything he'd ever heard before. Perhaps the gas of which the sea was composed was an extraordinarily good conductor of sound, with a property of diffusion that made the music seem to come from everywhere at once—softly at first, like something touched upon in a dream, and then, as he drew closer to the source, swelling into a racing, rippling flood of melody that wrapped itself around his nerves with a demoniac shiver of ecstasy.

The golden hounds began to fret with excitement, spreading their shining wings, driving him impatiently faster through the crystal branches.

Starke could feel the vibration growing in him—the very fibres of his muscles shuddering in sympathy with the unearthly harp. He guessed there was a lot of the music he couldn't hear. Too high, too low for his ears to register. But he could feel it.

He began to go faster, not because of the hounds, but because he wanted to. The deep quivering in his flesh excited him. He began to breathe harder, partly because of increased exertion, and some chemical quality of the mixture he breathed made him slightly drunk.

The thrumming harp-song stroked and stung him, waking a deeper, darker music, and suddenly he saw Beudag clearly—half-veiled and mystic in the candle light at Faolan's dun; smooth curving bronze, her hair loose fire about her throat. A great stab of agony went through him. He called her name, once, and the harp-song swept it up and away, and then suddenly there was no music any more, and no forest, and nothing but cold embers in Starke's heart.

He could see everything quite clearly in the time it took him to float from the top of the last tree to the floor of the plain. He had no idea how long a time that was. It didn't matter. It was one of those moments when time doesn't have any meaning.

The rim of the forest fell away in a long curve that melted glistening into the spark-shot sea. From it the plain stretched out, a level glassy floor of black obsidian, the spew of some long-dead volcano. Or was it dead? It seemed to Starke that the light here was redder, more vital, as though he were close to the source from which it sprang.

As he looked farther over the plain, the light seemed to coalesce into a shimmering curtain that wavered like the heat veils that dance along the Mercurian Twilight Belt at high noon. For one brief instant he glimpsed a picture on the curtain—a city, black, shining, fantastically turreted, the gigantic reflection of a Titan's dream. Then it was gone, and the immediate menace of the foreground took all of Starke's attention.

*****

He saw the flock, herded by more of the golden hounds. And he saw the shepherd, with the harp held silent between his hands.

The flock moved sluggishly, phosphorescently.

One hundred, two hundred silent, limply floating warriors drifting down the red dimness. In pairs, singly, or in pallid clusters they came. The golden hounds winged silently, leisurely around them, channeling them in tides that sluiced toward the fantastic ebon city.

The shepherd stood, a crop of obsidian, turning his shark-pale face. His sharp, aquamarine eyes found Starke. His silvery hand leapt beckoning over hard-threads, striking them a blow. Reverberations ran out, seized Starke, shook him. He dropped his crystal dagger.

Hot screens of fire exploded in his eyes, bubbles whirled and danced in his eardrums. He lost all muscular control. His dark head fell forward against the thick blackness of hair on his chest; his golden eyes dissolved into weak, inane yellow, and his mouth loosened. He wanted to fight, but it was useless. This shepherd was one of the sea-people he had come to see, and one way or another he would see him.

Dark blood filled his aching eyes. He felt himself led, nudged, forced first this way, then that. A golden hound slipped by, gave him a pressure which roiled him over into a current of sea-blood. It ran down past where the shepherd stood with only a harp for a weapon.

Starke wondered dimly whether these other warriors in the flock, drifting, were dead or alive like himself. He had another surprise coming.

They were all Rann's men. Men of Falga. Silver men with burning green hair. Rann's men. One of them, a huge warrior colored like powdered salt, wandered aimlessly by on another tide, his green eyes dull. He looked dead.

What business had the sea-people with the dead warriors of Falga? Why the hounds and the shepherd's harp? Questions eddied like lifted silt in Starke's tired, hanging head. Eddied and settled flat.

Starke joined the pilgrimage.

The hounds with deft flickerings of wings, ushered him into the midst of the flock. Bodies brushed against him. *Cold* bodies. He wanted to cry out. The cords of his neck constricted. In his mind the cry went forward:

"Are you alive, men of Falga?"

No answer; but the drift of scarred, pale bodies. The eyes in them knew nothing. They had forgotten Falga. They had forgotten Rann for whom they had lifted blade. Their tongues lolling in mouths asked nothing but sleep. They were getting it.

A hundred, two hundred strong they made a strange human river slipping toward the gigantic city wall. Starke-called-Conan and his bitter enemies going together. From the corners of his eyes, Starke saw the shepherd move. The shepherd was like Rann and her people who had years ago abandoned the sea to live on land. The shepherd seemed colder, more fish-like, though. There were small translucent webs between the thin fingers and spanning the long-toed feet. Thin, scar-like gills in the shadow of his tapered chin, lifted and sealed in the current, eating, taking sustenance from the blood-colored sea.

The harp spoke and the golden hounds obeyed. The harp spoke and the bodies twisted uneasily, as in a troubled sleep. A triple chord of it came straight at Starke. His fingers clenched.

"—and the dead shall walk again—"

Another ironic ripple of music.

"—and Rann's men will rise again, this time against her—"

Starke had time to feel a brief, bewildered shivering, before the current hurled him forward. Clamoring drunkenly, witlessly, all about him, the dead, muscleless warriors of Falga, tried to crush past him, all of them at once....

Long ago some vast sea Titan had dreamed of avenues struck from black stone. Each stone the size of three men tall. There had been a dream of walls going up and up until they dissolved into scarlet mist. There had been another dream of sea-gardens in which fish hung like erotic flowers, on tendrils of sensitive film-tissue. Whole beds of fish clung to garden base, like colonies of flowers aglow with sunlight. And on occasion a black amoebic presence filtered by, playing the gardener, weeding out an amber flower here, an amythystine bloom there.

And the sea Titan had dreamed of endless balustrades and battlements, of windowless turrets where creatures swayed like radium-skinned phantoms, carrying their green plumes of hair in their lifted palms and looked down with curious, insolent eyes from on high. Women with shimmering bodies like some incredible coral harvested and kept high over these black stone streets, each in its archway.

Starke was alone. Falga's warriors had gone off along a dim subterranean vent, vanished. Now the faint beckoning of harp and the golden hounds behind him, turned him down a passage that opened out into a large circular stone room, one end of which opened out into a hall. Around the ebon ceiling, slender schools of fish swam. It was their bright effulgence that gave light to the room. They had been there, breeding, eating, dying, a thousand years, giving light to the place, and they would be there, breeding and dying, a thousand more.

The harp faded until it was only a murmur.

Starke found his feet. Strength returned to him. He was able to see the man in the center of the room well. Too well.

The man hung in the fire tide. Chains of wrought bronze held his thin fleshless ankles so he couldn't escape. His body desired it. It floated up.

It had been dead a long time. It was gaseous with decomposition and it wanted to rise to the surface of the Red Sea. The chains prevented this. Its arms weaved like white scarves before a sunken white face. Black hair trembled on end.

*****

He was one of Faolan's men. One of the Rovers. One of those who had gone down at Falga because of Conan.

His name was Geil.

Starke remembered.

The part of him that was Conan remembered the name.

The dead lips moved.

"Conan. What luck is this! Conan. I make you welcome."

The words were cruel, the lips around them loose and dead. It seemed to Starke an anger and embittered wrath lay deep in those hollow eyes. The lips twitched again.

"I went down at Falga for you and Rann, Conan. Remember?"

Part of Starke remembered and twisted in agony.

"We're all here, Conan. All of us. Clev and Mannt and Bron and Aesur. Remember Aesur, who could shape metal over his spine, prying it with his fingers? Aesur is here, big as a sea-monster, waiting in a niche, cold and loose as string. The sea-shepherds collected us. Collected us for a purpose of irony. Look!"

The boneless fingers hung out, as in a wind, pointing.

Starke turned slowly, and his heart pounded an uneven, shattering drum beat. His jaw clinched and his eyes blurred. That part of him that was Conan cried out. Conan was so much of him and he so much of Conan it was impossible for a cleavage. They'd grown together like pearl material around sand-specule, layer on layer. Starke cried out.

In the hall which this circular room overlooked, stood a thousand men.

In lines of fifty across, shoulder to shoulder, the men of Crom Dhu stared unseeingly up at Starke. Here and there a face became shockingly familiar. Old memory cried their names.

"Bron! Clev! Mannt! Aesur!"

The collected decomposition of their bodily fluids raised them, drifted them above the flaggings. Each of them was chained, like Geil.

Geil whispered. "We have made a union with the men of Falga!"

Starke pulled back.

"Falga!"

"In death, all men are equals." He took his time with it. He was in no hurry. Dead bodies under-sea are never in a hurry. They sort of bump and drift and bide their time. "The dead serve those who give them a semblance of life. Tomorrow we march against Crom Dhu."

"You're crazy! Crom Dhu is *your* home! It's the place of Beudag and Faolan—"

"And—" interrupted the hanging corpse, quietly, "Conan? Eh?" He laughed. A crystal dribble of bubbles ran up from the slack mouth. "Especially Conan. Conan who sank us at Falga...."

Starke moved swiftly. Nobody stopped him. He had the corpse's short blade in an instant. Geil's chest made a cold, silent sheathe for it. The blade went like a fork through butter.

Coldly, without noticing this, Geil's voice spoke out:

"Stab me, cut me. You can't kill me any deader. Make sections of me. Play butcher. A flank, a hand, a heart! And while you're at it, I'll tell you the plan."

Snarling, Starke seized the blade out again. With blind violence he gave sharp blow after blow at the body, cursing bitterly, and the body took each blow, rocking in the red tide a little, and said with a matter-of-fact tone:

"We'll march out of the sea to Crom Dhu's gates. Romna and the others, looking down, recognizing us, will have the gates thrown wide to welcome us." The head tilted lazily, the lips peeled wide and folded down languidly over the words. "Think of the elation, Conan! The moment when Bron and Mannt and Aesur and I and yourself, yes, even yourself, Conan, return to Crom Dhu!"

*****

Starke saw it, vividly. Saw it like a tapestry woven for him. He stood back, gasping for breath, his nostrils flaring, seeing what his blade had done to Geil's body, and seeing the great stone gates of Crom Dhu crashing open. The deliberation. The happiness, the elation to Faolan and Romna to see old friends returned. Old Rovers, long thought dead. Alive again, come to help! It made a picture!

With great deliberation, Starke struck flat across before him.

Geil's head, severed from its lazy body, began, with infinite tiredness, to float toward the ceiling. As it traveled upward, now facing, now bobbling the back of its skull toward Starke, it finished its nightmare speaking:

"And then, once inside the gates, what then, Conan? Can you guess? Can you guess what we'll do, Conan?"

Starke stared at nothingness, the sword trembling in his fist. From far away he heard Geil's voice:

"—we will kill Faolan in his hall. He will die with surprised lips. Romna's harp will lie in his disemboweled stomach. His heart with its last pulsings will sound the strings. And as for Beudag—"

Starke tried to push the thoughts away, raging and helpless. Geil's body was no longer anything to look at. He had done all he could to it. Starke's face was bleached white and scraped down to the insane bone of it, "You'd kill your own people!"

Geil's separated head lingered at the ceiling, light-fish illuminating its ghastly features. "Our people? But we have no people! We're another race now. The dead. We do the biddings of the sea-shepherds."

Starke looked out into the hall, then he looked at the circular wall.

"Okay," he said, without tone in his voice. "Come out. Where ever you're hiding and using this voice-throwing act. Come on out and talk straight."

In answer, an entire section of ebon stones fell back on silent hingework. Starke saw a long slender black marble table. Six people sat behind it in carven midnight thrones.

They were all men. Naked except for film-like garments about their loins. They looked at Starke with no particular hatred or curiosity. One of them cradled a harp. It was the shepherd who'd drawn Starke through the gate. Amusedly, his webbed fingers lay on the strings, now and then bringing out a clear sound from one of the two hundred strands.

The shepherd stopped Starke's rush forward with a cry of that harp!

The blade in his hand was red hot. He dropped it.

The shepherd put a head on the story. "And then? And then we will march Rann's dead warriors all the way to Falga. There, Rann's people, seeing the warriors, will be overjoyed, hysterical to find their friends and relatives returned. They, too, will fling wide Falga's defenses. And death will walk in, disguised as resurrection."

Starke nodded, slowly, wiping his hand across his cheek. "Back on Earth we call that psychology. *Good* psychology. But will it fool Rann?"

"Rann will be with her ships at Crom Dhu. While she's gone, the innocent population will let in their lost warriors gladly." The shepherd had amused green eyes. He looked like a youth of some seventeen years. Deceptively young. If Starke guessed right, the youth was nearer to two centuries old. That's how you lived and looked when you were under the Red Sea. Something about the emanations of it kept part of you young.

Starke lidded his yellow hawks' eyes thoughtfully. "You've got all aces. You'll win. But what's Crom Dhu to you? Why not just Rann? She's one of you, you hate her more than you do the Rovers. Her ancestors came up on land, you never got over hating them for that—"

The shepherd shrugged. "Toward Crom Dhu we have little actual hatred. Except that they are by nature land-men, even if they do rove by boat, and pillagers. One day they might try their luck on the sunken devices of this city."

Starke put a hand out. "We're fighting Rann, too. Don't forget, we're on your side!"

"Whereas we are on no one's," retorted the green-haired youth, "Except our own. Welcome to the army which will attack Crom Dhu."

"Me! By the gods, over my dead body!"

"That," said the youth, amusedly, "is what we intend. We've worked many years, you see, to perfect the plan. We're not much good out on land. We needed bodies that could do the work for us. So, every time Faolan lost a ship or Rann lost a ship, we were there, with our golden hounds, waiting. Collecting. Saving. Waiting until we had enough of each side's warriors. They'll do the fighting for us. Oh, not for long, of course. The Source energy will give them a semblance of life, a momentary electrical ability of walk and combat, but once out of water they'll last only half an hour. But that should be time enough once the gates of Crom Dhu and Falga are open."

*****

Starke said, "Rann will find some way around you. Get her first. Attack Crom Dhu the following day."

The youth deliberated. "You're stalling. But there's sense in it. Rann is most important. We'll get Falga first, then. You'll have a bit of time in which to raise false hopes."

Starke began to get sick again. The room swam.

Very quietly, very easily, Rann came into his mind again. He felt her glide in like the merest touch of a sea fern weaving in a tide pool.

He closed his mind down, but not before she snatched at a shred of thought. Her aquamarine eyes reflected desire and inquiry.

"Hugh Starke, you're with the sea people?"

Her voice was soft. He shook his head.

"Tell me, Hugh Starke. How are you plotting against Falga?"

He said nothing. He thought nothing. He shut his eyes.

Her fingernails glittered, raking at his mind. "Tell me!"

His thoughts rolled tightly into a metal sphere which nothing could dent.

Rann laughed unpleasantly and leaned forward until she filled every dark horizon of his skull with her shimmering body. "All right. I *gave* you Conan's body. Now I'll take it away."

She struck him a combined blow of her eyes, her writhing lips, her bone-sharp teeth. "Go back to your old body, go back to your old body, Hugh Starke," she hissed. "Go back! Leave Conan to his idiocy. Go back to your old body!"

Fear had him. He fell down upon his face, quivering and jerking. You could fight a man with a sword. But how could you fight this thing in your brain? He began to suck sobbing breaths through his lips. He was screaming. He could not hear himself. Her voice rushed in from the dim outer red universe, destroying him.

"Hugh Starke! Go back to your old body!"

His old body was—dead!

And she was sending him back into it.

Part of him shot endwise through red fog.

He lay on a mountain plateau overlooking the harbor of Falga.

Red fog coiled and snaked around him. Flame birds dived eerily down at his staring, blind eyes.

His old body held him.

Putrefaction stuffed his nostrils. The flesh sagged and slipped greasily on his loosened structure. He felt small again and ugly. Flame birds nibbled, picking, choosing between his ribs. Pain gorged him. Cold, blackness, nothingness filled him. Back in his old body. Forever.

He didn't want that.

The plateau, the red fog vanished. The flame birds, too.

He lay once more on the floor of the sea shepherds, struggling.

"That was just a start," Rann told him. "Next time, I'll leave you up there on the plateau in that body. *Now*, will you tell the plans of the sea people?

And go on living in Conan? He's yours, if you tell." She smirked. "You don't want to be dead."

Starke tried to reason it out. Any way he turned was the wrong way. He grunted out a breath. "If I tell, you'll still kill Beudag."

"Her life in exchange for what you know, Hugh Starke."

Her answer was too swift. It had the sound of treachery. Starke did not believe. He would die. That would solve it. Then, at least, Rann would die when the sea people carried out their strategy. That much revenge, at least, damn it.

Then he got the idea.

He coughed out a laugh, raised his weak head to look at the startled sea shepherd. His little dialogue with Rann had taken about ten seconds, actually, but it had seemed a century. The sea shepherd stepped forward.

Starke tried to get to his feet. "Got—got a proposition for you. You with the harp. Rann's inside me. *Now.* Unless you guarantee Crom Dhu and Beudag's safety, I'll tell her some things she might want to be in on!"

The sea shepherd drew a knife.

Starke shook his head, coldly. "Put it away. Even if you get me I'll give the whole damned strategy to Rann."

The shepherd dropped his hand. He was no fool.

Rann tore at Starke's brain. "Tell me! Tell me their plan!"

He felt like a guy in a revolving door. Starke got the sea men in focus. He saw that they were afraid now, doubtful and nervous. "I'll be dead in a minute," said Starke. "Promise me the safety of Crom Dhu and I'll die without telling Rann a thing."

The sea shepherd hesitated, then raised his palm upward. "I promise," he said. "Crom Dhu will go untouched."

Starke sighed. He let his head fall forward until it hit the floor. Then he rolled over, put his hands over his eyes. "It's a deal. Go give Rann hell for me, will you, boys? Give her hell!"

As he drifted into mind darkness, Rann waited for him. Feebly, he told her. "Okay, duchess. You'd kill me even if I'd told you the idea. I'm ready. Try your god-awfullest to shove me back into that stinking body of mine. I'll fight you all the way there!"

Rann screamed. It was a pretty frustrated scream. Then the pains began. She did a lot of work on his mind in the next minute.

That part of him that was Conan held on like a clam holding to its precious contents.

The odor of putrid flesh returned. The blood mist returned. The flame birds fell down at him in spirals of sparks and blistering smoke, to winnow his naked ribs.

Starke spoke one last word before the blackness took him.

"Beudag."

*****

He never expected to awaken again.

He awoke just the same.

There was red sea all around him. He lay on a kind of stone bed, and the young sea shepherd sat beside him, looking down at him, smiling delicately.

Starke did not dare move for a while. He was afraid his head might fall off and whirl away like a big fish, using its ears as propellers. "Lord," he muttered, barely turning his head.

The sea creature stirred. "You won. You fought Rann, and won."

Starke groaned. "I feel like something passed through a wild-cat's intestines. She's gone. Rann's gone." He laughed. "That makes me sad. Somebody cheer me up. Rann's gone." He felt of his big, flat-muscled body. "She was bluffing. Trying to drive me batty. She knew she couldn't really tuck me back into that carcass, but she didn't want me to know. It was like a baby's nightmare before it's born. Or maybe you haven't got a memory like me." He rolled over, stretching. "She won't ever get in my head again. I've locked the gate and swallowed the key." His eyes dilated. "What's *your* name?"

"Linnl," said the man with the harp. "You didn't tell Rann our strategy?"

"What do *you* think?"

Linnl smiled sincerely. "I think I like you, man of Crom Dhu. I think I like your hatred for Rann. I think I like the way you handled the entire matter, wanted to kill Rann and save Crom Dhu, and being so willing to die to accomplish either."

"That's a lot of thinking. Yeah, and what about that promise you made?"

"It will be kept."

Starke gave him a hand. "Linnl, you're okay. If I ever get back to Earth, so help me, I'll never bait a hook again and drop it in the sea." It was lost to Linnl. Starke forgot it, and went on, laughing. There was an edge of hysteria to it. Relief. You got booted around for days, people milled in and out of your mind like it was a bargain basement counter, pawing over the treads and convolutions, yelling and fighting; the woman you loved was starved on a ship masthead, and as a climax a lady with green eyes tried to make you a filling for an accident-mangled body. And now you had an ally.

And you couldn't believe it.

He laughed in little starts and stops, his eyes shut.

"Will you let me take care of Rann when the time comes?"

His fingers groped hungrily upward, closed on an imaginary figure of her, pressed, tightened, choked.

Linnl said, "She's yours. I'd like the pleasure, but you have as much if not more of a revenge to take. Come along. We start now. You've been asleep for one entire period."

Starke let himself down gingerly. He didn't want to break a leg off. He felt if someone touched him he might disintegrate.

He managed to let the tide handle him, do all the work. He swam carefully after Linnl down three passageways where an occasional silver inhabitant of the city slid by.

Drifting below them in a vast square hall, each gravitating but imprisoned by leg-shackles, the warriors of Falga looked up with pale cold eyes at Starke and Linnl. Occasional discharges of light-fish from interstices in the walls, passed luminous, fleeting glows over the warriors. The light-fish flirted briefly in a long shining rope that tied knots around the dead faces and as quickly untied them. Then the light-fish pulsed away and the red color of the sea took over.

Bathed in wine, thought Starke, without humor. He leaned forward.

"Men of Falga!"

Linnl plucked a series of harp-threads.

"Aye." A deep suggestion of sound issued from a thousand dead lips.

"We go to sack Rann's citadel!"

"Rann!" came the muffled thunder of voices.

At the sound of another tune, the golden hounds appeared. They touched the chains. The men of Falga, released, danced through the red sea substance.

Siphoned into a valve mouth, they were drawn out into a great volcanic courtyard. Starke went close after. He stared down into a black ravine, at the bottom of which was a blazing caldera.

This was the Source Life of the Red Sea. Here it had begun a millennium ago. Here the savage cyclones of sparks and fire energy belched up, shaking titanic black garden walls, causing currents and whirlpools that threatened to suck you forward and shoot you violently up to the surface, in cannulas of force, thrust, in capillaries of ignited mist, in chutes of color that threatened to cremate but only exhilarated you, gave you a seething rebirth!

He braced his legs and fought the suction. An unbelievable sinew of fire sprang up from out the ravine, crackling and roaring.

The men of Falga did not fight the attraction.

They moved forward in their silence and hung over the incandescence.

The vitality of the Source grew upward in them. It seemed to touch their sandaled toes first, and then by a process of shining osmosis, climb up the limbs, into the loins, into the vitals, delineating their strong bone structure as mercury delineates the glass thermometer with a rise of temperature. The bones flickered like carved polished ivory through the momentarily film-like flesh. The ribs of a thousand men expanded like silvered spider legs, clenched, then expanded again. Their spines straightened, their shoulders flattened back. Their eyes, the last to take the fire, now were ignited and glowed like candles in refurbished sepulchers. The chins snapped up, the entire outer skins of their bodies broke into silver brilliance.

Swimming through the storm of energy like nightmare figments, entering cold, they reached the far side of the ravine resembling smelted metal from blast furnaces. When they brushed into one another, purple sparks sizzled, jumped from head to head, from hand to hand.

Linnl touched Starke's arm. "You're next."

"No thank you."

"Afraid?" laughed the harp-shepherd. "You're tired. It will give you new life. You're next."

*****

Starke hesitated only a moment. Then he let the tide drift him rapidly out. He was afraid. Damned afraid. A belch of fire caught him as he arrived in the core of the ravine. He was wrapped in layers of ecstasy. Beudag pressed against him. It was her consuming hair that netted him and branded him. It was her warmth that crept up his body into his chest and into his head. Somebody yelled somewhere in animal delight and unbearable passion. Somebody danced and threw out his hands and crushed that solar warmth deeper into his huge body. Somebody felt all tiredness, oldness flumed away, a whole new feeling of warmth and strength inserted.

That somebody was Starke.

Waiting on the other side of the ravine were a thousand men of Falga. What sounded like a thousand harps began playing now, and as Starke reached the other side, the harps began marching, and the warriors marched with them. They were still dead, but you would never know it. There were no minds inside those bodies. The bodies were being activated from outside. But you would never know it.

They left the city behind. In embering ranks, the soldier-fighters were led by golden hounds and distant harps to a place where a huge intra-coastal tide swept by.

They got on the tide for a free ride. Linnl beside him, using his harp, Starke felt himself sucked down through a deep where strange monsters sprawled. They looked at Starke with hungry eyes. But the harp wall swept them back.

Starke glanced about at the men. They don't know what they're doing, he thought. Going home to kill their parents and their children, to set the flame to Falga, and they don't know it. Their alive-but-dead faces tilted up, always upward, as though visions of Rann's citadel were there.

Rann. Starke let the wrath simmer in him. He let it cool. Then it was cold. Rann hadn't bothered him now for hours. Was there a chance she'd read his thought in the midst of that fighting nightmare? Did she know this plan for Falga? Was that an explanation for her silence now?

He sent his mind ahead, subtly. *Rann. Rann.* The only answer was the move of silver bodies through the fiery deeps.

Just before dawn they broke the surface of the sea.

Falga drowsed in the red-smeared fog silence. Its slave streets were empty and dew-covered. High up, the first light was bathing Rann's gardens and setting her citadel aglow.

Linnl lay in the shallows beside Starke. They both were smiling half-cruel smiles. They had waited long for this.

Linnl nodded. "This is the day of the carnival. Fruit, wine and love will be offered the returned soldiers of Rann. In the streets there'll be dancing."

Far over to the right lay a rise of mountain. At its blunt peak—Starke stared at it intently—rested a body of a little, scrawny Earthman, with flame-birds clustered on it. He'd climb that mountain later. When it was over and there was time.

"What are you searching for?" asked Linnl.

Starke's voice was distant. "Someone I used to know."

Filing out on the stone quays, their rustling sandals eroded by time, the men stood clean and bright. Starke paced, a caged animal, at their center, so his dark body would pass unnoticed.

They were seen.

The cliff guard looked down over the dirty slave dwellings, from their arrow galleries, and set up a cry. Hands waved, pointed frosty white in the dawn. More guards loped down the ramps and galleries, meeting, joining others and coming on.

Linnl, in the sea by the quay, suggested a theme on the harp. The other harps took it up. The shuddering music lifted from the water and with a gentle firmness, set the dead feet marching down the quays, upward through the narrow, stifling alleys of the slaves, to meet the guard.

Slave people peered out at them tiredly from their choked quarters. The passing of warriors was old to them, of no significance.

These warriors carried no weapons. Starke didn't like that part of it. A length of chain even, he wanted. But this emptiness of the hands. His teeth ached from too long a time of clenching his jaws tight. The muscles of his arms were feverish and nervous.

At the edge of the slave community, at the cliff base, the guard confronted them. Running down off the galleries, swords naked, they ran to intercept what they took to be an enemy.

The guards stopped in blank confusion.

*****

A little laugh escaped Starke's lips. It was a dream. With fog over, under and in between its parts. It wasn't real to the guard, who couldn't believe it. It wasn't real to these dead men either, who were walking around. He felt alone. He was the only live one. He didn't like walking with dead men.

The captain of the guard came down warily, his green eyes suspicious. The suspicion faded. His face fell apart. He had lain on his fur pelts for months thinking of his son who had died to defend Falga.

Now his son stood before him. Alive.

The captain forgot he was captain. He forgot everything. His sandals scraped over stones. You could hear the air go out of his lungs and come back in in a numbed prayer.

"My son! In Rann's name. They said you were slain by Faolan's men one hundred darknesses ago. My son!"

A harp tinkled somewhere.

The son stepped forward, smiling.

They embraced. The son said nothing. He couldn't speak.

This was the signal for the others. The whole guard, shocked and surprised, put away their swords and sought out old friends, brothers, fathers, uncles, sons!

They moved up the galleries, the guard and the returned warriors, Starke in their midst. Threading up the cliff, through passage after passage, all talking at once. Or so it seemed. The guards did the talking. None of the dead warriors replied. They only *seemed* to. Starke heard the music strong and clear everywhere.

They reached the green gardens atop the cliff. By this time the entire city was awake. Women came running, bare-breasted and sobbing, and throwing themselves forward into the ranks of their lovers. Flowers showered over them.

"So this is war," muttered Starke, uneasily.

They stopped in the center of the great gardens. The crowd milled happily, not yet aware of the strange silence from their men. They were too happy to notice.

"Now," cried Starke to himself. "Now's the time. Now!"

As if in answer, a wild skirling of harps out of the sky.

The crowd stopped laughing only when the returned warriors of Falga swept forward, their hands lifted and groping before them....

The crying in the streets was like a far siren wailing. Metal made a harsh clangor that was sheathed in silence at the same moment metal found flesh to lie in. A vicious pantomime was concluded in the green moist gardens.

Starke watched from Rann's empty citadel. Fog plumes strolled by the archways and a thick rain fell. It came like a blood squall and washed the garden below until you could not tell rain from blood.

The returned warriors had gotten their swords by now. First they killed those nearest them in the celebration. Then they took the weapons from the victims. It was very simple and very unpleasant.

The slaves had joined battle now. Swarming up from the slave town, plucking up fallen daggers and short swords, they circled the gardens, happening upon the arrogant shining warriors of Rann who had so far escaped the quiet, deadly killing of the alive-but-dead men.

Dead father killed startled, alive son. Dead brother garroted unbelieving brother. Carnival indeed in Falga.

An old man waited alone. Starke saw him. The old man had a weapon, but refused to use it. A young warrior of Falga, harped on by Linnl's harp, walked quietly up to the old man. The old man cried out. His mouth formed words. "Son! What *is* this?" He flung down his blade and made to plead with his boy.

The son stabbed him with silent efficiency, and without a glance at the body, walked onward to find another.

Starke turned away, sick and cold.

A thousand such scenes were being finished.

He set fire to the black spider-silk tapestries. They whispered and talked with flame. The stone echoed his feet as he searched room after room. Rann had gone, probably last night. That meant that Crom Dhu was on the verge of falling. Was Faolan dead? Had the people of Crom Dhu, seeing Beudag's suffering, given in? Falga's harbor was completely devoid of ships, except for small fishing skiffs.

The fog waited him when he returned to the garden. Rain found his face.

The citadel of Rann was fire-encrusted and smoke shrouded as he looked up at it.

A silence lay in the garden. The fight was over.

The men of Falga, still shining with Source-Life, hung their blades from uncomprehending fingers, the light beginning to leave their green eyes. Their skin looked dirty and dull.

Starke wasted no time getting down the galleries, through the slave quarter, and to the quays again.

Linnl awaited him, gently petting the obedient harp.

"It's over. The slaves will own what's left. They'll be our allies, since we've freed them."

Starke didn't hear. He was squinting off over the Red Sea.

Linnl understood. He plucked two tones from the harp, which pronounced the two words uppermost in Starke's thought.

"Crom Dhu."

"If we're not too late." Starke leaned forward. "If Faolan lives. If Beudag still stands at the masthead."

Like a blind man he walked straight ahead, until he fell into the sea.

*****

It was not quite a million miles to Crom Dhu. It only seemed that far.

A sweep of tide picked them up just off shore from Falga and siphoned them rapidly, through deeps along coastal latitudes, through crystal forests. He cursed every mile of the way.

He cursed the time it took to pause at the Titan's city to gather fresh men. To gather Clev and Mannt and Aesur and Bruce. Impatiently, Starke watched the whole drama of the Source-Fire and the bodies again. This time it was the bodies of Crom Dhu men, hung like beasts on slow-turned spits, their limbs and vitals soaking through and through, their skins taking bronze color, their eyes holding flint-sparks. And then the harps wove a garment around each, and the garment moved the men instead of the men the garment.

In the tidal basilic now, Starke twisted. Coursing behind him were the new bodies of Clev and Aesur! The current elevated them, poked them through obsidian needle-eyes like spider-silk threads.

There was good irony in this. Crom Dhu's men, fallen at Falga under Conan's treachery, returned now under Conan, to exonerate that treachery.

Suddenly they were in Crom Dhu's outer basin. Shadows swept over them. The long dark falling shadows of Falga's longboats lying in that harbor. Shadows like black culling-nets let down. The school of men cleaved the shadow nets. The tide ceased here, eddied and distilled them.

Starke glared up at the immense silver bottom of a Falgian ship. He felt his face stiffen and his throat tighten. Then, flexing knees, he rammed upward, night air broke dark red around his head.

The harbor held flare torches on the rims of long ships. On the neck of land that led from Crom Dhu to the mainland the continuing battle sounded. Faint cries and clashing made their way through the fog veils. They sounded like echoes of past dreams.

Linnl let Starke have the leash. Starke felt something pressed into his fist. A coil of slender green woven reeds, a rope with hooked weights on the end of it. He knew how to use it without asking. But he wished for a knife, now, even though he realized carrying a knife in the sea was all but impossible if you wanted to move fast.

He saw the sleek naked figurehead of Rann's best ship a hundred yards away, a floating silhouette, its torches hanging fire like Beudag's hair.

He swam toward it, breathing quietly. When at last the silvered figurehead with the mocking green eyes and the flag of shoal-shallow hair hung over him, he felt the cool white ship metal kiss his fingers.

The smell of torch-smoke lingered. A rise of faint shouts from the land told of another rush upon the Gate. Behind him—a ripple. Then—a thousand ripples.

The resurrected men of Crom Dhu rose in dents and stirrings of sparkling wine. They stared at Crom Dhu and maybe they knew what it was and maybe they didn't. For one moment, Starke felt apprehension. Suppose Linnl was playing a game. Suppose, once these men had won the battle, they went on into Crom Dhu, to rupture Romna's harp and make Faolan the blinder? He shook the thought away. That would have to be handled in time. On either side of him Clev and Mannt appeared. They looked at Crom Dhu, their lips shut. Maybe they saw Faolan's eyrie and heard a harp that was more than these harps that sang them to blade and plunder—Romna's instrument telling bard-tales of the rovers and the coastal wars and the old, living days. Their eyes looked and looked at Crom Dhu, but saw nothing.

The sea shepherds appeared now; the followers of Linnl, each with his harp and the harp music began, high. So high you couldn't hear it. It wove a tension on the air.

Silently, with a grim certainty, the dead-but-not-dead gathered in a bronze circle about Rann's ship. The very silence of their encirclement made your skin crawl and sweat break cold on your cheeks.

A dozen ropes went raveling, looping over the ship side. They caught, held, grapnelled, hooked.

Starke had thrown his, felt it bite and hold. Now he scrambled swiftly, cursing, up its length, kicking and slipping at the silver hull.

He reached the top.

Beudag was there.

Half over the low rail he hesitated, just looking at her.

*****

Torchlight limned her, shadowed her. She was still erect; her head was tired and her eyes were closed, her face thinned and less brown, but she was still alive. She was coming out of a deep stupor now, at the whistle of ropes and the grate of metal hooks on the deck.

She saw Starke and her lips parted. She did not look away from him. His breath came out of him, choking.

It almost cost him his life, his standing there, looking at her.

A guard, with flesh like new snow, shafted his bow from the turret and let it loose. A chain lay on deck. Thankfully, Starke took it.

Clev came over the rail beside Starke. His chest took the arrow. The shaft burst half through and stopped, held. Clev kept going after the man who had shot it. He caught up with him.

Beudag cried out. "Behind you, Conan!"

Conan! In her excitement, she gave the old name.

Conan he *was*. Whirling, he confronted a wiry little fellow, chained him brutally across the face, seized the man's falling sword, used it on him. Then he walked in, got the man's jaw, unbalanced him over into the sea.

The ship was awake now. Most of the men had been down below, resting from the battles. Now they came pouring up, in a silver spate. Their yelling was in strange contrast to the calm silence of Crom Dhu's men. Starke found himself busy.

Conan had been a healthy animal, with great recuperative powers. Now his muscles responded to every trick asked of them. Starke leaped cleanly across the deck, watching for Rann, but she was no where to be seen. He engaged two blades, dispatched one of them. More ropes raveled high and snaked him. Every ship in the harbor was exploding with violence. More men swarmed over the rail behind Starke, silently.

Above the shouting, Beudag's voice came, at sight of the fighting men. "Clev! Mannt! Aesur!"

Starke was a god, anything he wanted he could have. A man's head? He could have it. It meant acting the guillotine with knife and wrist and lunged body. Like—*this*! His eyes were smoking amber and there were deep lines of grim pleasure tugging at his lips. An enemy cannot fight without hands. One man, facing Starke, suddenly displayed violent stumps before his face, not believing them.

Are you watching, Faolan, cried Starke inside himself, delivering blows. Look here, Faolan! God, no, you're blind. *Listen* then! Hear the ring of steel on steel. Does the smell of hot blood and hot bodies reach you? Oh, if you could see this tonight, Faolan. Falga would be forgotten. This is Conan, out of idiocy, with a guy named Starke wearing him and telling him where to go!

It was not safe on deck. Starke hadn't particularly noticed before, but the warriors of Crom Dhu didn't care whom they attacked now. They were beginning to do surgery to one another. They excised one another's shoulders, severed limbs in blind instantaneous obedience. This was no place for Beudag and himself.

He cut her free of the masthead, drew her quickly to the rail.

Beudag was laughing. She could do nothing but laugh. Her eyes were shocked. She saw dead men alive again, lashing out with weapons; she had been starved and made to stand night and day, and now she could only laugh.

Starke shook her.

She did not stop laughing.

"Beudag! You're all right. You're free."

She stared at nothing. "I'll—I'll be all right in a minute."

He had to ward off a blow from one of his own men. He parried the thrust, then got in and pushed the man off the deck, over into the sea. That was the only thing to do. You couldn't kill them.

Beudag stared down at the tumbling body.

"Where's Rann?" Starke's yellow eyes narrowed, searching.

"She *was* here." Beudag trembled.

Rann looked out of her eyes. Out of the tired numbness of Beudag, an echo of Rann. Rann was nearby, and this was her doing.

Instinctively, Starke raised his eyes.

Rann appeared at the masthead, like a flurry of snow. Her green-tipped breasts were rising and falling with emotion. Pure hatred lay in her eyes. Starke licked his lips and readied his sword.

Rann snapped a glance at Beudag. Stooping, as in a dream, Beudag picked up a dagger and held it to her own breast.

Starke froze.

Rann nodded, with satisfaction. "Well, Starke? How will it be? Will you come at me and have Beudag die? Or will you let me go free?"

Starke's palms felt sweaty and greasy. "There's no place for you to go. Falga's taken. I can't guarantee your freedom. If you want to go over the side, into the sea, that's your chance. You might make shore and your own men."

"Swimming? With the sea-*beasts* waiting?" She accented the *beasts* heavily. She was one of the sea-*people*. They, Linnl and his men, were sea-*beasts*. "No, Hugh Starke. I'll take a skiff. Put Beudag at the rail where I can watch her all the way. Guarantee my passage to shore and my own men there, and Beudag lives."

Starke waved his sword. "Get going."

He didn't want to let her go. He had other plans, good plans for her. He shouted the deal down at Linnl. Linnl nodded back, with much reluctance.

Rann, in a small silver skiff, headed toward land. She handled the boat and looked back at Beudag all the while. She passed through the sea-beasts and touched the shore. She lifted her hand and brought it smashing down.

Whirling, Starke swung his fist against Beudag's jaw. Her hand was already striking the blade into her breast. Her head flopped back. His fist carried through. She fell. The blade clattered. He kicked it overboard. Then he lifted Beudag. She was warm and good to hold. The blade had only pricked her breast. A small rivulet of blood ran.

On the shore, Rann vanished upward on the rocks, hurrying to find her men.

In the harbor the harp music paused. The ships were taken. Their crews lay filling the decks. Crom Dhu's men stopped fighting as quickly as they'd started. Some of the bright shining had dulled from the bronze of their arms and bare torsos. The ships began to sink.

Linnl swam below, looking up at Starke. Starke looked back at him and nodded at the beach. "Swell. Now, let's go get that she-devil," he said.

*****

Faolan waited on his great stone balcony, overlooking Crom Dhu. Behind him the fires blazed high and their eating sound of flame on wood filled the pillared gloom with sound and furious light.

Faolan leaned against the rim, his chest swathed in bandage and healing ointment, his blind eyes flickering, looking down again and again with a fixed intensity, his head tilted to listen.

Romna stood beside him, filled and refilled the cup that Faolan emptied into his thirsty mouth, and told him what happened. Told of the men pouring out of the sea, and Rann appearing on the rocky shore. Sometimes Faolan leaned to one side, weakly, toward Romna's words. Sometimes he twisted to hear the thing itself, the thing that happened down beyond the Gate of besieged Falga.

Romna's harp lay untouched. He didn't play it. He didn't need to. From below, a great echoing of harps, more liquid than his, like a waterfall drenched the city, making the fog sob down red tears.

"Are those harps?" cried Faolan.

"Yes, harps!"

"What was that?" Faolan listened, breathing harshly, clutching for support.

"A skirmish," said Romna.

"Who won?"

"*We* won."

"And *that*?" Faolan's blind eyes tried to see until they watered.

"The enemy falling back from the Gate!"

"And that sound, and that sound!" Faolan went on and on, feverishly, turning this way and that, the lines of his face agonized and attentive to each eddy and current and change of tide. The rhythm of swords through fog and body was a complicated music whose themes he must recognize. "Another fell! I heard him cry. And another of Rann's men!"

"Yes," said Romna.

"But why do our warriors fight so quietly? I've heard nothing from their lips. So quiet."

Romna scowled. "Quiet. Yes—quiet."

"And where did they come from? All our men are in the city?"

"Aye." Romna shifted. He hesitated, squinting. He rubbed his bulldog jaw. "Except those that died at—Falga."

Faolan stood there a moment. Then he rapped his empty cup.

"More wine, bard. More wine."

He turned to the battle again.

"Oh, gods, if I could see it, if I could only see it!"

Below, a ringing crash. A silence. A shouting, a pouring of noise.

"The Gate!" Faolan was stricken with fear. "We've lost! My sword!"

"Stay, Faolan!" Romna laughed. Then he sighed. It was a sigh that did not believe. "In the name of ten thousand mighty gods. Would that I were blind now, or could see better."

Faolan's hand caught, held him. "What *is* it? Tell!"

"Clev! And Tlan! And Conan! And Blucc! And Mannt! Standing in the gate, like wine visions! Swords in their hands!"

Faolan's hand relaxed, then tightened. "Speak their names again, and speak them slowly. And tell the truth." His skin shivered like that of a nervous animal. "You said—Clev? Mannt? Blucc?"

"And Tlan! And Conan! Back from Falga. They've opened the Gate and the battle's won. It's over, Faolan. Crom Dhu will sleep tonight."

Faolan let him go. A sob broke from his lips. "I will get drunk. Drunker than ever in my life. Gloriously drunk. Gods, but if I could have seen it. Been in it. Tell me again of it, Romna...."

*****

Faolan sat in the great hall, on his carved high-seat, waiting.

The pad of sandals on stone, outside, the jangle of chains.

A door flung wide, red fog sluiced in, and in the sluice, people walking. Faolan started up. "Clev? Mannt? Aesur!"

Starke came forward into the firelight. He pressed his right hand to the open mouth of the wound on his thigh. "No, Faolan. Myself and two others."

"Beudag?"

"Yes." And Beudag came wearily to him.

Faolan stared. "Who's the other? It walks light. It's a woman."

Starke nodded. "Rann."

Faolan rose carefully from his seat. He thought the name over. He took a short sword from a place beside the high seat. He stepped down. He walked toward Starke. "You brought Rann alive to me?"

Starke pulled the chain that bound Rann. She ran forward in little steps, her white face down, her eyes slitted with animal fury.

"Faolan's blind," said Starke. "I let you live for one damned good reason, Rann. Okay, go ahead."

Faolan stopped walking, curious. He waited.

Rann did nothing.

Starke took her hand and wrenched it behind her back. "I said 'go ahead.' Maybe you didn't hear me."

"I will," she gasped, in pain.

Starke released her. "Tell me what happens, Faolan."

Rann gazed steadily at Faolan's tall figure there in the light.

Faolan suddenly threw his hands to his eyes and choked.

Beudag cried out, seized his arm.

"I can see!" Faolan staggered, as if jolted. "I can see!" First he shouted it, then he whispered it. "*I can see.*"

Starke's eyes blurred. He whispered to Rann, tightly. "Make him see it, Rann or you die now. Make him see it!" to Faolan. "What do you see?"

Faolan was bewildered, he swayed. He put out his hands to shape the vision. "I—I see Crom Dhu. It's a good sight. I see the ships of Rann. Sinking!" He laughed a broken laugh. "I—see the fight beyond the gate!"

Silence swam in the room, over their heads.

Faolan's voice went alone, and hypnotized, into that silence.

He put out his big fists, shook them, opened them. "I see Mannt, and Aesur and Clev! Fighting as they always fought. I see Conan as he was. I see Beudag wielding steel again, on the shore! I see the enemy killed! I see men pouring out of the sea with brown skins and dark hair. Men I knew a long darkness ago. Men that roved the sea with me. *I see Rann captured!*" He began to sob with it, his lungs filling and releasing it, sucking in on it, blowing it out. Tears ran down from his vacant, blazing eyes. "I see Crom Dhu as it was and is and shall be! *I see, I see, I see!*"

Starke felt the chill on the back of his neck.

"I see Rann captured and held, and her men dead around her on the land before the Gate. I see the Gate thrown open—" Faolan halted. He looked at Starke. "Where are Clev and Mannt? Where is Blucc and Aesur?"

Starke let the fires burn on the hearths a long moment. Then he replied.

"They went back into the sea, Faolan."

Faolan's fingers fell emptily. "Yes," he said, heavily. "They had to go back, didn't they? They couldn't stay, could they? Not even for one night of food on the table, and wine in the mouth, and women in the deep warm furs before the hearth. Not even for one toast." He turned. "A drink, Romna. A drink for everyone."

Romna gave him a full cup. He dropped it, fell down to his knees, clawed at his breasts. "My heart!"

"Rann, you sea-devil!"

Starke held her instantly by the throat. He put pressure on the small raging pulses on either side of her snow-white neck. "Let him go, Rann!" More pressure. "*Let him go!*" Faolan grunted. Starke held her until her white face was dirty and strange with death.

It seemed like an hour later when he released her. She fell softly and did not move. She wouldn't move again.

Starke turned slowly to look at Faolan.

"You saw, didn't you, Faolan?" he said.

Faolan nodded blindly, weakly. He roused himself from the floor, groping. "I saw. For a moment, I saw everything. And Gods! but it made good seeing! Here, Hugh-Starke-Called-Conan, give this other side of me something to lean on."

*****

Beudag and Starke climbed the mountain above Falga the next day. Starke went ahead a little way, and with his coming the flame birds scattered, glittering away.

He dug the shallow grave and did what had to be done with the body he found there, and then when the grave was covered with thick grey stones he went back for Beudag. They stood together over it. He had never expected to stand over a part of himself, but here he was, and Beudag's hand gripped his.

He looked suddenly a million years old standing there. He thought of Earth and the Belt and Jupiter, of the joy streets in the Jekkara Low Canals of Mars. He thought of space and the ships going through it, and himself inside them. He thought of the million credits he had taken in that last job. He laughed ironically.

"Tomorrow, I'll have the sea creatures hunt for a little metal box full of credits." He nodded solemnly at the grave. "He wanted that. Or at least he thought. He killed himself getting it. So if the sea people find it, I'll send it up here to the mountain and bury it down under the rocks in his fingers. I guess that's the best place."

Beudag drew him away. They walked down the mountain toward Falga's harbor where a ship waited them. Walking, Starke lifted his face. Beudag was with him, and the sails of the ship were rising to take the wind, and the Red Sea waited for them to travel it. What lay on its far side was something for Beudag and Faolan-of-the-Ships and Romna and Hugh-Starke-Called-Conan to discover. He felt damned good about it. He walked on steadily, holding Beudag near.

And on the mountain, as the ship sailed, the flame birds soared down fitfully and frustratedly to beat at the stone mound; ceased, and mourning shrilly, flew away.

The Creatures That Time Forgot

Mad, impossible world! Sun-blasted by day, cold-wracked by night—and life condensed by radiation into eight days! Sim eyed the Ship—if he only dared reach it and escape! ... but it was more than half an hour distant—the limit of life itself!

*****

During the night, Sim was born. He lay wailing upon the cold cave stones. His blood beat through him a thousand pulses each minute. He grew, steadily.

Into his mouth his mother with feverish hands put the food. The nightmare of living was begun. Almost instantly at birth his eyes grew alert, and then, without half understanding why, filled with bright, insistent terror. He gagged upon the food, choked and wailed. He looked about, blindly.

There was a thick fog. It cleared. The outlines of the cave appeared. And a man loomed up, insane and wild and terrible. A man with a dying face. Old, withered by winds, baked like adobe in the heat. The man was crouched in a far corner of the cave, his eyes whitening to one side of his face, listening to the far wind trumpeting up above on the frozen night planet.

Sim's mother, trembling, now and again, staring at the man, fed Sim pebble-fruits, valley-grasses and ice-nipples broken from the cavern entrances, and eating, eliminating, eating again, he grew larger, larger.

The man in the corner of the cave was his father! The man's eyes were all that was alive in his face. He held a crude stone dagger in his withered hands and his jaw hung loose and senseless.

Then, with a widening focus, Sim saw the old people sitting in the tunnel beyond this living quarter. And as he watched, they began to die.

Their agonies filled the cave. They melted like waxen images, their faces collapsed inward on their sharp bones, their teeth protruded. One minute their faces were mature, fairly smooth, alive, electric. The next minute a desication and burning away of their flesh occurred.

Sim thrashed in his mother's grasp. She held him. "No, no," she soothed him, quietly, earnestly, looking to see if this, too, would cause her husband to rise again.

With a soft swift padding of naked feet, Sim's father ran across the cave. Sim's mother screamed. Sim felt himself torn loose from her grasp. He fell upon the stones, rolling, shrieking with his new, moist lungs!

The webbed face of his father jerked over him, the knife was poised. It was like one of those prenatal nightmares he'd had while still in his mother's flesh. In the next few blazing, impossible instants questions flicked through his brain. The knife was high, suspended, ready to destroy him. But the whole question of life in this cave, the dying people, the withering and the insanity, surged through Sim's new, small head. How was it that he understood? A newborn child? Can a newborn child think, see, understand, interpret? No. It was wrong! It was impossible. Yet it was happening! To him. He had been alive an hour now. And in the next instant perhaps dead!

His mother flung herself upon the back of his father, and beat down the weapon. Sim caught the terrific backwash of emotion from both their conflicting minds. "Let me kill him!" shouted the father, breathing harshly, sobbingly. "What has he to live for?"

"No, no!" insisted the mother, and her body, frail and old as it was, stretched across the huge body of the father, tearing at his weapon. "He must live! There may be a future for him! He may live longer than us, and be young!"

The father fell back against a stone crib. Lying there, staring, eyes glittering, Sim saw another figure inside that stone crib. A girl-child, quietly feeding itself, moving its delicate hands to procure food. His sister.

The mother wrenched the dagger from her husband's grasp, stood up, weeping and pushing back her cloud of stiffening gray hair. Her mouth trembled and jerked. "I'll kill you!" she said, glaring down at her husband. "Leave my children alone."

The old man spat tiredly, bitterly, and looked vacantly into the stone crib, at the little girl. "One-eighth of *her* life's over, already," he gasped. "And she doesn't know it. What's the use?"

As Sim watched, his own mother seemed to shift and take a tortured, smoke-like form. The thin bony face broke out into a maze of wrinkles. She was shaken with pain and had to sit by him, shuddering and cuddling the knife to her shriveled breasts. She, like the old people in the tunnel, was aging, dying.

Sim cried steadily. Everywhere he looked was horror. A mind came to meet his own. Instinctively he glanced toward the stone crib. Dark, his sister, returned his glance. Their minds brushed like straying fingers. He relaxed somewhat. He began to learn.

The father sighed, shut his lids down over his green eyes. "Feed the child," he said, exhaustedly. "Hurry. It is almost dawn and it is our last day of living, woman. Feed him. Make him grow."

Sim quieted, and images, out of the terror, floated to him.

This was a planet next to the sun. The nights burned with cold, the days were like torches of fire. It was a violent, impossible world. The people lived in the cliffs to escape the incredible ice and the day of flame. Only at dawn and sunset was the air breath-sweet, flower-strong, and then the cave peoples brought their children out into a stony, barren valley. At dawn the ice thawed into creeks and rivers, at sunset the day-fires died and cooled. In the intervals of even, livable temperature the people lived, ran, played, loved, free of the caverns; all life on the planet jumped, burst into life. Plants grew instantly, birds were flung like pellets across the sky. Smaller, legged animal life rushed frantically through the rocks; everything tried to get its living down in the brief hour of respite.

It was an unbearable planet. Sim understood this, a matter of hours after birth. Racial memory bloomed in him. He would live his entire life in the caves, with two hours a day outside. Here, in stone channels of air he would talk, talk incessantly with his people, sleep never, think, think and lie upon his back, dreaming; but never sleeping.

And he would live exactly eight days.

*****

The violence of this thought evacuated his bowels. Eight days. Eight *short* days. It was wrong, impossible, but a fact. Even while in his mother's flesh some racial knowledge had told him he was being formed rapidly, shaped and propelled out swiftly.

Birth was quick as a knife. Childhood was over in a flash. Adolescence was a sheet of lightning.

Manhood was a dream, maturity a myth, old age an inescapably quick reality, death a swift certainty.

Eight days from now he'd stand half-blind, withering, dying, as his father now stood, staring uselessly at his own wife and child.

This day was an eighth part of his total life! He must enjoy every second of it. He must search his parents' thoughts for knowledge.

Because in a few hours they'd be dead.

This was so impossibly unfair. Was this all of life? In his prenatal state hadn't he dreamed of *long* lives, valleys not of blasted stone but green foliage and temperate clime? Yes! And if he'd dreamed then there must be truth in the visions. How could he seek and find the long life? Where? And how could he accomplish a life mission that huge and depressing in eight short, vanishing days?

How had his people gotten into such a condition?

As if at a button pressed, he saw an image. Metal seeds, blown across space from a distant green world, fighting with long flames, crashing on this bleak planet. From their shattered hulls tumble men and women.

When? Long ago. Ten thousand days. The crash victims hid in the cliffs from the sun. Fire, ice and floods washed away the wreckage of the huge metal seeds. The victims were shaped and beaten like iron upon a forge. Solar radiations drenched them. Their pulses quickened, two hundred, five hundred, a thousand beats a minute. Their skins thickened, their blood changed. Old age came rushing. Children were born in the caves. Swifter, swifter, swifter the process. Like all this world's wild life, the men and women from the crash lived and died in a week, leaving children to do likewise.

So this is life, thought Sim. It was not spoken in his mind, for he knew no words, he knew only images, old memory, an awareness, a telepathy that could penetrate flesh, rock, metal. So I'm the five thousandth in a long line of futile sons? What can I do to save myself from dying eight days from now? Is there escape?

His eyes widened, another image came to focus.

Beyond this valley of cliffs, on a low mountain lay a perfect, unscarred metal seed. A metal ship, not rusted or touched by the avalanches. The ship was deserted, whole, intact. It was the only ship of all these that had crashed that was still a unit, still usable. But it was so far away. There was no one in it to help. This ship, then, on the far mountain, was the destiny toward which he would grow. There was his only hope of escape.

His mind flexed.

In this cliff, deep down in a confinement of solitude, worked a handful of scientists. To these men, when he was old enough and wise enough, he must go. They, too, dreamed of escape, of long life, of green valleys and temperate weathers. They, too, stared longingly at that distant ship upon its high mountain, its metal so perfect it did not rust or age.

The cliff groaned.

Sim's father lifted his eroded, lifeless face.

"Dawn's coming," he said.

*****

II

Morning relaxed the mighty granite cliff muscles. It was the time of the Avalanche.

The tunnels echoed to running bare feet. Adults, children pushed with eager, hungry eyes toward the outside dawn. From far out, Sim heard a rumble of rock, a scream, a silence. Avalanches fell into valley. Stones that had been biding their time, not quite ready to fall, for a million years let go their bulks, and where they had begun their journey as single boulders they smashed upon the valley floor in a thousand shrapnels and friction-heated nuggets.

Every morning at least one person was caught in the downpour.

The cliff people dared the avalanches. It added one more excitement to their lives, already too short, too headlong, too dangerous.

Sim felt himself seized up by his father. He was carried brusquely down the tunnel for a thousand yards, to where the daylight appeared. There was a shining insane light in his father's eyes. Sim could not move. He sensed what was going to happen. Behind his father, his mother hurried, bringing with her the little sister, Dark. "Wait! Be careful!" she cried to her husband.

Sim felt his father crouch, listening.

High in the cliff was a tremor, a shivering.

"Now!" bellowed his father, and leaped out.

An avalanche fell down at them!

Sim had accelerated impressions of plunging walls, dust, confusion. His mother screamed! There was a jolting, a plunging.

With one last step, Sim's father hurried him forward into the day. The avalanche thundered behind him. The mouth of the cave, where mother and Dark stood back out of the way, was choked with rubble and two boulders that weighed a hundred pounds each.

The storm thunder of the avalanche passed away to a trickle of sand. Sim's father burst out into laughter. "Made it! By the Gods! Made it alive!" And he looked scornfully at the cliff and spat. "Pagh!"

Mother and sister Dark struggled through the rubble. She cursed her husband. "Fool! You might have killed Sim!"

"I may yet," retorted the father.

Sim was not listening. He was fascinated with the remains of an avalanche afront of the next tunnel. A blood stain trickled out from under a rise of boulders, soaking into the ground. There was nothing else to be seen. Someone else had lost the game.

Dark ran ahead on lithe, supple feet, naked and certain.

The valley air was like a wine filtered between mountains. The heaven was a restive blue; not the pale scorched atmosphere of full day, nor the bloated, bruised black-purple of night, a-riot with sickly shining stars.

This was a tide pool. A place where waves of varying and violent temperatures struck, receded. Now the tide pool was quiet, cool, and its life moved abroad.

Laughter! Far away, Sim heard it. Why laughter? How could any of his people find time for laughing? Perhaps later he would discover why.

The valley suddenly blushed with impulsive color. Plant-life, thawing in the precipitant dawn, shoved out from most unexpected sources. It flowered as you watched. Pale green tendrils appeared on scoured rocks. Seconds later, ripe globes of fruit twitched upon the blade-tips. Father gave Sim over to mother and harvested the momentary, volatile crop, thrust scarlet, blue, yellow fruits into a fur sack which hung at his waist. Mother tugged at the moist new grasses, laid them on Sim's tongue.

His senses were being honed to a fine edge. He stored knowledge thirstily. He understood love, marriage, customs, anger, pity, rage, selfishness, shadings and subtleties, realities and reflections. One thing suggested another. The sight of green plant life whirled his mind like a gyroscope, seeking balance in a world where lack of time for explanations made a mind seek and interpret on its own. The soft burden of food gave him knowledge of his system, of energy, of movement. Like a bird newly cracking its way from a shell, he was almost a unit, complete, all-knowing. Heredity had done all this for him. He grew excited with his ability.

*****

They walked, mother, father and the two children, smelling the smells, watching the birds bounce from wall to wall of the valley like scurrying pebbles and suddenly the father said a strange thing:

"Remember?"

Remember what? Sim lay cradled. Was it any effort for them to remember when they'd lived only seven days!

The husband and wife looked at each other.

"Was it only three days ago?" said the woman, her body shaking, her eyes closing to think. "I can't believe it. It is so unfair." She sobbed, then drew her hand across her face and bit her parched lips. The wind played at her gray hair. "Now is my turn to cry. An hour ago it was you!"

"An hour is half a life."

"Come," she took her husband's arm. "Let us look at everything, because it will be our last looking."

"The sun'll be up in a few minutes," said the old man. "We must turn back now."

"Just one more moment," pleaded the woman.

"The sun will catch us."

"Let it catch me then!"

"You don't mean that."

"I mean nothing, nothing at all," cried the woman.

The sun was coming fast. The green in the valley burnt away. Searing wind blasted from over the cliffs. Far away where sun bolts hammered battlements of cliff, the huge stone faces shook their contents; those avalanches not already powdered down, were now released and fell like mantles.

"Dark!" shouted the father. The girl sprang over the warm floor of the valley, answering, her hair a black flag behind her. Hands full of green fruits, she joined them.

The sun rimmed the horizon with flame, the air convulsed dangerously with it, and whistled.

The cave people bolted, shouting, picking up their fallen children, bearing vast loads of fruit and grass with them back to their deep hideouts. In moments the valley was bare. Except for one small child someone had forgotten. He was running far out on the flatness, but he was not strong enough, and the engulfing heat was drifting down from the cliffs even as he was half across the valley.

Flowers were burnt into effigies, grasses sucked back into rocks like singed snakes, flower seeds whirled and fell in the sudden furnace blast of wind, sown far into gullies and crannies, ready to blossom at sunset tonight, and then go to seed and die again.

Sim's father watched that child running, alone, out on the floor of the valley. He and his wife and Dark and Sim were safe in the mouth of their tunnel.

"He'll never make it," said father. "Do not watch him, woman. It's not a good thing to watch."

They turned away. All except Sim, whose eyes had caught a glint of metal far away. His heart hammered in him, and his eyes blurred. Far away, atop a low mountain, one of those metal seeds from space reflected a dazzling ripple of light! It was like one of his intra-embryo dreams fulfilled! A metal space seed, intact, undamaged, lying on a mountain! There was his future! There was his hope for survival! There was where he would go in a few days, when he was—strange thought—a grown man!

The sun plunged into the valley like molten lava.

The little running child screamed, the sun burned, and the screaming stopped.

Sim's mother walked painfully, with sudden age, down the tunnel, paused, reached up, broke off two last icicles that had formed during the night. She handed one to her husband, kept the other. "We will drink one last toast. To you, to the children."

"To *you*," he nodded to her. "To the children." They lifted the icicles. The warmth melted the ice down into their thirsty mouths.

*****

All day the sun seemed to blaze and erupt into the valley. Sim could not see it, but the vivid pictorials in his parents' minds were sufficient evidence of the nature of the day fire. The light ran like mercury, sizzling and roasting the caves, poking inward, but never penetrating deeply enough. It lighted the caves. It made the hollows of the cliff comfortably warm.

Sim fought to keep his parents young. But no matter how hard he fought with mind and image, they became like mummies before him. His father seemed to dissolve from one stage of oldness to another. This is what will happen to me soon, though Sim in terror.

Sim grew upon himself. He felt the digestive-eliminatory movements of his body. He was fed every minute, he was continually swallowing, feeding. He began to fit words to images and processes. Such a word was love. It was not an abstraction, but a process, a stir of breath, a smell of morning air, a flutter of heart, the curve of arm holding him, the look in the suspended face of his mother. He saw the processes, then searched behind her suspended face and there was the word, in her brain, ready to use. His throat prepared to speak. Life was pushing him, rushing him along toward oblivion.

He sensed the expansion of his fingernails, the adjustments of his cells, the profusion of his hair, the multiplication of his bones and sinew, the grooving of the soft pale wax of his brain. His brain at birth as clear as a circle of ice, innocent, unmarked, was, an instant later, as if hit with a thrown rock, cracked and marked and patterned in a million crevices of thought and discovery.

His sister, Dark, ran in and out with other little hothouse children, forever eating. His mother trembled over him, not eating, she had no appetite, her eyes were webbed shut.

"Sunset," said his father, at last.

The day was over. The light faded, a wind sounded.

His mother arose. "I want to see the outside world once more ... just once more...." She stared blindly, shivering.

His father's eyes were shut, he lay against the wall.

"I cannot rise," he whispered faintly. "I cannot."

"Dark!" The mother croaked, the girl came running. "Here," and Sim was handed to the girl. "Hold to Sim, Dark, feed him, care for him." She gave Sim one last fondling touch.

Dark said not a word, holding Sim, her great green eyes shining wetly.

"Go now," said the mother. "Take him out into the sunset time. Enjoy yourselves. Pick foods, eat. Play."

Dark walked away without looking back. Sim twisted in her grasp, looking over her shoulder with unbelieving, tragic eyes. He cried out and somehow summoned from his lips the first word of his existence.

"Why...?"

He saw his mother stiffen. "The child spoke!"

"Aye," said his father. "Did you hear what he said?"

"I heard," said the mother quietly.

The last thing Sim saw of his living parents was his mother weakly, swayingly, slowly moving across the floor to lie beside her silent husband. That was the last time he ever saw them move.

*****

IV

The night came and passed and then started the second day.

The bodies of all those who had died during the night were carried in a funeral procession to the top of a small hill. The procession was long, the bodies numerous.

Dark walked in the procession, holding the newly walking Sim by one hand. Only an hour before dawn Sim had learned to walk.

At the top of the hill, Sim saw once again the far off metal seed. Nobody ever looked at it, or spoke of it. Why? Was there some reason? Was it a mirage? Why did they not run toward it? Worship it? Try to get to it and fly away into space?

The funeral words were spoken. The bodies were placed upon the ground where the sun, in a few minutes, would cremate them.

The procession then turned and ran down the hill, eager to have their few minutes of free time running and playing and laughing in the sweet air.

Dark and Sim, chattering like birds, feeding among the rocks, exchanged what they knew of life. He was in his second day, she in her third. They were driven, as always, by the mercurial speed of their lives.

Another piece of his life opened wide.

Fifty young men ran down from the cliffs, holding sharp stones and rock daggers in their thick hands.

Shouting, they ran off toward distant black, low lines of small rock cliffs.

"War!"

The thought stood in Sim's brain. It shocked and beat at him. These men were running to fight, to kill, over there in those small black cliffs where other people lived.

But why? Wasn't life short enough without fighting, killing?

From a great distance he heard the sound of conflict, and it made his stomach cold. "Why, Dark, why?"

Dark didn't know. Perhaps they would understand tomorrow. Now, there was the business of eating to sustain and support their lives. Watching Dark was like seeing a lizard forever flickering its pink tongue, forever hungry.

Pale children ran on all sides of them. One beetle-like boy scuttled up the rocks, knocking Sim aside, to take from him a particularly luscious red berry he had found growing under an outcrop.

The child ate hastily of the fruit before Sim could gain his feet. Then Sim hurled himself unsteadily, the two of them fell in a ridiculous jumble, rolling, until Dark pried them, squalling, apart.

Sim bled. A part of him stood off, like a god, and said, "This should not be. Children should not be this way. It is wrong!"

Dark slapped the little intruding boy away. "Get on!" she cried. "What's your name, bad one?"

"Chion!" laughed the boy. "Chion, Chion, Chion!"

Sim glared at him with all the ferocity in his small, unskilled features. He choked. This was his enemy. It was as if he'd waited for an enemy of person as well as scene. He had already understood the avalanches, the heat, the cold, the shortness of life, but these were things of places, of scene—mute, extravagant manifestations of unthinking nature, not motivated save by gravity and radiation. Here, now, in this stridulent Chion he recognized a thinking enemy!

Chion darted off, turned at a distance, tauntingly crying:

"Tomorrow I will be big enough to kill you!"

And he vanished around a rock.

More children ran, giggling, by Sim. Which of them would be friends, enemies? How could friends and enemies come about in this impossible, quick life time? There was no time to make either, was there?

Dark, as if knowing his thoughts, drew him away. As they searched for desired foods, she whispered fiercely in his ear. "Enemies are made over things like stolen foods; gifts of long grasses make friends. Enemies come, too, from opinions and thoughts. In five seconds you've made an enemy for life. Life's so short enemies must be made quickly." And she laughed with an irony strange for one so young, who was growing older before her rightful time. "You must fight to protect yourself. Others, superstitious ones, will try killing you. There is a belief, a ridiculous belief, that if one kills another, the murderer partakes of the life energy of the slain, and therefore will live an extra day. You see? As long as that is believed, you're in danger."

But Sim was not listening. Bursting from a flock of delicate girls who tomorrow would be tall, quieter, and who day after that would gain breasts and the next day take husbands, Sim caught sight of one small girl whose hair was a violet blue flame.

She ran past, brushed Sim, their bodies touched. Her eyes, white as silver coins, shone at him. He knew then that he'd found a friend, a love, a wife, one who'd a week from now lie with him atop the funeral pyre as sunlight undressed their flesh from bone.

Only the glance, but it held them in mid-motion, one instant.

"Your name?" he shouted after her.

"Lyte!" she called laughingly back.

"I'm Sim," he answered, confused and bewildered.

"Sim!" she repeated it, flashing on. "I'll remember!"

Dark nudged his ribs. "Here, *eat*," she said to the distracted boy. "Eat or you'll never get big enough to catch her."

From nowhere, Chion appeared, running by. "Lyte!" he mocked, dancing malevolently along and away. "Lyte! I'll remember Lyte, too!"

Dark stood tall and reed slender, shaking her dark ebony clouds of hair, sadly. "I see your life before you, little Sim. You'll need weapons soon to fight for this Lyte one. Now, hurry—the sun's coming!"

They ran back to the caves.

*****

One-fourth of his life was over! Babyhood was gone. He was now a young boy! Wild rains lashed the valley at nightfall. He watched new river channels cut in the valley, out past the mountain of the metal seed. He stored the knowledge for later use. Each night there was a new river, a bed newly cut.

"What's beyond the valley?" wondered Sim.

"No one's ever been beyond it," explained Dark. "All who tried to reach the plain were frozen to death or burnt. The only land we know's within half an hour's run. Half an hour out and half an hour back."

"No one has ever reached the metal seed, then?"

Dark scoffed. "The Scientists, they try. Silly fools. They don't know enough to stop. It's no use. It's too far."

The Scientists. The word stirred him. He had almost forgotten the vision he had short hours after birth. His voice was eager. "Where are the Scientists?" he demanded.

Dark looked away from him, "I wouldn't tell you if I knew. They'd kill you, experimenting! I don't want you joining them! Live your life, don't cut it in half trying to reach that silly metal thing on the mountain."

"I'll find out where they are from someone else, then!"

"No one'll tell you! They hate the Scientists. You'll have to find them on your own. And then what? Will you save us? Yes, save us, little boy!" Her face was sullen; already half her life was gone, her breasts were beginning to shape. Tomorrow she must divine how best to live her youth, her love, and she knew no way to fully plumb the depths of passion in so short a space.

"We can't sit and talk and eat," he protested. "And *nothing* else."

"There's always love," she retorted acidly. "It helps one forget. Gods, yes," she spat it out. "Love!"

*****

Sim ran through the tunnels, seeking. Sometimes he half imagined where the Scientists were. But then a flood of angry thought from those around him, when he asked the direction to the Scientists' cave, washed over him in confusion and resentment. After all, it was the Scientists' fault that they had been placed upon this terrible world! Sim flinched under the bombardment of oaths and curses.

Quietly he took his seat in a central chamber with the children to listen to the grown men talk. This was the time of education, the Time of Talking. No matter how he chafed at delay, or how great his impatience, even though life slipped fast from him and death approached like a black meteor, he knew his mind needed knowledge. Tonight, then, was the night of school. But he sat uneasily. Only *five* more days of life.

Chion sat across from Sim, his thin-mouthed face arrogant.

Lyte appeared between the two. The last few hours had made her firmer footed, gentler, taller. Her hair shone brighter. She smiled as she sat beside Sim, ignoring Chion. And Chion became rigid at this and ceased eating.

The dialogue crackled, filled the room. Swift as heart beats, one thousand, two thousand words a minute. Sim learned, his head filled. He did not shut his eyes, but lapsed into a kind of dreaming that was almost intra-embryonic in lassitude and drowsy vividness.

In the faint background the words were spoken, and they wove a tapestry of knowledge in his head.

*****

He dreamed of green meadows free of stones, all grass, round and rolling and rushing easily toward a dawn with no taint of freezing, merciless cold or smell of boiled rock or scorched monument. He walked across the green meadow. Overhead the metal seeds flew by in a heaven that was a steady, even temperature. Things were slow, slow, slow.

Birds lingered upon gigantic trees that took a hundred, two hundred, five thousand days to grow. Everything remained in its place, the birds did not flicker nervously at a hint of sun, nor did the trees suck back frightenedly when a ray of sunlight poured over them.

In this dream people strolled, they rarely ran, the heart rhythm of them was evenly languid, not jerking and insane. Their kisses were long and lingering, not the parched mouthings and twitchings of lovers who had eight days to live. The grass remained, and did not burn away in torches. The dream people talked always of tomorrow and living and not tomorrow and dying. It all seemed so familiar that when Sim felt someone take his hand he thought it simply another part of the dream.

Lyte's hand lay inside his own. "Dreaming?" she asked.

"Yes."

"Things are balanced. Our minds, to even things, to balance the unfairness of our living, go back in on ourselves, to find what there is that is good to see."

He beat his hand against the stone floor again and again. "It does not make things fair! I hate it! It reminds me that there is something better, something I have missed! Why can't we be ignorant! Why can't we live and die without knowing that this is an abnormal living?" And his breath rushed harshly from his half-open, constricted mouth.

"There is purpose in everything," said Lyte. "This gives us purpose, makes us work, plan, try to find a way."

His eyes were hot emeralds in his face. "I walked up a hill of grass, very slowly," he said.

"The same hill of grass I walked an hour ago?" asked Lyte.

"Perhaps. Close enough to it. The dream is better than the reality." He flexed his eyes, narrowed them. "I watched people and they did not eat."

"Or talk?"

"Or talk, either. And we always are eating, always talking. Sometimes those people in the dream sprawled with their eyes shut, not moving a muscle."

As Lyte stared down into his face a terrible thing happened. He imagined her face blackening, wrinkling, twisting into knots of agedness. The hair blew out like snow about her ears, the eyes were like discolored coins caught in a web of lashes. Her teeth sank away from her lips, the delicate fingers hung like charred twigs from her atrophied wrists. Her beauty was consumed and wasted even as he watched, and when he seized her, in terror, he cried out, for he imagined his own hand corroded, and he choked back a cry.

"Sim, what's wrong?"

The saliva in his mouth dried at the taste of the words.

"Five more days...."

"The Scientists."

Sim started. Who'd spoken? In the dim light a tall man talked. "The Scientists crashed us on this world, and now have wasted thousands of lives and time. It's no use. It's no use. Tolerate them but give them none of your time. You only live once, remember."

Where were these hated Scientists? Now, after the Learning, the Time of Talking, he was ready to find them. Now, at least, he knew enough to begin his fight for freedom, for the ship!

"Sim, where're you going?"

But Sim was gone. The echo of his running feet died away down a shaft of polished stone.

*****

It seemed that half the night was wasted. He blundered into a dozen dead ends. Many times he was attacked by the insane young men who wanted his life energy. Their superstitious ravings echoed after him. The gashes of their hungry fingernails covered his body.

He found what he looked for.

A half dozen men gathered in a small basalt cave deep down in the cliff lode. On a table before them lay objects which, though unfamiliar, struck harmonious chords in Sim.

The Scientists worked in sets, old men doing important work, young men learning, asking questions; and at their feet were three small children. They were a process. Every eight days there was an entirely new set of scientists working on any one problem. The amount of work done was terribly inadequate. They grew old, fell dead just when they were beginning their creative period. The creative time of any one individual was perhaps a matter of twelve hours out of his entire span. Three-quarters of one's life was spent learning, a brief interval of creative power, then senility, insanity, death.

The men turned as Sim entered.

"Don't tell me we have a recruit?" said the eldest of them.

"I don't believe it," said another, younger one. "Chase him away. He's probably one of those war-mongers."

"No, no," objected the elder one, moving with little shuffles of his bare feet toward Sim. "Come in, come in, boy." He had friendly eyes, slow eyes, unlike those of the swift inhabitants of the upper caves. Grey and quiet. "What do you want?"

Sim hesitated, lowered his head, unable to meet the quiet, gentle gaze. "I want to live," he whispered.

The old man laughed quietly. He touched Sim's shoulder. "Are you a new breed? Are you sick?" he queried of Sim, half-seriously. "Why aren't you playing? Why aren't you readying yourself for the time of love and marriage and children? Don't you know that tomorrow night you'll be an adolescent? Don't you realize that if you are not careful you'll miss all of life?" He stopped.

Sim moved his eyes back and forth with each query. He blinked at the instruments on the table top. "Shouldn't I be here?" he asked, naively.

"Certainly," roared the old man, sternly. "But it's a miracle you are. We've had no volunteers from the rank and file for a thousand days! We've had to breed our own scientists, a closed unit! Count us! Six! Six men! And three children! Are we not overwhelming?" The old man spat upon the stone floor. "We ask for volunteers and the people shout back at us, 'Get someone else!' or 'We have no time!' And you know why they say that?"

"No." Sim flinched.

"Because they're selfish. They'd like to live longer, yes, but they know that anything they do cannot possibly insure their *own* lives any extra time. It might guarantee longer life to some future offspring of theirs. But they won't give up their love, their brief youth, give up one interval of sunset or sunrise!"

Sim leaned against the table, earnestly. "I understand."

"You do?" The old man stared at him blindly. He sighed and slapped the child's thigh, gently. "Yes, of course, you do. It's too much to expect anyone to understand, any more. You're rare."

The others moved in around Sim and the old man.

"I am Dienc. Tomorrow night Cort here will be in my place. I'll be dead by then. And the night after that someone else will be in Cort's place, and then you, if you work and believe—but first, I give you a chance. Return to your playmates if you want. There is someone you love? Return to her. Life is short. Why should you care for the unborn to come? You have a right to youth. Go now, if you want. Because if you stay you'll have no time for anything but working and growing old and dying at your work. But it is good work. Well?"

Sim looked at the tunnel. From a distance the wind roared and blew, the smells of cooking and the patter of naked feet sounded, and the laughter of lovers was an increasingly good thing to hear. He shook his head, impatiently, and his eyes were wet.

"I will stay," he said.

*****

VI

The third night and third day passed. It was the fourth night. Sim was drawn into their living. He learned about that metal seed upon the top of the far mountain. He heard of the original seeds—things called "ships" that crashed and how the survivors hid and dug in the cliffs, grew old swiftly and in their scrabbling to barely survive, forgot all science. Knowledge of mechanical things had no chance of survival in such a volcanic civilization. There was only NOW for each human.

Yesterday didn't matter, tomorrow stared them vividly in their very faces. But somehow the radiations that had forced their aging had also induced a kind of telepathic communication whereby philosophies and impressions were absorbed by the new born. Racial memory, growing instinctively, preserved memories of another time.

"Why don't we go to that ship on the mountain?" asked Sim.

"It is too far. We would need protection from the sun," explained Dienc.

"Have you tried to make protection?"

"Salves and ointments, suits of stone and bird-wing and, recently, crude metals. None of which worked. In ten thousand more life times perhaps we'll have made a metal in which will flow cool water to protect us on the march to the ship. But we work so slowly, so blindly. This morning, mature, I took up my instruments. Tomorrow, dying, I lay them down. What can one man do in one day? If we had ten thousand men, the problem would be solved...."

"I will go to the ship," said Sim.

"Then you will die," said the old man. A silence had fallen on the room at Sim's words. Then the men stared at Sim. "You are a very selfish boy."

"Selfish!" cried Sim, resentfully.

The old man patted the air. "Selfish in a way I like. You want to live longer, you'll do anything for that. You will try for the ship. But I tell you it is useless. Yet, if you want to, I cannot stop you. At least you will not be like those among us who go to war for an extra few days of life."

"War?" asked Sim. "How can there be war here?"

And a shudder ran through him. He did not understand.

"Tomorrow will be time enough for that," said Dienc. "Listen to me, now."

The night passed.

*****

VII

It was morning. Lyte came shouting and sobbing down a corridor, and ran full into his arms. She had changed again. She was older, again, more beautiful. She was shaking and she held to him. "Sim, they're coming after you!"

Bare feet marched down the corridor, surged inward at the opening. Chion stood grinning there, taller, too, a sharp rock in either of his hands. "Oh, there you are, Sim!"

"Go away!" cried Lyte savagely whirling on him.

"Not until we take Sim with us," Chion assured her. Then, smiling at Sim. "*If* that is, he is with us in the fight."

Dienc shuffled forward, his eye weakly fluttering, his bird-like hands fumbling in the air. "Leave!" he shrilled angrily. "This boy is a Scientist now. He works with us."

Chion ceased smiling. "There is better work to be done. We go now to fight the people in the farthest cliffs." His eyes glittered anxiously. "Of course, you will come with us, Sim?"

"No, no!" Lyte clutched at his arm.

Sim patted her shoulder, then turned to Chion. "Why are you attacking these people?"

"There are three extra days for those who go with us to fight."

"Three extra days! Of living?"

Chion nodded firmly. "If we win, we live eleven days instead of eight. The cliffs they live in, something about the mineral in it! Think of it, Sim, three long, good days of life. Will you join us?"

Dienc interrupted. "Get along without him. Sim is my pupil!"

Chion snorted. "Go die, old man. By sunset tonight you'll be charred bone. Who are you to order us? We are young, we want to live longer."

Eleven days. The words were unbelievable to Sim. Eleven days. Now he understood why there was war. Who wouldn't fight to have his life lengthened by almost half its total. So many more days of youth and love and seeing and living! Yes. Why not, indeed!

"Three extra days," called Dienc, stridently, "*if* you live to enjoy them. If you're not killed in battle. *If. If!* You have never won yet. You have always lost!"

"But this time," Chion declared sharply, "We'll win!"

Sim was bewildered. "But we are all of the same ancestors. Why don't we all share the best cliffs?"

Chion laughed and adjusted a sharp stone in his hand. "Those who live in the best cliffs think they are better than us. That is always man's attitude when he has power. The cliffs there, besides, are smaller, there's room for only three hundred people in them."

Three extra days.

"I'll go with you," Sim said to Chion.

"Fine!" Chion was very glad, much too glad at the decision.

Dienc gasped.

Sim turned to Dienc and Lyte. "If I fight, and win, I will be half a mile closer to the Ship. And I'll have three extra days in which to strive to reach the Ship. That seems the only thing for me to do."

Dienc nodded, sadly. "It *is* the only thing. I believe you. Go along now."

"Good-bye," said Sim.

The old man looked surprised, then he laughed as at a little joke on himself. "That's right—I won't see you again, will I? Good-bye, then." And they shook hands.

They went out, Chion, Sim, and Lyte, together, followed by the others, all children growing swiftly into fighting men. And the light in Chion's eyes was not a good thing to see.

*****

Lyte went with him. She chose his rocks for him and carried them. She would not go back, no matter how he pleaded. The sun was just beyond the horizon and they marched across the valley.

"Please, Lyte, go back!"

"And wait for Chion to return?" she said. "He plans that when you die I will be his mate." She shook out her unbelievable blue-white curls of hair defiantly. "But I'll be with you. If you fall, I fall."

Sim's face hardened. He was tall. The world had shrunk during the night. Children packs screamed by hilarious in their food-searching and he looked at them with alien wonder: could it be only four days ago he'd been like these? Strange. There was a sense of many days in his mind, as if he'd really lived a thousand days. There was a dimension of incident and thought so thick, so multi-colored, so richly diverse in his head that it was not to be believed so much could happen in so short a time.

The fighting men ran in clusters of two or three. Sim looked ahead at the rising line of small ebon cliffs. This, then, he said to himself, is my fourth day. And still I am no closer to the Ship, or to anything, not even—he heard the light tread of Lyte beside him—not even to her who bears my weapons and picks me ripe berries.

One-half of his life was gone. Or a third of it—IF he won this battle. *If.*

He ran easily, lifting, letting fall his legs. This is the day of my physical awareness, as I run I feed, as I feed I grow and as I grow I turn eyes to Lyte with a kind of dizzying vertigo. And she looks upon me with the same gentleness of thought. This is the day of our youth. Are we wasting it? Are we losing it on a dream, a folly?

Distantly he heard laughter. As a child he'd questioned it. Now he understood laughter. This particular laughter was made of climbing high rocks and plucking the greenest blades and drinking the headiest vintage from the morning ices and eating of the rock-fruits and tasting of young lips in new appetite.

They neared the cliffs of the enemy.

He saw the slender erectness of Lyte. The new surprise of her white breasts; the neck where if you touched you could time her pulse; the fingers which cupped in your own were animate and supple and never still; the....

Lyte snapped her head to one side. "Look ahead!" she cried. "See what is to come—look only ahead."

He felt that they were racing by part of their lives, leaving their youth on the pathside, without so much as a glance.

"I am blind with looking at stones," he said, running.

"Find new stones, then!"

"I see stones—" His voice grew gentle as the palm of her hand. The landscape floated under him. Everything was like a fine wind, blowing dreamily. "I see stones that make a ravine that lies in a cool shadow where the stone-berries are thick as tears. You touch a boulder and the berries fall in silent red avalanches, and the grass is very tender...."

"I do not see it!" She increased her pace, turning her head away.

He saw the floss upon her neck, like the small moss that grows silvery and light on the cool side of pebbles, that stirs if you breathe the lightest breath upon it. He looked upon himself, his hands clenched as he heaved himself forward toward death. Already his hands were veined and youth-swollen.

They were the hands of a young boy whose fingers are made for touching, which are suddenly sensitive and with more surface, and are nervous, and seem not a part of him because they are so big for the slender lengths of his arms. His neck, through which the blood ached and pumped, was building out with age, too, with tiny blue tendrils of veins imbedded and flaring in it.

Lyte handed him food to eat.

"I am not hungry," he said.

"Eat, keep your mouth full," she commanded sharply. "So you will not talk to me this way!"

"If I could only kiss you," he pleaded. "Just one time."

"After the battle there may be time."

"Gods!" He roared, anguished. "Who cares for battles!"

Ahead of them, rocks hailed down, thudding. A man fell with his skull split wide. The war was begun.

Lyte passed the weapons to him. They ran without another word until they entered the killing ground. Then he spoke, not looking at her, his cheeks coloring. "Thank you," he said.

She ducked as a slung stone shot by her head. "It was not an easy thing for me," she admitted. "Sim! Be careful!"

The boulders began to roll in a synthetic avalanche from the battlements of the enemy!

*****

Only one thought was in his mind now. To kill, to lessen the life of someone else so he could live, to gain a foothold here and live long enough to make a stab at the ship. He ducked, he weaved, he clutched stones and hurled them up. His left hand held a flat stone shield with which he diverted the swiftly plummeting rocks. There was a spatting sound everywhere. Lyte ran with him, encouraging him. Two men dropped before him, slain, their breasts cleaved to the bone, their blood springing out in unbelievable founts.

It was a useless conflict. Sim realized instantly how insane the venture was. They could never storm the cliff. A solid wall of rocks rained down. A dozen men dropped with shards of ebony in their brains, a half dozen more showed drooping, broken arms. One screamed and the upthrust white joint of his knee was exposed as the flesh was pulled away by two successive blows of well-aimed granite. Men stumbled over one another.

The muscles in his cheeks pulled tight and he began to wonder why he had ever come. But his raised eyes, as he danced from side to side, weaving and bobbing, sought always the cliffs. He wanted to live there so intensely, to have his chance. He would have to stick it out. But the heart was gone from him.

Lyte screamed piercingly. Sim, his heart panicking, twisted and saw that her hand was loose at the wrist, with an ugly wound bleeding profusely on the back of the knuckles. She clamped it under her armpit to soothe the pain. The anger rose in him and exploded. In his fury he raced forward, throwing his missiles with deadly accuracy. He saw a man topple and flail down, falling from one level to another of the caves, a victim of his shot. He must have been screaming, for his lungs were bursting open and closed and his throat was raw, and the ground spun madly under his racing feet.

The stone that clipped his head sent him reeling and plunging back. He ate sand. The universe dissolved into purple whorls. He could not get up. He lay and knew that this was his last day, his last time. The battle raged around him, dimly he felt Lyte over him. Her hands cooled his head, she tried to drag him out of range, but he lay gasping and telling her to leave him.

"Stop!" shouted a voice. The whole war seemed to give pause. "Retreat!" commanded the voice swiftly. And as Sim watched, lying upon his side, his comrades turned and fled back toward home.

"The sun is coming, our time is up!" He saw their muscled backs, their moving, tensing, flickering legs go up and down. The dead were left upon the field. The wounded cried for help. But there was no time for the wounded. There was only time for swift men to run the gauntlet home and, their lungs aching and raw with heated air, burst into their tunnels before the sun burnt and killed them.

The sun!

Sim saw another figure racing toward him. It was Chion! Lyte was helping Sim to his feet, whispering helpfully to him. "Can you walk?" she asked. And he groaned and said, "I think so." "Walk then," she said.

"Walk slowly, and then faster and faster. We'll make it. Walk slowly, start carefully. We'll make it, I know we will."

Sim got to his feet, stood swaying. Chion raced up, a strange expression cutting lines in his cheeks, his eyes shining with battle. Pushing Lyte abruptly aside he seized upon a rock and dealt Sim a jolting blow upon his ankle that laid wide the flesh. All of this was done quite silently.

Now he stood back, still not speaking, grinning like an animal from the night mountains, his chest panting in and out, looking from the thing he had done, to Lyte, and back. He got his breath. "He'll never make it," he nodded at Sim. "We'll have to leave him here. Come along, Lyte."

Lyte, like a cat-animal, sprang upon Chion, searching for his eyes, shrieking through her exposed, hard-pressed teeth. Her fingers stroked great bloody furrows down Chion's arms and again, instantly, down his neck. Chion, with an oath, sprang away from her. She hurled a rock at him. Grunting, he let it miss him, then ran off a few yards. "Fool!" he cried, turning to scorn her. "Come along with me. Sim will be dead in a few minutes. Come along!"

Lyte turned her back on him. "I will go if you carry me."

Chion's face changed. His eyes lost their gleaming. "There is no time. We would both die if I carried you."

Lyte looked through and beyond him. "Carry me, then, for that's how I wish it to be."

Without another word, glancing fearfully at the sun, Chion fled. His footsteps sped away and vanished from hearing. "May he fall and break his neck," whispered Lyte, savagely glaring at his form as it skirted a ravine. She returned to Sim. "Can you walk?"

*****

Agonies of pain shot up his leg from the wounded ankle. He nodded ironically. "We could make it to the cave in two hours, walking. I have an idea, Lyte. Carry me." And he smiled with the grim joke.

She took his arm. "Nevertheless we'll walk. Come."

"No," he said. "We're staying here."

"But why?"

"We came to seek a home here. If we walk we will die. I would rather die here. How much time have we?"

Together they measured the sun. "A few minutes," she said, her voice flat and dull. She held close to him.

He looked at her. Lyte, he thought. Tomorrow I would have been a man. My body would have been strong and full and there would have been time with you, a kissing and a touching. Damn, but what kind of life is this where every last instant is drenched with fear and alert with death? Am I to be denied even some bit of real life?

The black rocks of the cliff were paling into deep purples and browns as the sun began to flood the world.

What a fool he was! He should have stayed and worked with Dienc, and thought and dreamed, and at least one time cupped Lyte's mouth with his own.

With the sinews of his neck standing out defiantly he bellowed upward at the cliff holes.

"Send me down one man to do battle!"

Silence. His voice echoed from the cliff. The air was warm.

"It's no use," said Lyte, "They'll pay no attention."

He shouted again. "Hear me!" He stood with his weight on his good foot, his injured left leg throbbing and pulsating with pain. He shook a fist. "Send down a warrior who is no coward! I will not turn and run home! I have come to fight a fair fight! Send a man who will fight for the right to his cave! Him I will surely kill!"

More silence. A wave of heat passed over the land, receded.

"Oh, surely," mocked Sim, hands on naked hips, head back, mouth wide, "surely there's one among you not afraid to fight a cripple!" Silence. "No?" Silence.

"Then I have miscalculated you. I'm wrong. I'll stand here, then, until the sun shucks the flesh off my bone in black scraps, and call you the filthy names you deserve."

He got an answer.

"I do not like being called names," replied a man's voice.

Sim leaned forward, forgetting his crippled foot.

A huge man appeared in a cave mouth on the third level.

"Come down," urged Sim. "Come down, fat one, and kill me."

The man scowled seriously at his opponent a moment, then lumbered slowly down the path, his hands empty of any weapons. Immediately every cave above clustered with heads. An audience for this drama.

The man approached Sim. "We will fight by the rules, if you know them."

"I'll learn as we go," replied Sim.

This pleased the man and he looked at Sim warily, but not unkindly. "This much I will tell you," offered the man generously. "If you die, I will give your mate shelter and she will live, as she pleases, because she is the wife of a good man."

Sim nodded swiftly. "I am ready," he said.

"The rules are simple. We do not touch each other, save with stones. The stones and the sun will do either of us in. Now is the time—"

*****

VIII

A tip of the sun showed on the horizon. "My name is Nhoj," said Sim's enemy, casually fingering up a handful of pebbles and stones, weighing them. Sim did likewise. He was hungry. He had not eaten for many minutes. Hunger was the curse of this planet's peoples—a perpetual demanding of empty stomachs for more, more food. His blood flushed weakly, shot tinglingly through veins in jolting throbs of heat and pressure, his ribcase shoved out, went in, shoved out again, impatiently.

"Now!" roared the three hundred watchers from the cliffs. "Now!" they clamored, the men and women and children balanced, in turmoil on the ledges. "Now! Begin!"

As if at a cue, the sun leaped high. It smote them a blow as with a flat, sizzling stone. The two men staggered under the molten impact, sweat broke from their naked thighs and loins, under their arms and on their faces was a glaze like fine glass.

Nhoj shifted his huge weight and looked at the sun as if in no hurry to fight. Then, silently, with no warning, he kanurcked out a pebble with a startling trigger-flick of thumb and forefinger. It caught Sim flat on the cheek, staggered him back, so that a rocket of unbearable pain climbed up his crippled foot and burst into nervous explosion at the pit of his stomach. He tasted blood from his bleeding cheek.

Nhoj moved serenely. Three more flickers of his magical hands and three tiny, seemingly harmless bits of stone flew like whistling birds. Each of them found a target, slammed it. The nerve centers of Sim's body! One hit his stomach so that ten hours' eating almost slid up his throat. A second got his forehead, a third his neck. He collapsed to the boiling sand. His knee made a wrenching sound on the hard earth. His face was colorless and his eyes, squeezed tight, were pushing tears out from the hot, quivering lids. But even as he had fallen he had let loose, with wild force, his handful of stones!

The stones purred in the air. One of them, and only one, struck Nhoj. Upon the left eyeball. Nhoj moaned and laid his hands in the next instant to his shattered eye.

Sim choked out a bitter, sighing laugh. This much triumph he had. The eye of his opponent. It would give him ... Time. Oh, gods, he thought, his stomach retching sickly, fighting for breath, this is a world of time. Give me a little more, just a trifle!

Nhoj, one-eyed, weaving with pain, pelted the writhing body of Sim, but his aim was off now, the stones flew to one side or if they struck at all they were weak and spent and lifeless.

Sim forced himself half erect. From the corners of his eyes he saw Lyte, waiting, staring at him, her lips breathing words of encouragement and hope. He was bathed in sweat, as if a rain spray had showered him down.

*****

The sun was now fully over the horizon. You could smell it. Stones glinted like mirrors, the sand began to roil and bubble. Illusions sprang up everywhere in the valley. Instead of one warrior Nhoj he was confronted by a dozen, each in an upright position, preparing to launch another missile. A dozen irregular warriors who shimmered in the golden menace of day, like bronze gongs smitten, quivered in one vision!

Sim was breathing desperately. His nostrils flared and sucked and his mouth drank thirstily of flame instead of oxygen. His lungs took fire like silk torches and his body was consumed. The sweat spilled from his pores to be instantly evaporated. He felt himself shriveling, shriveling in on himself, he imagined himself looking like his father, old, sunken, slight, withered! Where was the sand? Could he move? Yes. The world wriggled under him, but now he was on his feet.

There would be no more fighting.

A murmur from the cliff told this. The sunburnt faces of the high audience gaped and jeered and shouted encouragement to their warrior. "Stand straight, Nhoj, save your strength now! Stand tall and perspire!" they urged him. And Nhoj stood, swaying lightly, swaying slowly, a pendulum in an incandescent fiery breath from the skyline. "Don't move, Nhoj, save your heart, save your power!"

"The Test, The Test!" said the people on the heights. "The test of the sun."

And this was the worst part of the fight. Sim squinted painfully at the distorted illusion of cliff. He thought he saw his parents; father with his defeated face, his green eyes burning, mother with her hair blowing like a cloud of grey smoke in the fire wind. He must get up to them, live for and with them!

Behind him, Sim heard Lyte whimper softly. There was a whisper of flesh against sand. She had fallen. He did not dare turn. The strength of turning would bring him thundering down in pain and darkness.

His knees bent. If I fall, he thought, I'll lie here and become ashes. Where was Nhoj? Nhoj was there, a few yards from him, standing bent, slick with perspiration, looking as if he were being hit over the spine with great hammers of destruction.

"Fall, Nhoj! Fall!" screamed Sim, mentally. "Fall, fall! Fall and die so I can take your place!"

But Nhoj did not fall. One by one the pebbles in his half-loose left hand plummeted to the broiling sands and Nhoj's lips peeled back, the saliva burned away from his lips and his eyes glazed. But he did not fall. The will to live was strong in him. He hung as if by a wire.

Sim fell to one knee!

"Ahh!" wailed the knowing voices from the cliff. They were watching death. Sim jerked his head up, smiling mechanically, foolishly as if caught in the act of doing something silly. "No, no," he insisted drowsily, and got back up again. There was so much pain he was all one ringing numbness. A whirring, buzzing, frying sound filled the land. High up, an avalanche came down like a curtain on a drama, making no noise. Everything was quiet except for a steady humming. He saw fifty images of Nhoj now, dressed in armours of sweat, eyes puffed with torture, cheeks sunken, lips peeled back like the rind of a drying fruit. But the wire still held him.

"Now," muttered Sim, sluggishly, with a thick, baked tongue between his blazing teeth. "Now I'll fall and lie and dream." He said it with slow, thoughtful pleasure. He planned it. He knew how it must be done. He would do it accurately. He lifted his head to see if the audience was watching.

They were gone!

The sun had driven them back in. All save one or two brave ones. Sim laughed drunkenly and watched the sweat gather on his dead hands, hesitate, drop off, plunge down toward sand and turn to steam half way there.

Nhoj fell.

The wire was cut. Nhoj fell flat upon his stomach, a gout of blood kicked from his mouth. His eyes rolled back into a white, senseless insanity.

Nhoj fell. So did his fifty duplicate illusions.

All across the valley the winds sang and moaned and Sim saw a blue lake with a blue river feeding it and low white houses near the river with people going and coming in the houses and among the tall green trees. Trees taller than seven men, beside the river mirage.

"Now," explained Sim to himself at last, "Now I can fall. Right—into—that—lake."

He fell forward.

He was shocked when he felt the hands eagerly stop him in mid-plunge, lift him, hurry him off, high in the hungry air, like a torch held and waved, ablaze.

"How strange is death," he thought, and blackness took him.

*****

He wakened to the flow of cool water on his cheeks.

He opened his eyes fearfully. Lyte held his head upon her lap, her fingers were moving food to his mouth. He was tremendously hungry and tired, but fear squeezed both of these things away. He struggled upward, seeing the strange cave contours overhead.

"What time is it?" he demanded.

"The same day as the contest. Be quiet," she said.

"The same day!"

She nodded amusedly. "You've lost nothing of your life. This is Nhoj's cave. We are inside the black cliff. We will live three extra days. Satisfied? Lie down."

"Nhoj is dead?" He fell back, panting, his heart slamming his ribs. He relaxed slowly. "I won. Gods, I won," he breathed.

"Nhoj is dead. So were we, almost. They carried us in from outside only in time."

He ate ravenously. "We have no time to waste. We must get strong. My leg—" He looked at it, tested it. There was a swathe of long yellow grasses around it and the ache had died away. Even as he watched the terrific pulsings of his body went to work and cured away the impurities under the bandages. It *has* to be strong by sunset, he thought. It *has* to be.

He got up and limped around the cave like a captured animal. He felt Lyte's eyes upon him. He could not meet her gaze. Finally, helplessly, he turned.

She interrupted him. "You want to go on to the ship?" she asked, softly. "Tonight? When the sun goes down?"

He took a breath, exhaled it. "Yes."

"You couldn't possibly wait until morning?"

"No."

"Then I'll go with you."

"No!"

"If I lag behind, let me. There's nothing here for me."

They stared at each other a long while. He shrugged wearily.

"All right," he said, at last. "I couldn't stop you, I know that. We'll go together."

*****

IX

They waited in the mouth of their new cave. The sun set. The stones cooled so that one could walk on them. It was almost time for the leaping out and the running toward the distant, glittering metal seed that lay on the far mountain.

Soon would come the rains. And Sim thought back over all the times he had watched the rains thicken into creeks, into rivers that cut new beds each night. One night there would be a river running north, the next a river running north-east, the third night a river running due west. The valley was continually cut and scarred by the torrents. Earthquakes and avalanches filled the old beds. New ones were the order of the day. It was this idea of the river and the directions of the river that he had turned over in his head for many hours. It might possibly—Well, he would wait and see.

He noticed how living in this new cliff had slowed his pulse, slowed everything. A mineral result, protection against the solar radiations. Life was still swift, but not as swift as before.

"Now, Sim!" cried Lyte, testing the valley air.

They ran. Between the hot death and the cold one. Together, away from the cliffs, out toward the distant, beckoning ship.

Never had they run this way in their lives. The sound of their feet running was a hard, insistent clatter over vast oblongs of rock, down into ravines, up the sides, and on again. They raked the air in and out their lungs. Behind them the cliffs faded away into things they could never turn back to now.

They did not eat as they ran. They had eaten to the bursting point in the cave, to save time. Now it was only running, a lifting of legs, a balancing of bent elbows, a convulsion of muscles, a slaking in of air that had been fiery and was now cooling.

"Are they watching us?"

Lyte's breathless voice snatched at his ears, above the pound of his heart.

Who? But he knew the answer. The cliff peoples, of course. How long had it been since a race like this one? A thousand days? Ten thousand? How long since someone had taken the chance and sprinted with an entire civilization's eyes upon their backs, into gullies, across cooling plain. Were there lovers pausing in their laughter back there, gazing at the two tiny dots that were a man and woman running toward destiny? Were children eating of new fruits and stopping in their play to see the two people racing against time? Was Dienc still living, narrowing hairy eyebrows down over fading eyes, shouting them on in a feeble, rasping voice, shaking a twisted hand? Were there jeers? Were they being called fools, idiots? And in the midst of the name calling, were people praying them on, hoping they would reach the ship? Yes, under all the cynicism and pessimism, some of them, all of them, must be praying.

Sim took a quick glance at the sky, which was beginning to bruise with the coming night. Out of nowhere clouds materialized and a light shower trailed across a gully two hundred yards ahead of them. Lightning beat upon distant mountains and there was a strong scent of ozone on the disturbed air.

"The halfway mark," panted Sim, and he saw Lyte's face half turn, longingly looking back at the life she was leaving. "Now's the time, if we want to turn back, we still have time. Another minute—"

*****

Thunder snarled in the mountains. An avalanche started out small and ended up huge and monstrous in a deep fissure. Light rain dotted Lyte's smooth white skin. In a minute her hair was glistening and soggy with rain.

"Too late now," she shouted over the patting rhythm of her own naked feet. "We've got to go ahead!"

And it was too late. Sim knew, judging the distances, that there was no turning back now.

His leg began to pain him a little. He favored it, slowing. A wind came up swiftly. A cold wind that bit into the skin. But it came from the cliffs behind them, helped rather than hindered them. An omen? he wondered. No.

For as the minutes went by it grew upon him how poorly he had estimated the distance. Their time was dwindling out, but they were still an impossible distance from the ship. He said nothing, but the impotent anger at the slow muscles in his legs welled up into bitterly hot tears in his eyes.

He knew that Lyte was thinking the same as himself. But she flew along like a white bird, seeming hardly to touch ground. He heard her breath go out and in her throat, like a clean, sharp knife in its sheathe.

Half the sky was dark. The first stars were peering through lengths of black cloud. Lightning jiggled a path along a rim just ahead of them. A full thunderstorm of violent rain and exploding electricity fell upon them.

They slipped and skidded on moss-smooth pebbles. Lyte fell, scrambled up again with a burning oath. Her body was scarred and dirty. The rain washed over her.

The rain came down and cried on Sim. It filled his eyes and ran in rivers down his spine and he wanted to cry with it.

Lyte fell and did not rise, sucking her breath, her breasts quivering.

He picked her up and held her. "Run, Lyte, please, run!"

"Leave me, Sim. Go ahead!" The rain filled her mouth. There was water everywhere. "It's no use. Go on without me."

He stood there, cold and powerless, his thoughts sagging, the flame of hope blinking out. All the world was blackness, cold falling sheathes of water, and despair.

"We'll walk, then," he said. "And keep walking, and resting."

They walked for fifty yards, easily, slowly, like children out for a stroll. The gully ahead of them filled with water that went sliding away with a swift wet sound, toward the horizon.

Sim cried out. Tugging at Lyte he raced forward. "A new channel," he said, pointing. "Each day the rain cuts a new channel. Here, Lyte!" He leaned over the flood waters.

He dived in, taking her with him.

The flood swept them like bits of wood. They fought to stay upright, the water got into their mouths, their noses. The land swept by on both sides of them. Clutching Lyte's fingers with insane strength, Sim felt himself hurled end over end, saw flicks of lightning on high, and a new fierce hope was born in him. They could no longer run, well, then they would let the water do the running for them.

With a speed that dashed them against rocks, split open their shoulders, abraded their legs, the new, brief river carried them. "This way!" Sim shouted over a salvo of thunder and steered frantically toward the opposite side of the gully. The mountain where the ship lay was just ahead. They must not pass it by. They fought in the transporting liquid and were slammed against the far side. Sim leaped up, caught at an overhanging rock, locked Lyte in his legs, and drew himself hand over hand upward.

As quickly as it had come, the storm was gone. The lightning faded. The rain ceased. The clouds melted and fell away over the sky. The wind whispered into silence.

"The ship!" Lyte lay upon the ground. "The ship, Sim. This is the mountain of the ship!"

Now the cold came. The killing cold.

They forced themselves drunkenly up the mountain. The cold slid along their limbs, got into their arteries like a chemical and slowed them.

Ahead of them, with a fresh-washed sheen, lay the ship. It was a dream. Sim could not believe that they were actually so near it. Two hundred yards. One hundred and seventy yards. Gods, but it was cold.

The ground became covered with ice. They slipped and fell again and again. Behind them the river was frozen into a blue-white snake of cold solidity. A few last drops of rain from somewhere came down as hard pellets.

Sim fell against the bulk of the ship. He was actually touching it. Touching it! He heard Lyte whimpering in her constricted throat. This was the metal, the ship. How many others had touched it in the long days? He and Lyte had made it!

He touched it lovingly. Then, as cold as the air, his veins were chilled.

Where was the entrance?

You run, you swim, you almost drown, you curse, you sweat, you work, you reach a mountain, you go up it, you hammer on metal, you shout with relief, you reach the ship, and then—you can't find the entrance.

*****

He fought to keep himself from breaking down. Slowly, he told himself, but not too slowly, go around the ship. The metal slid under his searching hands, so cold that his hands, sweating, almost froze to it. Now, far around to the side. Lyte moved with him. The cold held them like a fist. It began to squeeze.

The entrance.

Metal. Cold, immutable metal. A thin line of opening at the sealing point. Throwing all caution aside, he beat at it. He felt his stomach seething with cold. His fingers were numb, his eyes were half frozen in their sockets. He began to beat and search and scream against the metal door. "Open up! Open up!" He staggered.

The air-lock sighed. With a whispering of metal on rubber beddings, the door swung softly sidewise and vanished back.

He saw Lyte run forward, clutch at her throat, and drop inside a small shiny chamber. He shuffled after her, blankly.

The air-lock door sealed shut behind him.

He could not breathe. His heart began to slow, to stop.

They were trapped inside the ship now, and something was happening. He sank down to his knees and choked for air.

The ship he had come to for salvation was now slowing his pulse, darkening his brain, poisoning him. With a starved, faint kind of expiring terror, he realized that he was dying.

Blackness.

*****

He had a dim sense of time passing, of thinking, struggling, to make his heart go quick, quick.... To make his eyes focus. But the fluid in his body lagged quietly through his settling veins and he heard his temple pulses thud, pause, thud, pause and thud again with lulling intermissions.

He could not move, not a hand or leg or finger. It was an effort to lift the tonnage of his eyelashes. He could not shift his face even, to see Lyte lying beside him.

From a distance came her irregular breathing. It was like the sound a wounded bird makes with his dry, unraveled pinions. She was so close he could almost feel the heat of her; yet she seemed a long way removed.

I'm getting cold! he thought. Is this death? This slowing of blood, of my heart, this cooling of my body, this drowsy thinking of thoughts?

Staring at the ship's ceiling he traced its intricate system of tubes and machines. The knowledge, the purpose of the ship, its actions, seeped into him. He began to understand in a kind of revealing lassitude just what these things were his eyes rested upon. Slow. Slow.

There was an instrument with a gleaming white dial.

Its purpose?

He drudged away at the problem, like a man underwater.

People had used the dial. Touched it. People had repaired it. Installed it. People had dreamed of it before the building, before the installing, before the repairing and touching and using. The dial contained memory of use and manufacture, its very shape was a dream-memory telling Sim why and for what it had been built. Given time, looking at anything, he could draw from it the knowledge he desired. Some dim part of him reached out, dissected the contents of things, analyzed them.

This dial measured time!

Millions of days of time!

But how could that be? Sim's eyes dilated, hot and glittering. Where were humans who needed such an instrument?

Blood thrummed and beat behind his eyes. He closed them.

Panic came to him. The day was passing. I am lying here, he thought, and my life slips away. I cannot move. My youth is passing. How long before I can move?

Through a kind of porthole he saw the night pass, the day come, the day pass, and again another night. Stars danced frostily.

I will lie here for four or five days, wrinkling and withering, he thought. This ship will not let me move. How much better if I had stayed in my home cliff, lived, enjoyed this short life. What good has it done to come here? I'm missing all the twilights and dawns. I'll never touch Lyte, though she's here at my side.

Delirium. His mind floated up. His thoughts whirled through the metal ship. He smelled the razor sharp smell of joined metal. He heard the hull contract with night, relax with day.

Dawn.

Already—another dawn!

Today I would have been mature. His jaw clenched. I must get up. I must move. I must enjoy my time of maturity.

But he didn't move. He felt his blood pump sleepily from chamber to red chamber in his heart, on down and around through his dead body, to be purified by his folding and unfolding lungs. Then the circuit once more.

The ship grew warm. From somewhere a machine clicked. Automatically the temperature cooled. A controlled gust of air flushed the room.

Night again. And then another day.

He lay and saw four days of his life pass.

He did not try to fight. It was no use. His life was over.

He didn't want to turn his head now. He didn't want to see Lyte with her face like his tortured mother's—eyelids like gray ash flakes, eyes like beaten, sanded metal, cheeks like eroded stones. He didn't want to see a throat like parched thongs of yellow grass, hands the pattern of smoke risen from a fire, breasts like desiccated rinds and hair stubbly and unshorn as moist gray weeds!

And himself? How did *he* look? Was his jaw sunken, the flesh of his eyes pitted, his brow lined and age-scarred?

*****

His strength began to return. He felt his heart beating so slow that it was amazing. One hundred beats a minute. Impossible. He felt so cool, so thoughtful, so easy.

His head fell over to one side. He stared at Lyte. He shouted in surprise.

She was young and fair.

She was looking at him, too weak to say anything. Her eyes were like tiny silver medals, her throat curved like the arm of a child. Her hair was blue fire eating at her scalp, fed by the slender life of her body.

Four days had passed and still she was young ... no, younger than when they had entered the ship. She was still adolescent.

He could not believe it.

Her first words were, "How long will this last?"

He replied, carefully. "I don't know."

"We are still young."

"The ship. Its metal is around us. It cuts away the sun and the things that came from the sun to age us."

Her eyes shifted thoughtfully. "Then, if we stay here—"

"We'll remain young."

"Six more days? Fourteen more? Twenty?"

"More than that, maybe."

She lay there, silently. After a long time she said, "Sim?"

"Yes."

"Let's stay here. Let's not go back. If we go back now, you know what'll happen to us...?"

"I'm not certain."

"We'll start getting old again, won't we?"

He looked away. He stared at the ceiling and the clock with the moving finger. "Yes. We'll grow old."

"What if we grow old—instantly. When we step from the ship won't the shock be too much?"

"Maybe."

Another silence. He began to move his limbs, testing them. He was very hungry. "The others are waiting," he said.

Her next words made him gasp. "The others are dead," she said. "Or will be in a few hours. All those we knew back there are old and worn."

He tried to picture them old. Dark, his sister, bent and senile with time. He shook his head, wiping the picture away. "They may die," he said. "But there are others who've been born."

"People we don't even know," said Lyte, flatly.

"But, nevertheless, *our* people," he replied. "People who'll live only eight days, or eleven days unless we help them."

"But we're *young*, Sim! We're young! We can *stay* young!"

He didn't want to listen. It was too tempting a thing to listen to. To stay here. To live. "We've already had more time than the others," he said. "I need workers. Men to heal this ship. We'll get on our feet now, you and I, and find food, eat, and see if the ship is movable. I'm afraid to try to move it myself. It's so big. I'll need help."

"But that means running back all that distance!"

"I know." He lifted himself weakly. "But I'll do it."

"How will you get the men back here?"

"We'll use the river."

"*If* it's there. It *may* be somewhere else."

"We'll wait until there *is* one, then. I've got to go back, Lyte. The son of Dienc is waiting for me, my sister, your brother, are old people, ready to die, and waiting for some word from us—"

After a long while he heard her move, dragging herself tiredly to him. She put her head upon his chest, her eyes closed, stroking his arm. "I'm sorry. Forgive me. You have to go back. I'm a selfish fool."

He touched her cheek, clumsily. "You're human. I understand you. There's nothing to forgive."

*****

They found food. They walked through the ship. It was empty. Only in the control room did they find the remains of a man who must have been the chief pilot. The others had evidently bailed out into space in emergency lifeboats. This pilot, sitting at his controls, alone, had landed the ship on a mountain within sight of other fallen and smashed crafts. Its location on high ground had saved it from the floods. The pilot himself had died, probably of heart failure, soon after landing. The ship had remained here, almost within reach of the other survivors, perfect as an egg, but silent, for—how many thousand days? If the pilot had lived, what a different thing life might have been for the ancestors of Sim and Lyte. Sim, thinking of this—felt the distant, ominous vibration of war. How had the war between worlds come out? Who had won? Or had both planets lost and never bothered trying to pick up survivors? Who had been right? Who was the enemy? Were Sim's people of the guilty or innocent side? They might never know.

He checked the ship hurriedly. He knew nothing of its workings, yet as he walked its corridors, patted its machines, he learned from it. It needed only a crew. One man couldn't possibly set the whole thing running again. He laid his hand upon one round, snout-like machine. He jerked his hand away, as if burnt.

"Lyte!"

"What is it?"

He touched the machine again, caressed it, his hand trembled violently, his eyes welled with tears, his mouth opened and closed, he looked at the machine, loving it, then looked at Lyte.

"With this machine—" he stammered, softly, incredulously. "With—with this machine I can—"

"What, Sim?"

He inserted his hand into a cup-like contraption with a lever inside. Out of porthole in front of him he could see the distant line of cliffs. "We were afraid there might never be another river running by this mountain, weren't we?" he asked, exultantly.

"Yes, Sim, but—"

"There *will* be a river. And I *will* come back, tonight! And I'll bring men with me. Five hundred men! Because with this machine I can blast a river bottom all the way to the cliffs, down which the waters will rush, giving myself and the men a swift, sure way of traveling back!" He rubbed the machine's barrel-like body. "When I touched it, the life and method of it shot into me! Watch!" He depressed the lever.

A beam of incandescent fire lanced out from the ship, screaming.

Steadily, accurately, Sim began to cut away a river bed for the storm waters to flow in. The night was turned to day by its hungry eating.

*****

The return to the cliffs was to be carried out by Sim alone. Lyte was to remain in the ship, in case of any mishap. The trip back seemed, at first glance, to be impossible. There would be no river rushing to cut his time, to sweep him along toward his destination. He would have to run the entire distance in the dawn, and the sun would get him, catch him before he'd reached safety.

"The only way to do it is to start *before* sunrise."

"But you'd be frozen, Sim."

"Here." He made adjustments on the machine that had just finished cutting the river bed in the rock floor of the valley. He lifted the smooth snout of the gun, pressed the lever, left it down. A gout of fire shot toward the cliffs. He fingered the range control, focused the flame end three miles from its source. Done. He turned to Lyte. "But I don't understand," she said.

He opened the air-lock door. "It's bitter cold out, and half an hour yet till dawn. If I run parallel to the flame from the machine, close enough to it, there'll not be much heat but enough to sustain life, anyway."

"It doesn't sound safe," Lyte protested.

"*Nothing* does, on this world." He moved forward. "I'll have a half hour start. That should be enough to reach the cliffs."

"But if the machine should fail while you're still running near its beam?"

"Let's not think of that," he said.

A moment later he was outside. He staggered as if kicked in the stomach. His heart almost exploded in him. The environment of his world forced him into swift living again. He felt his pulse rise, kicking through his veins.

The night was cold as death. The heat ray from the ship sliced across the valley, humming, solid and warm. He moved next to it, very close. One misstep in his running and—

"I'll be back," he called to Lyte.

He and the ray of light went together.

*****

In the early morning the peoples in the caves saw the long finger of orange incandescence and the weird whitish apparition floating, running along beside it. There was muttering and superstition.

So when Sim finally reached the cliffs of his childhood he saw alien peoples swarming there. There were no familiar faces. Then he realized how foolish it was to expect familiar faces. One of the older men glared down at him. "Who're you?" he shouted. "Are you from the enemy cliff? What's your name?"

"I am Sim, the son of Sim!"

"Sim!"

An old woman shrieked from the cliff above him. She came hobbling down the stone pathway. "Sim, Sim, it *is* you!"

He looked at her, frankly bewildered. "But I don't know you," he murmured.

"Sim, don't you recognize me? Oh, Sim, it's me! Dark!"

"Dark!"

He felt sick at his stomach. She fell into his arms. This old, trembling woman with the half-blind eyes, his sister.

Another face appeared above. That of an old man. A cruel, bitter face. It looked down at Sim and snarled. "Drive him away!" cried the old man. "He comes from the cliff of the enemy. He's lived there! He's still young! Those who go there can never come back among us. Disloyal beast!" And a rock hurtled down.

Sim leaped aside, pulling the old woman with him.

A roar came from the people. They ran toward Sim, shaking their fists. "Kill him, kill him!" raved the old man, and Sim did not know who he was.

"Stop!" Sim held out his hands. "I come from the ship!"

"The ship?" The people slowed. Dark clung to him, looking up into his young face, puzzling over its smoothness.

"Kill him, kill him, kill him!" croaked the old man, and picked up another rock.

"I offer you ten days, twenty days, thirty more days of life!"

The people stopped. Their mouths hung open. Their eyes were incredulous.

"Thirty days?" It was repeated again and again. "How?"

"Come back to the ship with me. Inside it, one can live forever!"

The old man lifted high a rock, then, choking, fell forward in an apoplectic fit, and tumbled down the rocks to lie at Sim's feet.

Sim bent to peer at the ancient one, at the bleary, dead eyes, the loose, sneering lips, the crumpled, quiet body.

"Chion!"

"Yes," said Dark behind him, in a croaking, strange voice. "Your enemy. Chion."

*****

That night a thousand warriors started for the ship as if going to war. The water ran in the new channel. Five hundred of them were drowned or lost behind in the cold. The others, with Sim, got through to the ship.

Lyte awaited them, and threw wide the metal door.

The weeks passed. Generations lived and died in the cliffs, while the five hundred workers labored over the ship, learning its functions and its parts.

On the last day they disbanded. Each ran to his station. Now there was a destiny of travel who still remained behind.

Sim touched the control plates under his fingers.

Lyte, rubbing her eyes, came and sat on the floor next to him, resting her head against his knee, drowsily. "I had a dream," she said, looking off at something far away. "I dreamed I lived in caves in a cliff on a cold-hot planet where people grew old and died in eight days and were burnt."

"What an impossible dream," said Sim. "People couldn't possibly live in such a nightmare. Forget it. You're awake now."

He touched the plates gently. The ship rose and moved into space. Sim was right. The nightmare was over at last.

*****

[Transcriber's Note: No Section III or V heading in original text.]

Asleep in Armageddon

Avoid Planetoid 787. Lush and sunny, with fine air and no dangerous beasts, it'll tempt you to curve in for some nice solid-ground sleep. DON'T!

*****

You don't want death and you don't expect death. Something goes wrong, your rocket tilts in space, a planetoid jumps up, blackness, movement, hands over the eyes, a violent pulling back of available power in the fore-jets, the crash....

The darkness. In the darkness, the senseless pain. In the pain, the nightmare.

He was not unconscious.

Your name? asked hidden voices. *Sale*, he replied in whirling nausea. *Leonard Sale. Occupation*, cried the voices. *Spaceman!* he cried, alone in the night. *Welcome*, said the voices. *Welcome, welcome.* They faded.

He stood up in the wreckage of his ship. It lay like a folded, tattered garment around him.

The sun rose and it was morning.

Sale pried himself out the small air-lock and stood breathing the atmosphere. Luck. Sheer luck. The air was breathable. An instant's checking showed him that he had two month's supply of food with him.

Fine, fine! And this—he fingered at the wreckage. Miracle of miracles! The radio was intact.

He stuttered out the message on the sending key. CRASHED ON PLANETOID 787. SALE. SEND HELP. SALE. SEND HELP.

The reply came instantly: HELLO, SALE. THIS IS ADDAMS IN MARSPORT. SENDING RESCUE SHIP LOGARITHM. WILL ARRIVE PLANETOID 787 IN SIX DAYS. HANG ON.

Sale did a little dance.

It was simple as that. One crashed. One had food. One radioed for help. Help came. *La!* He clapped his hands.

The sun rose and was warm. He felt no sense of mortality. Six days would be no time at all. He would eat, he would read, he would sleep. He glanced at his surroundings. No dangerous animals; a tolerable oxygen supply. What more could one ask. Beans and bacon, was the answer. The happy smell of breakfast filled the air.

After breakfast he smoked a cigarette slowly, deeply, blowing out. He nodded contentedly. What a life! Not a scratch on him. Luck. Sheer luck.

His head nodded. Sleep, he thought.

Good idea. Forty winks. Plenty of time to sleep, take it easy. Six whole long, luxurious days of idling and philosophizing. Sleep.

He stretched himself out, tucked his arm under his head, and shut his eyes.

*****

Insanity came in to take him. The voices whispered.

Sleep, yes, sleep, said the voices. *Ah, sleep, sleep.*

He opened his eyes. The voices stopped. Everything was normal. He shrugged. He shut his eyes casually, fitfully. He settled his long body.

Eeeeeeeeeee, sang the voices, far away.

Ahhhhhhhh, sang the voices.

Sleep, sleep, sleep, sleep, sleep, sang the voices.

Die, die, die, die, die, sang the voices.

Oooooooooooooo, cried the voices.

Mmmmmmmmmmmmmm, a bee ran through his brain.

He sat up. He shook his head. He put his hands to his ears. He blinked at the crashed ship. Hard metal. He felt the solid rock under his fingers. He saw the real sun warming the blue sky.

Let's try sleeping on our back, he thought. He adjusted himself, lying back down. His watch ticked on his wrist. The blood burned in his veins.

Sleep, sleep, sleep, sleep, sleep, sang the voices.

Ohhhhhhhhhhhhhh, sang the voices.

Ahhhhhhhhhhhhhhh, sang the voices.

Die, die, die, die, die. Sleep, sleep, die, sleep, die, sleep, die! Oohhh. Ahhhhh. Eeeeeeeeeeeeeee!

Blood tapped in his ears. The sound of the wind rising.

Mine, mine, said a voice. *Mine, mine, he's mine!*

No, mine, mine, said another voice. *No, mine, mine; he's* mine!

No, ours, ours, sang ten voices. *Ours, ours, he's* ours!

His fingers twitched. His jaws spasmed. His eyelids jerked.

At last, at last, sang a high voice. *Now, now. The long time, the waiting. Over, over*, sang the high voice. *Over, over at last!*

It was like being undersea. Green songs, green visions, green time. Bubbled voices drowning in deep liquors of sea tide. Far away choruses chanting senseless rhymes. Leonard Sale stirred in agony.

Mine, mine, cried a loud voice. *Mine, mine!* shrieked another. *Ours, ours!* shrieked the chorus.

The din of metal, the crash of sword, the conflict, the battle, the fight, the war. All of it exploding, his mind fiercely torn apart!

Eeeeeeeeeeeee!

He leaped up, screaming. The landscape melted and flowed.

A voice said, "I am Tylle of Rathalar. Proud Tylle, Tylle of the Blood Mound and the Death Drum. Tylle of Rathalar, Killer of Men!"

Another spoke, "I am Iorr of Wendillo, Wise Iorr, Destroyer of Infidels!"

The chorus chanted. "And we the warriors, we the steel, we the warriors, we the red blood rushing, the red blood falling, the red blood steaming in the sun—"

Leonard Sale staggered under the burden. "Go away!" he cried. "Leave me, in God's name, leave me!"

Eeeeeeeeeee, shrieked the high sound of steel hot on steel.

Silence.

*****

He stood with the sweat boiling out of him. He was trembling so violently he could not stand. Insane, he thought. Absolutely insane. Raving insane. Insane.

He jerked the food kit open, did something to a chemical packet. Hot coffee was ready in an instant. He mouthed it, spilled gushes of it down his shirt. He shivered. He sucked in raw gulps of breath.

Let's be logical, he thought, sitting down heavily. The coffee seared his tongue. No record of insanity in the family for two hundred years. All healthy, well-balanced. No reason for insanity now. Shock? Silly. No shock. I'm to be rescued in six days. No shock to that. No danger. Just an ordinary planetoid. Ordinary, ordinary place. No reason for insanity. I'm sane.

Oh? cried a small metal voice within. An echo. Fading.

"Yes!" he cried, beating his fists together. "Sane!"

Hahahahahahahahahah. Somewhere a vanishing laughter.

He whirled about. "Shut up, you!" he cried.

We didn't say anything, said the mountains. We didn't say anything, said the sky. We didn't say anything, said the wreckage.

"All right then," he said, swaying. "See that you don't."

Everything was normal.

*****

The pebbles were getting hot. The sky was big and blue. He looked at his fingers and saw the way the sun burned on every black hair. He looked at his boots and the dust on them. Suddenly he felt very happy because he made a decision. I won't go to sleep, he thought. I'm having nightmares, so why sleep. There's your solution.

He made a routine. From nine o'clock in the morning, which was this minute, until twelve, he would walk around and see the planetoid. He would write on a pad with a yellow pencil everything he saw. Then he would sit down and open a can of oily sardines and some canned fresh bread with good butter on it. From twelve thirty until four he would read nine chapters of *War and Peace*. He took the book from the wreckage, and laid it where he might find it later. There was a book of T. S. Eliot's poetry, too. That might be nice.

Supper would come at five-thirty and then from six until ten he would listen to the radio from Earth. There would be a couple of bad comedians telling jokes and a bad singer singing some song, and the latest news flashes, signing off at midnight with the UN anthem.

After that?

He felt sick.

I'll play solitaire until dawn, he thought. I'll sit up and drink hot black coffee and play solitaire, no cheating, until sunrise.

Ho ho, he thought.

"What did you say?" he asked himself.

"I said 'Ha ha'," he replied. "*Some* time, you'll have to sleep."

"I'm wide awake," he said.

"Liar," he retorted, enjoying the conversation.

"I feel fine," he said.

"Hypocrite," he replied.

"I'm not afraid of the night, or sleep, or anything," he said.

"*Very* funny," he said.

He felt bad. He wanted to sleep. And the fact that he was afraid of sleep made him want to lie down all the more and shut his eyes and curl up. "Comfy-cozy?" asked his ironic censor.

"I'll just walk and look at the rocks and the geological formations and think how good it is to be alive," he said.

"Ye gods," cried his censor. "William Saroyan!"

You'll go on, he thought, maybe one day, maybe one night, but what about the next night and the next, and the *next*? Can you stay awake *all* that time, for six nights? Until the rescue ship comes? Are you *that* good, *that* strong?

The answer was no.

What are you afraid of? I don't know. Those voices. Those sounds. But they can't hurt you, can they?

They *might*. You've got to face them some time. Must I? Brace up to it, old man. Chin up, and all that rot.

He sat down on the hard ground. He felt very much like crying. He felt as if life was over and he was entering new and unknown territory. It was such a deceiving day, with the sun warm; physically, he felt able and well, one might fish on such a day as this, or pick flowers or kiss a woman or anything. But in the midst of a lovely day, what did one get?

Death.

Well, hardly *that*.

Death, he insisted.

He lay down and closed his eyes. He was tired of messing around.

All right, he thought, if you *are* death, come get me. I want to know what all this damned nonsense is about.

Death came.

*****

Eeeeeeeeeeeeee, said a voice.

Yes, I know, said Leonard Sale, lying there. But what else?

Ahhhhhhhhhhhhhh, said a voice.

I know that, also, said Leonard Sale, irritably. He turned cold. His mouth hung open wildly.

"I am Tylle of Rathalar, Killer of Men!"

"I am Iorr of Wendillo, Destroyer of Infidels!"

What is this place? asked Leonard Sale, struggling against horror.

"Once a mighty planet!" said Tylle of Rathalar.

"Once a place of battles!" said Iorr of Wendillo.

"Now dead," said Tylle.

"Now silent," said Iorr.

"Until *you* came," said Tylle.

"To give us life again," said Iorr.

You're dead, insisted Leonard Sale, flesh writhing. You're nothing but empty wind.

"We live, through you."

"And fight, through *you*!"

So that's it, thought Leonard Sale. I'm to be a battleground, am I? Are you friends?

"Enemies!" cried Iorr.

"Foul enemies!" cried Tylle.

*****

Leonard smiled a rictal smile. He felt ghastly. How long have you waited? he demanded.

"How long is *time*?" Ten thousand years? "Perhaps." Ten million years? "Perhaps."

What are you? Thoughts, spirits, ghosts? "All of those, and more." Intelligences? "Precisely." How did you survive?

Eeeeeeeeeeeeeee, sang the chorus, far away.

Ahhhhhhhhhhhhh, sang another army, waiting to fight.

"Once upon a time, this was fertile land, a rich planet. And there were two nations, strong nations, led by two strong men. I, Iorr. And he, that one who calls himself Tylle. And the planet declined and gave way to nothingness. The peoples and the armies languished in the midst of a great war which had lasted five thousand years. We lived long lives and loved long loves, drank much, slept much, fought much. And when the planet died, our bodies withered, and, only in time, and with much science, did we survive."

Survive, wondered Leonard Sale. But there is nothing of you!

"Our *minds*, fool, our *minds*! What is a body without a mind?"

What is a mind without a *body*, laughed Leonard Sale. I've got you there. Admit it, I've *got* you!

"True," said the cruel voice. "One is useless lacking the other. But survival is survival even when unconscious. The minds of our nations, through science, through wonder, survived."

But without senses, lacking eyes, ears, lacking touch, smell, and the rest? "Lacking all those, yes. We were vapors, merely. For a long time. Until today."

And now I am here, thought Leonard Sale. "You are here," said the voice. "To give substance to our mentalities. To give us our needed body."

I'm only one, thought Sale. "Nevertheless, you are of use."

I'm an individual, thought Sale. I resent your intrusion.

"He resents our intrusion! Did you hear him, Iorr? He resents!"

"As if he had a right to resent!"

Be careful, warned Sale. I'll blink my eyes and you'll be gone, phantoms! I'll wake up and rub you out!

"But you'll have to sleep again, *some* time!" cried Iorr. "And when you do, we'll be here, waiting, waiting, waiting. For you."

What do you want? "Solidity. Mass. Sensation again." You can't *both* have it. "We'll fight that out between us."

A hot clamp twisted his skull. It was as if a spike had been thrust and beaten down between the bivalvular halves of his brain.

Now it was terribly clear. Horribly, magnificently clear. He was their universe. The world of his thoughts, his brain, his skull, divided into two camps, that of Iorr, that of Tylle. They were *using* him!

Pennants flung up on a pink mind sky! Brass shields caught the sun. Grey animals shifted and came rushing in bristling tides of sword and plume and trumpet.

Eeeeeeeeeeeeeeee! The rushing.

Ahhhhhhhhhhhhh! The roaring.

Nowwwwwwwwwww! the whirling.

Mmmmmmmmmmmm——

Ten thousand men hurtled across the small hidden stage. Ten thousand men floated on the shellacked inner ball of his eye. Ten thousand javelins hissed between the small bone hulls of his head. Ten thousand jeweled guns exploded. Ten thousand voices chanted in his ears. Now his body was riven and extended, shaken and rolled, he was screaming, writhing, the plates of his skull threatened to burst asunder. The gabbling, the shrilling, as, across bone plains of mind and continent of inner marrow, through gullies of vein, down hills of artery, over rivers of melancholy, came armies and armies, one army, two armies, swords flashed in the sun, bearing down upon each other, fifty thousand minds snatching, scrabbling, cutting at him, demanding, using. In a moment, the hard collision, one army on another, the rush, the blood, the sound, the fury, the death, the insanity!

Like cymbals, the armies struck!

He leaped up, raving. He ran across the desert. He ran and ran and did not stop running.

He sat down and cried. He sobbed until his lungs ached. He cried very hard and long. Tears ran down his cheeks and into his upraised, trembling fingers. "God, God, help me, oh God, help me," he said.

All was normal again.

*****

It was four o'clock in the afternoon. The rocks were baked by the sun. He managed, after a time, to cook himself a few hot biscuits, which he ate with strawberry jam. He wiped his stained fingers on his shirt, blindly, trying not to think.

"At least I know what I'm up against," he thought. "Oh, Lord, what a world. What an innocent looking world, and what a monster it really is. It's good no one ever explored it before. Or *did* they?" He shook his aching head. Pity them, who ever crashed here before, if any ever did. Warm sun, hard rocks, not a sign of hostility. A lovely world.

Until you shut your eyes and relaxed your mind.

And the night and the voices and the insanity and the death padded in on soft feet.

"I'm all right now, though," he said, proudly. "Look at that." He displayed his hand. By a supreme effort of will, it was no longer shaking. "I'll show you who in hell's ruler here," he announced to the innocent sky. "*I am.*" He tapped his chest.

To think that *thought* could live that long! A million years, perhaps, all these thoughts of death and disorder and conquest, lingering in the innocent but poisonous air of the planet, waiting for a real man to give them a channel through which they might issue again in all their senseless virulence.

Now that he was feeling better, it was all silly. All I have to do, he thought, is stay awake six nights. They won't bother me that way. When I'm awake, I'm dominant. I'm stronger than those crazy monarchs and their silly tribes of sword-flingers and shield-bearers and horn-blowers. I'll stay awake.

But *can* you? he wondered. Six whole nights? Awake?

There's coffee and medicine and books and cards.

But I'm tired *now*, so tired, he thought. Can I hold out?

Well, if not. There's always the gun.

Where will these silly monarchs be if you put a bullet through their stage? All the world's a stage? No. *You*, Leonard Sale, are the small stage. And they the players. And what if you put a bullet through the wings, tearing down scenes, destroying curtains, ruining lines! Destroy the stage, the players, all, if they aren't careful!

First of all, he must radio through to Marsport, again. If there was any way they could rush the rescue ship sooner, then maybe he could hang on. Anyway, he must warn them what sort of planet this was, this so innocent seeming spot of nightmare and fever vision—

He tapped on the radio key for a minute. His mouth tightened. The radio was dead.

It had sent through the proper rescue message, received a reply, and then extinguished itself.

The proper touch of irony, he thought. There was only one thing to do. Draw a plan.

This he did. He got a yellow pencil and delineated his six day plan of escape.

Tonight, he wrote, read six more chapters of *War and Peace*. At four in the morning have hot black coffee. At four-fifteen take cards from pack and play ten games of solitaire. This should take until six-thirty when—more coffee. At seven o'clock, listen to early morning programs from Earth, if the receiving equipment on the radio works at all. Does it?

He tried the radio receiver. It was dead.

Well, he wrote, from seven o'clock until eight, sing all the songs you remember, make your own entertainment. From eight until nine think about

Helen King. Remember Helen. On second thought, think about Helen right now.

He marked that out with his pencil.

The rest of the days were set down in minute detail.

He checked the medical kit. There were several packets of tablets that would keep you awake. One tablet an hour every hour for six days. He felt quite confident.

"Here's mud in your evil eye, Iorr, Tylle!"

He swallowed one of the stay-wake tablets with a scalding mouth of black coffee.

*****

Well, with one thing and another it was Tolstoy or Balzac, gin-rummy, coffee, tablets, walking, more Tolstoy, more Balzac, more gin-rummy, more solitaire. The first day passed, as did the second and the third.

On the fourth day he lay quietly in the shade of a rock, counting to a thousand by fives, then by tens, to keep his mind occupied and awake. His eyes were so tired he had to bathe them frequently in cool water. He couldn't read, he was bothered with splitting headaches. He was so exhausted he couldn't move. He was numb with medicine. He resembled a waxen dummy, stuffed with things to preserve him in a state of horrified wakefulness. His eyes were glass, his tongue a rusted pike, his fingers felt as if they were gloved in needles and fur.

He followed the hand of his watch. One second less to wait, he thought. Two seconds, three seconds, four, five, ten, thirty seconds. A whole minute. Now an hour less time to wait. Oh, ship, hurry on thy appointed round!

He began to laugh softly.

What would happen if he just gave up, drifted off into sleep? Sleep, ah, sleep; perchance to dream. All the world a stage.... What if he gave up the unequal struggle, lapsed down?

Eeeeeeeeeee, the high, shrill warning sound of battle metal.

He shivered. His tongue moved in his dry, burry mouth.

Iorr and Tylle would battle out their ancient battle.

Leonard Sale would become quite insane.

And whichever won the battle, would take this ruin of an insane man, the shaking, laughing wild body, and wander it across the face of this world for ten, twenty years, occupying it, striding in it, pompous, holding court, making grand gestures, ordering heads severed, calling on inward unseen dancing girls. Leonard Sale, what remained of him, would be led off to some hidden cave, there to be infested with wars and worms of wars for twenty insane years, occupied and prostituted by old and outlandish thoughts.

When the rescue ship arrived it would find nothing. Sale would be hidden somewhere by a triumphant army in his head. Hidden in some cleft of rock, placed there like a nest for Iorr to lie upon in evil occupation.

The thought of it almost broke him in half.

Twenty years of insanity. Twenty years of torture, doing what you don't want to do. Twenty years of wars raging and being split apart, twenty years of nausea and trembling.

His head sank down between his knees. His eyes snapped and cracked and made soft noises. His eardrum popped tiredly.

Sleep, sleep, sang soft sea voices.

I'll—I'll make a proposition with you, listen, thought Leonard Sale. You, Iorr, you, too, Tylle! Iorr, you can occupy me on Mondays, Wednesdays and Fridays. Tylle, you can take me over on Sundays, Tuesdays and Saturdays. Thursday is maid's night out. Okay?

Eeeeeeeeeeeee, sang the sea tides, seething in his brain.

Ohhhhhhhhhhhhhh, sang the distant voices softly, soft.

What'll you say, is it a *bargain*, Iorr, Tylle?

No, said a voice.

No, said another.

Greedy, both of you, greedy! complained Sale. A pox on both your houses!

He slept.

*****

He *was* Iorr, jeweled rings on his hands. He arose beside his rocket and held out his fingers, commanding blind armies. He was Iorr, ancient ruler of jeweled warriors.

He *was* Tylle, lover of women, killer of dogs!

With some hidden bit of awareness, his hand crept to the holster at his hip. The sleeping hand withdrew the gun there. The hand lifted, the gun pointed.

The armies of Tylle and Iorr gave battle.

The gun exploded.

The bullet tore across Sale's forehead, wakening him.

He stayed awake for another six hours, getting over his latest siege. He knew it to be hopeless now. He washed and bandaged the wound he had given himself. He wished he had aimed straighter and it was all over. He watched the sky. Two more days. Two more. Come on, ship, come on. He was heavy with sleeplessness.

No use. At the end of six hours he was raving badly. He took the gun up and put it down and took it up again, put it against his head, tightened his hand on the trigger, changed his mind, looked at the sky again.

Night settled. He tried to read, threw the book away. He tore it up and burned it, just to have something to do.

So tired. In another hour, he decided. If nothing happens, I'll kill myself. This is for certain now. I'll *do* it, this time.

He got the gun ready and laid it on the ground next to himself.

He was very calm now, though tired. It would be over and done. He would be dead.

He watched the minute hand of his watch. One minute, five minutes, twenty-five minutes.

The flame appeared on the sky.

It was so unbelievable he started to cry. "A rocket," he said, standing up. "A rocket!" he cried, rubbing his eyes. He ran forward.

The flame brightened, grew, came down.

He waved frantically, running forward, leaving his gun, his supplies, everything behind. "You *see* that, Iorr, Tylle! You savages, you monsters, I beat you! I *won*! They're coming to rescue me now! I've won, damn you."

He laughed harshly at the rocks and the sky and the backs of his hands.

The rocket landed. Leonard Sale stood swaying, waiting for the door to lid open.

"Goodbye, Iorr, goodbye, Tylle!" he shouted in triumph, grinning, eyes hot.

Eeeeee, sang a diminishing roar in time.

Ahhhhhh, voices faded.

The rocket flipped wide its air-lock. Two men jumped out.

"Sale?" they called. "We're Ship ACDN13. Intercepted your SOS and decided to pick you up ourselves. The Marsport ship won't get through until day after tomorrow. We want a spot of rest ourselves. Thought it'd be good to spend the night here, pick you up, and go on."

"No," said Sale, face melting with terror. "No spend night—"

He couldn't talk. He fell to the ground.

"Quick," said a voice, in the bleary vortex over him. "Give him a shot of food liquid, another of sedative. He needs sustenance and rest."

"No rest!" screamed Sale.

"Delirious," said one man softly.

"No sleep!" screamed Sale.

"There, there," said the man gently. A needle poked into Sale's arm.

Sale thrashed. "No sleep, go!" he mouthed horribly. "Oh, go!"

"Delirious," said one man. "Shock."

"No *sedative*!" screamed Sale.

The sedative flowed into him.

Eeeeeeeeeee, sang the ancient winds.

Ahhhhhhhhhhh, sang the ancient seas.

"No sedative, no sleep, please, don't, don't, *don't*!" screamed Sale, trying to get up. "You don't—understand!"

"Take it easy, old man, you're safe among us now, nothing to worry about," said the rescuer above him.

Leonard Sale slept. The two men stood over him.

As they watched, Sale's features changed violently. He groaned and cried and snarled in his sleep. His face was riven with emotion. It was the face of a saint, a sinner, a fiend, a monster, a darkness, a light, one, many, an army, a vacuum, all, all!

He writhed in his sleep.

Eeeeeeeeee! the sound burst from his mouth. *Ahhhhhhhhhh!* he screamed.

"What's wrong with him?" asked one of the two rescuers.

"I don't know. More sedative?"

"More sedative. Nerves. He needs more sleep."

They stuck the needle in his arm. Sale writhed and spat and moaned.

Then, suddenly, he was dead.

He lay there, the two men over him. "What a shame," said one of them. "Can you figure that?"

"Shock. Poor guy. What a pity." They covered his face. "Did you ever see a face like that?"

"Totally insane."

"Loneliness. Shock."

"Yes. Lord, what an expression. I hope never to see a face like *that* again."

"What a shame, waiting for us, and we arrive, and he dies anyway."

They glanced around. "What shall we do? Shall we spend the night?"

"Yes. It's good to be out of the ship."

"We'll bury him first, of course."

"Naturally."

"And spend the night in the open, with good air, right? Good to be in the open again. After two weeks in that damned ship."

"Right. I'll find a spot for him. You start supper, eh?"

"Done."

"Should be good sleeping tonight."

"Fine, fine."

They made a grave and said a word over it. They drank their evening coffee silently. They smelled the sweet air of the planet and looked at the lovely sky and the bright and beautiful stars.

"What a night," they said, lying down.

"Pleasant dreams," said one, rolling over.

And the other replied, "Pleasant dreams."

They slept.

Defense Mech

Halloway stared down at Earth, and his brain tore loose and screamed, Man, man, how'd you

get in a mess like this, in a rocket a million miles past the moon, shooting for Mars and danger and terror and maybe death.

*****

Oh, my god, do you realize how far from Earth we are? Do you really *think* about it? It's enough to scare the guts from a man. Hold me up. *Do* something. Give me sedatives or hold my hand or run call mama. A million cold miles up. See all the flickering stars? Look at my hands tremble. Feel my heart whirling like a hot pinwheel!

The captain comes toward me, a stunned expression on his small, tight face. He takes my arm, looking into my eyes. Hello, captain. I'm sick, if that's what you want to know. I've a right to be scared—just look at all that space! Standing here a moment ago, I stared down at Earth so round and cloud-covered and asleep on a mat of stars, and my brain tore loose and screamed, man, man, how'd you get in a mess like this, in a rocket a million miles past the moon, shooting for Mars with a crew of fourteen others! I can hardly stand up, my knees, my hands, my heart, are shaking apart. Hold me up, sir.

What are hysterics like? The captain unprongs the inter-deck audio and speaks swiftly, scowling, into it. I hope he's phoning the psychiatrist. I need something. Oh, dammit, dammit!

The psychiatrist descends the ladder in immaculate salt-white uniform and walks toward me in a dream. Hello, doctor. You're the one for me. Please, sir, turn this damned rocket around and fly back to New York. I'll go crazy with all this space and distance!

The psychiatrist and the captain's voices murmur and blend, with here and there an emphasis, a toss of head, a gesture:

"Young Halloway here's on a fear-jag, doctor. Can you help him?"

"I'll try. Good man, Halloway is. Imagine you'll need him and his muscles when we land."

"With the crew as small as it is, every man's worth his weight in uranium. He's *got* to be cured."

The psychiatrist shakes his head.

"Might have to squirt him full of drugs to keep him quiet the rest of the expedition."

The captain explodes, saying that is impossible. Blood drums in my head. The doctor moves closer, smelling clean, sharp and white.

"Please, understand, captain, this man is definitely psychotic about going home. His talk is almost a reversion to childhood. I can't refuse his demands, and his fear seems too deeply based for reasoning. However, I think I've an idea. Halloway?"

Yes, sir? Help me, doctor. I want to go home. I want to see popcorn exploding into a buttered avalanche inside a glass cube, I want to roller skate, I want to climb into the old cool wet ice-wagon and go *chikk-chikk-chikk* on the ice with a sharp pick, I want to take long sweating hikes in the country, see big brick buildings and bright-faced people, fight the old gang, anything but this—*awful*!

The psychiatrist rubs his chin.

"All right, son. You can go back to Earth, now, tonight."

Again the captain explodes.

"You can't tell him *that*. We're landing on Mars *today*!"

The psychiatrist pats down the captain patiently.

"Please, captain. Well, Halloway, back to New York for you. How does it sound?"

I'm not not so scared now. We're going down on the moving ladder and here is the psychiatrist's cubicle.

He's pouring lights into my eyes. They revolve like stars on a disc. Lots of strange machines around, attachments to my head, my ears. Sleepy. Oh, so sleepy. Like under warm water. Being pushed around. Laved. Washed. Quiet. Oh, gosh. Sleepy.

"—listen to me, Halloway—"

Sleepy. Doctor's talking. Very soft, like feathers. Soft, soft.

"—you're going to land on earth. No matter what they tell you, you're landing on Earth ... no matter what happens you'll be on Earth ... everything you see and do will be like on Earth ... remember that ... remember that ... you won't be afraid because you'll be on Earth ... remember that ... over and over ... you'll land on Earth in an hour ... home ... home again ... no matter what anyone says...."

Oh, yes, sir, home again. Sleepy. Home again. Drifting, sleeping, oh thank you, sir, thank you from the bottom of my drowsy, sleepy soul. Yes, sir. Yes, sir. Sleepy. Drifting.

*****

I'm awake!

Hey, everybody, come look! Here comes Earth! Right at us, like a green moss ball off a bat! Coming at us on a curve!

"Check stations! Mars landing!"

"Get into bulgers! Test atmosphere!"

Get into your *what* did he say?

"Your baseball uniform, Halloway. Your baseball uniform."

Yes, sir. My baseball uniform. Where'd I put it? Over here. Head into, legs into, feet into it. There. Ha, this is great! Pitch her in here, old boy, old boy! *Smack!* Yow!

Yes, sir, it's over in that metal locker. I'll take it out. Head, arms, legs into it—I'm dressed. Baseball uniform. Ha! This is great! Pitch 'er in here, ole boy, ole boy! *Smack!* Yow!

"Adjust bulger helmets, check oxygen."

What?

"Put on your catcher's mask, Halloway."

Oh. The mask slides down over my face. Like that. The captain comes rushing up, eyes hot green and angry.

"Doctor, what's this infernal nonsense?"

"You wanted Halloway able to do his work, didn't you, captain?"

"Yes, but what in hell've you done to him?"

Strange. As they talk, I hear their words flow over my head like a wave dashed on a sea-stone, but the words drain off, leaving no imprint. As soon as some words invade my head, something eats and digests them and I think the words are something else entirely.

The psychiatrist nods at me.

"I couldn't change his basic desire. Given time, yes, a period of months, I could have. But you need him *now*. So, against all the known ethics of my profession, which say one must never lie to a patient, I've followed along in his own thought channel. I didn't dare frustrate him. He wanted to go home, so I *let* him. I've given him a fantasy. I've set up a protective defense mechanism in his mind that refuses to believe certain realities, that evaluates all things from its own desire for security and home. His mind will automatically block any thought or image that endangers that security."

The captain stares wildly.

"Then, then Halloway's insane!"

"Would you have him mad with fear, or able to work on Mars hindered by only a slight 'tetched' condition? Coddle him and he'll do fine. Just remember, we're landing on Earth, *not* Mars."

"Earth, Mars, you'll have *me* raving next!"

The doctor and the captain certainly talk weirdly. Who cares? Here comes Earth! Green, expanding like a moist cabbage underfoot!

"Mars landing! Air-lock opened! Use bulger oxygen."

Here we go, gang! Last one out is a pink chimpanzee!

"Halloway, come back, you damn fool! You'll kill yourself!"

Feel the good sweet Earth! Home again! Praise the Lord! Let's dance, sing off-key, laugh! Ha! Oh, boy!

In the door of the house stands the captain, his face red and wrinkled, waving his fists.

"Halloway, come back! Look behind you, you fool!"

I whirl about and cry out, happily.

Shep! Shep, old dog! He comes running to meet me, long fur shining amber in the sunshine. Barking. Shep, I haven't seen you in years. Good old pooch. Come 'ere, Shep. Let me pet you.

The captain shrieks:

"Don't pet it! It looks like a carnivorous Martian worm. Man, the jaws on that thing! Halloway, use your knife!"

Shep snarls and shows his teeth. Shep, what's wrong? That's no way to greet me. Come on, Shep. Hey! I pull back my fingers as his swift jaws snap. Shep circles me, swiftly. You haven't rabies, have you, Shep? He darts in, snatches my ankle with strong, locking white teeth! Lord, Shep, you're crazy! I can't let this go on. And you used to be such a fine, beautiful dog. Remember all the hikes we took into the lazy corn country, by the red barns and deep wells? Shep clenches tight my ankle. I'll give him one more chance. Shep, *let go*! Where did this long knife come from in my hand, like magic? Sorry to do this, Shep, but—*there*!

Shep screams, thrashing, screams again. My arm pumps up and down, my gloves are freckled with blood-flakes.

Don't scream, Shep. I *said* I was sorry, didn't I?

"Get out there, you men, and bury that beast immediately."

I glare at the captain. Don't talk that way about Shep.

The captain stares at my ankle.

"Sorry, Halloway. I meant, bury that 'dog,' you men. Give him full honors. You were lucky, son, another second and those knife-teeth'd bored through your ankle-cuff metal."

I don't know what he means. I'm wearing sneakers, sir.

"Oh, yeah, so you are. Yeah. Well, I'm sorry, Halloway. I know how you must feel about—Shep. He was a fine dog."

I think about it a moment and my eyes fill up, wet.

*****

There'll be a picnic and a hike; the captain says. Three hours now the boys have carried luggage from the metal house. The way they talk, this'll be some picnic. Some seem afraid, but who worries about copperheads and water-moccasins and crawfish? Not me. No, sir. Not me.

Gus Bartz, sweating beside me on some apparatus, squints at me.

"What's eatin' you, Halloway?"

I smile. Me? Nothing. Why?

"You and that act with that Martian worm."

What're you talking about? What worm?

The captain interrupts, nervously.

"Bartz, lay off Halloway. The doctor'll explain why. Ask him."

Bartz goes away, scratching his head.

The captain pats my shoulder.

"You're our strong-arm man, Halloway. You've got muscles from working on the rocket engines. So keep alert today, eh, on your hike to look over the territory? Keep your—b.b. gun—ready."

Beavers, do you think, sir?

The captain swallows hard and blinks.

"Unh—oh, beavers, yeah, beavers. Sure. Beavers! Maybe. Mountain lions and Indians, too, I hear. Never can tell. Be careful."

Mountain lions and Indians in New York in this day and age? Aw, sir.

"Let it go. Keep alert, anyhow. Smoke?"

I don't smoke, sir. A strong mind in a healthy body, you know the old rule.

"The old rule. Oh, *yes*. The *old* rule. Only joking. I don't want a smoke anyway. Like hell."

What was that last, sir?

"Nothing, Halloway, carry on, carry on."

I help the others work, now. Are we taking the yellow street-car to the edge of town, Gus?

"We're using propulsion belts, skimming low over the dead seas."

How's that again, Gus?

"I said, we're takin' the yellow street-car to the end of the line, yeah."

We're ready. Everyone's packed, spreading out. We're going in groups of four. Down Main Street past the pie factory, over the bridge, through the tunnel, past the circus grounds and we'll rendezvous, says the captain, at a place he points to on a queer, disjointed map.

Whoosh! We're off! I forgot to pay my fare.

"That's okay, I paid it."

Thanks, captain. We're really traveling. The cypresses and the maples flash by. *Kaawhoom!* I wouldn't admit this to anyone but you, sir, but momentarily, there, I didn't see this street-car. Suddenly we moved in empty space, nothing supporting us, and I didn't see any car. But *now* I see it, sir.

The captain gazes at me as at a nine-day miracle.

"You do, eh?"

Yes, sir. I clutch upward. Here's the strap. I'm holding it.

"You look pretty funny sliding through the air with your hand up like that, Halloway."

How's that, sir?

"Ha, ha, ha!"

Why are the others laughing at me, sir?

"Nothing, son, nothing. Just happy, that's all."

Ding Ding. Ding Ding. Canal Street and Washington. *Ding Ding. Whoosh.* This is real traveling. Funny, though, the captain and his men keep moving, changing seats, never stay seated. It's a long street-car. I'm way in back now. They're up front.

By the large brown house on the next corner stands a popcorn wagon, yellow and red and blue. I can taste the popcorn in my mind. It's been a long time since I've eaten some ... if I ask the captain's permission to stop and buy a bag, he'll refuse. I'll just sneak off the car at the next stop. I can get back on the next car and catch up with the gang later.

*****

How do you stop this car? My fingers fumble with my baseball outfit, doing something I don't want to know about. The car is stopping! Why's that. Popcorn is more important.

I'm off the car, walking. Here's the popcorn machine with a man behind it, fussing with little silver metal knobs.

"*—murr—lokk—loc—cor—iz—*"

Tony! Tony, bambino! What are you doing here?

"*Click.*"

It can't be, but it is. Tony, who died ten long years ago, when I was a freckled kid! Alive and selling popcorn again. Oh, Tony, it's good to see you. His black moustache's so waxed, so shining, his dark hair like burnt oily shavings, his dark shining happy eyes, his smiling red cheeks! He shimmers in my eyes like in a cold rain. Tony! Let me shake your hand! Gimme a bag of popcorn, senor!

"*Click-click-click—sput-click—reeeeee-eeeeeeee—*"

The captain didn't see you, Tony, you were hidden so well, only *I* saw you. Just a moment while I search for my nickel.

"*Reeeeeee.*"

Whew, I'm dizzy. It's very hot. My heads spins like a leaf on a storm wind. Let me hold onto your wagon, Tony, quick, I'm shivering and I've got sharp needle head pains....

"*Reeeeeeee.*"

I'm running a temperature. I feel as if I have a torch hung flaming in my head.

Hotter. Pardon me for criticizing you, Tony, but I think its your popper turned up too high. Your face looks afraid, contorted, and your hands move so rapidly, why? Can't you shut it off? I'm hot. Everything melts. My knees sag.

Warmer still. He'd better turn that thing off, I can't take any more. I can't find my nickel anyhow. Please, snap it off, Tony, I'm sick. My uniform glows orange. I'll take fire!

Here, I'll turn it off for you, Tony.

You *hit* me!

Stop hitting me, stop clicking those knobs! It's hot, I tell you. Stop, or I'll—

Tony. Where are you? Gone.

Where did that purple flame shoot from? That loud blast, what was it? The flame seemed to stream from my hand, out of my scout flashlight. Purple flame—eating!

I smell a sharp bitter odor.

Like hamburger fried overlong.

I feel better now. Cool as winter. But—

Like a fly buzzing in my ears, a voice comes, faint, far off,

"Halloway, damn it, Halloway, where are you?"

Captain! It's his voice, sizzling. I don't see you, sir!

"Halloway, we're on the dead sea bottom near an ancient Martian city and—oh, never mind, dammit, if you hear me, press your boy-scout badge and yell!"

I press the badge intensely, sweating. Hey, captain!

"Halloway! Glory. You're *not* dead. Where are you?"

I stopped for popcorn, sir. I can't see you. How do I hear you?

"It's an echo. Let it go. If you're okay, grab the next street-car."

That's very opportune. Because here comes a big red street-car now, around the corner of the drug store.

"*What!*"

Yes, sir, and its chock full of people. I'll climb aboard.

"Wait a minute! Hold on! Murder! What *kind* of people, dammit?"

It's the West Side gang. Sure. The whole bunch of tough kids.

"West side gang, hell, those are Martians, get the hell outa there! Transfer to another car—take the subway! Take the elevated!"

Too late. The car's stopped. I'll have to get on. The conductor looks impatient.

"Impatient," he says. "You'll be massacred!"

Oh, oh. Everybody's climbing from the street-car, looking angry at me. Kelly and Grogan and Tompkins and the others. I guess there'll be a fight.

The captain's voice stabs my ears, but I don't see him anywhere:

"Use your r-gun, your blaster, your blaster. Hell, use your slingshot, or throw spitballs, or whatever the devil you imagine you got holstered there, but *use* it! Come on, men, about face and back!"

I'm outnumbered. I bet they'll gang me and give me the bumps, the bumps, the bumps. I bet they'll truss me to a maple tree, maple tree, maple tree and tickle me. I bet they'll ink-tattoo their initials on my forehead. Mother won't like this.

The captain's voice opens up louder, driving nearer:

"And Poppa ain't happy! Get outa there, Halloway!"

They're hitting me, sir! We're battling!

"Keep it up, Halloway!"

I knocked one down, sir, with an upper-cut. I'm knocking another down now. Here goes a third! Someone's grabbed my ankle. I'll kick him! *There!* I'm stumbling, falling! Lights in my eyes, purple ones, big purple lightning bolts sizzling the air!

Three of them vanished, just like that!

I think they fell down a manhole.

I'm sorry. I didn't mean to hurt them bad.

They stole my flashlight.

"Get it back, Halloway! We're coming. Get your flash and use it!" That's silly.

"Silly," he says. "Silly. Silly."

*****

I got my flashlight back, broken, no good. We're wrestling. There are so many of them, I'm weak. They're climbing all over me, hitting. It's not fair, I'm falling down, kicking, screaming!

"Up speed, men, full power!"

They're binding me up. I can't move. They're rushing me into the street-car now. Now I won't be able to go on that hike. And I planned on it so hard, too.

"*Here we are, Halloway! Blast 'em, men! Oh, my Lord, look at the horrible faces on those creatures! Guh!*"

Watch out, captain! They'll get you, too, and the others! *Ahh!* Somebody struck me on the back of my head. Darkness. Dark. Dark.

Rockabye baby on the tree-top ... when the wind blows....

"Okay, Halloway, *any* time. Just any old time you want to come to."

Dark. A voice talking. Dark as a whale's insides. Ouch, my head. I'm flat on my back, I can feel rocks under me.

"Good morning, *dear* Mr. Halloway."

That you, captain, over in that dark corner?

"It ain't the president of the United States!"

Where is this cave?

"Suppose *you* tell us, you got us into this mess with your eternally blasted popcorn! Why'd you get off the street-car?"

Did the West Side gang truss us up like this, captain?

"West Side gang, *goh*! Those faces, those inhuman, weird, unsavory and horrible faces. All loose-fleshed and—gangrenous. Aliens, the whole rotting clutch of 'em."

What a funny way to talk.

"Listen, you parboiled idiot, in about an hour we're going to be fried, gutted, iced, killed, slaughtered, murdered, we will be, ipso facto, dead. Your 'friends' are whipping up a little blood-letting jamboree. Can't I shove it through your thick skull, we're on Mars, about to be sliced and hammered by a lousy bunch of Martians!"

"Captain, sir?"

"Yes, Berman?"

"The cave door is opening, sir. I think the Martians are ready to have at us again, sir. Some sort of test or other, no doubt."

"Let go a me, you one-eyed monster! I'm coming, don't push!"

We're outside the cave. They're cutting our bonds. See, captain, they aren't hurting us, after all. Here's the brick alley. There's Mrs. Haight's underwear waving on the clothes-line. See all the people from the beer hall—what're they waiting for?

"To see us die."

"Captain, what's wrong with Halloway, he's acting queer—"

"At least he's better off than us. He can't see these creatures' faces and bodies. It's enough to turn a man's stomach. This must be their amphitheatre. That looks like an obstacle course. I gather from their sign lingo that if we make it through the obstacles, we're free. Footnote: nobody's ever gotten through alive yet. Seems they want you to go first, Berman. Good luck, boy."

"So long, captain. So long, Gus. So long, Halloway."

Berman's running down-alley with an easy, long-muscled stride. I hear him yelling high and clear, even though he's getting far away.

Here comes an automobile!

Berman! Ahh! It hit him! He's fallen!

Berman, get up, get up!

"Stay here, Halloway, it's not your turn yet."

My turn? What do you mean? Someone's gotta help Berman.

"Halloway, come back! Oh, man, I don't want to see this!"

*****

Lift up my legs, put them down, breathe out, breathe in, swing arms, swing legs, chew my tongue, blink my eyes, Berman, here I come, gee, things are crazy-funny, here comes an ice-wagon trundling along, it's coming right at *me*! I can't see to get around it, it's coming so fast, I'll jump inside it, jump, jump, cool, ice, ice-pick, *chikk-chikk-chikk*, I hear the captain screaming off a million hot miles gone, *chikk-chikk-chikk* around the ice perimeter, the ice wagon is thundering, rioting, jouncing, shaking, rolling on big rusty iron wheels, smelling of sour ammonia, bouncing on a corduroy dirt and brick alley-road, the rear end of it seems to be snapping shut with many ice-prongs, I feel intense pain in my left leg, *chikk-chikk-chikk-chikk*! piece of ice, cold square, cold cube, a shuddering and convulsing, a temblor, the wagon wheels stop rolling, I jump down and run away from the wrecked wagon, did the wagon roll over Berman, I hope not, a fence here, I'll jump over it, another popcorn machine, very warm, very hot, all flame and red fire and burning metal knobs....

Oops, I didn't mean to strike the popcorn man down, hello, Berman, what're you doing in my arms, how'd you get here, did I pick you up, and why? an obstacle race at the high-school? you're heavy, I'm tired, dogs nipping at my heels, how far am I supposed to carry you? I hear the captain screaming me on, for why, for why? here comes the big bad truant officer with a club in his hand to take me back to school, he looks mean and broad....

I kicked the truant officer's shins and kicked him in the face ... Mama won't like that ... yes, mommy ... no mommy ... that's unfair ... that's not ethical fighting ... something went squish ... hmm ... let's forget about it, shall we?

Breathing hard. Here comes the gang after me, all the rough, bristly Irishmen and scarred Norwegians and stubborn Italians ... hit, kick, wrestle ... here comes a swift car, fast, fast! I hope I can duck, with you, Berman ... here comes another car from the opposite way!... If I work things right ... uh ... stop screaming, Berman!

The cars crashed into each other.

The cars still roll, tumbling, like two animals tearing at each other's throats.

Not far to go now, Berman, to the end of the alley. Just ahead. I'll sleep for forty years when this is over ... where'd I get this flashlight in my hand? from one of those guys I knocked down? from the popcorn man? I'll poke it in front of me ... people run away ... maybe they don't like its light in their eyes.... The end of the alley! There's the green valley and my house, and there's Mom and Pop waiting! Hey, let's sing, let's dance, we're going home!

"Halloway, you so-and-so, you did it!"

Dark. Sleep. Wake up slow. Listen.

"—and Halloway ran down that amphitheatre nonchalant as a high-school kid jumping hurdles. A big saffron Martian beast with a mouth so damn big it looked like the rear end of a delivery truck, lunged forward square at Halloway—"

"What'd Halloway do?"

"Halloway jumped right inside the monster's mouth—right inside!"

"What happened then?"

"The animal looked dumbfounded. It tried to spit out. Then, to top it all, what did Halloway do, I ask you, I ask you, what did he do? He drew forth his boy-scout blade and went *chikk-chikk-chikk* all around the bloody interior, pretending like he's holed up in an ice-wagon, chipping himself off pieces of ice."

"No?"

"On my honor! The monster, after taking a bit of this *chikk-chikk-chikk* business, leaped around, cavorting, floundering, rocking, tossing, and then, with a spout of blood, out popped Halloway, grinning like a kid, and on he ran, dodging spears and pretending they were pebbles, leaping a line of crouched warriors and saying they're a picket fence. Then he lifted Berman and trotted with him until he met a three hundred pound Martian wrestler. Halloway supposed that it was the truant officer and promptly kicked him in the face. Then he knocked down another guy working furiously at the buttons of a paralysis machine which looked, to Halloway, like a popcorn wagon! After which two gigantic black Martian leopards attacked, resembling to him nothing more than two very bad drivers in dark automobiles. Halloway sidestepped. The two 'cars' crashed and tore each other apart, fighting. Halloway pumped on, shooting people with his 'flashlight' which he retrieved from the 'popcorn' man. Pointing the flash at people, he was amazed when they vanished and—oh, oh, Halloway's waking up, I saw his eyelids flicker. Quiet, everyone. Halloway, you awake?"

Yeah. I been listening to you talk for five minutes. I still don't understand. Nothing happened at all. How long I been asleep?

"Two days. Nothing happened, eh? Nothing, except you got the Martians kow-towing, that's all, brother. Your spectacular performance impressed people. The enemy suddenly decided that if *one* earthman could do what you did, what would happen if a million more came?"

Everybody keeps on with this joking, this lying about Mars. Stop it. Where am I?

"Aboard the rocket, about to take off."

Leave Earth? No, no, I don't want to leave Earth, good green Earth! Let go! I'm afraid! Let go of me! Stop the ship!

"Halloway, *this* is Mars—we're going back *to* Earth."

Liars, all of you! I don't want to go to Mars, I want to stay here, on Earth!

"Holy cow, here we go again. Hold him down, Gus. Hey, doctor, on the double! Come help Halloway change his mind back, willya!"

Liars! You can't do this! Liars! Liars!

Lazarus Come Forth

The Morgue Ship had gleaned information from
space that would end the three hundred year war,
knowledge that would defeat the aggressor Martians—if Brandon could carry it to Earth.

*****

Logan's way of laughing was bad. "There's a new body up in the air-lock, Brandon. Climb the rungs and have a look."

Logan's eyes had a green shine to them, eager and intent. They were ugly, obscene.

Brandon swore under his breath. This room of the Morgue Ship was crowded with their two personalities. Besides that, there were scores of cold shelves of bodies freezing quietly, and the insistent vibration of the coroner tables, machinery spinning under them. And Logan was like a little machine that never stopped talking.

"Leave me alone." Brandon rose up, tall and thinned by the years, looking as old as a pocked meteor. "Just keep quiet."

Logan sucked his cigarette. "Scared to go upstairs? Scared it might be your son we just picked up?"

Brandon reached Logan in about one stride, and while the Morgue Ship slipped on through space, he clenched the coroner's blue uniform with the small bones inside it and hung it up against the wall, pressing inward until Logan couldn't breathe. Logan blew air, his eyes looked helpless. He tried to speak and could only grunt like a stuck pig. He waved his short arms, flapping.

Brandon kept him there, crucified on a fist.

"I told you. Let me search for my own son's body in my own way. I don't need your tongue."

Logan's eyes were losing their shine, were getting blind and glazed. Brandon stepped back, releasing the little assistant. Logan bumped softly against metal flooring, his mouth hungry for air, his nostrils flaring for breath. Brandon watched the little face of Logan over the crouched, gasping body, with red color and anger shooting up into it with every passing second.

"Coward!" he threw it out of himself, Logan did. "Got yellow—neon-tubing—for your spine. Coward. Never went to war. Never did anything for Earth against Mars."

Brandon said the words in slow motion. "Shut up."

"Why?" Logan crept back, inching up the metal hull. The blood pumps under the skirts of the tables pulsed across the warm silence. "Does it hurt, the truth? Your son'd be proud of you, okay. Ha!" He coughed and spat. "He was so damn ashamed of you he went and signed up for space combat. So he got lost from his ship during a battle." Logan licked his lips very carefully. "So, to make up for it, you signed on a Morgue Ship. Try to find his body. Try to make amends. I know you. You wouldn't join the Space Warriors to fight. No guts for that. Had to get a nice easy job on a morgue ship—"

Lines appeared in Brandon's gaunt cheeks, his eyes were closed, the lids pale. He said, and tried to believe it himself, "Someone has to pick up the bodies after the battle. They can't go flying on forever in their own orbits. They deserve burial."

The bitterness of Logan struck even deeper. "Who are you tryin' to convince?" He was on his feet now. "Me, it's different. I got a right to running this ship. I was in the other war."

"You're a liar," Brandon retorted. "You hunted radium in the asteroids with a mineral tug. You took this Morgue Ship job so you could go right on hunting radium, picking up bodies on the side."

Logan laughed softly, but not humorously. "So what? Least I'm no coward. I'll burn anybody gets in my way." He thought it over. "Unless," he added, "they give me a little money."

Brandon turned away, feeling ill. He forced himself to climb up the rungs toward that air-lock, where that fresh body lay, newly still-born from space by the retrieving-claw. His palms let wet shining prints on the rungs. His climbing feet made a soft noise in the cold metal silence.

The body lay in the cold air-lock's center, as thousands had lain before. Its posture was one of easy slumber, relaxed and not speaking ever again.

*****

Brandon took in his breath. Numbly he realized it was not his son. Every time a new body was found he feared and yet hoped it would be Richard. Richard of the easy laughter and good smile and dark curly hair. Richard who was now floating off somewhere toward some far eternity.

Brandon's eyes dilated. He went to his knees and with efficient darts of his eyes, he covered the vital points of this strange uniform with the young body inside it. His heart pounded briefly, and when he got up again he acted like he had been struck in the face. He walked unsteadily to the rungs.

"Logan," he called down the hole in a numbed voice. "Logan, come up here. Quick."

Logan climbed lazily up, emitting grunts and smoke.

"Look here," said Brandon, kneeling again by the body.

Logan looked and didn't believe it. "Where in hell'd you get that?"

Lying there, the face of the body was like snow framed by the ebon-black of the hair. The eyes were blue jewels caught in the snow. There were slender fingers reclining against the hips. But, most important of all, was the cut of the silver metal uniform, the grey leather belt and the bronze triangle over the silent heart with the numerals 51 on it.

Logan held onto the rungs. "Three hundred years old," he whispered it. "Three hundred years old," he said.

"Yes." The Numerals 51 were enough for Brandon. "After all these centuries, and in perfect condition. Look how calm he is. Most corpse faces aren't—pretty. Something happened, three hundred years ago, and he's been drifting, alone, ever since. I—" Brandon caught his breath.

"What's wrong?" snapped Logan.

"This man," said Brandon, wonderingly, "committed suicide."

"How do you figure?"

"There's not a mark of decompression, centrifugal force, disintegrator or ray-burn on him. He simply *stepped* out of a ship. Why should a Scientist of the 51 Circle commit suicide?"

"They had wars back there, too," said Logan. "But this is the first time I ever seen a stiff from one of them. It can't happen. He shoulda been messed up by meteors."

A strange prickling crept over Brandon. "When I was a kid, I remember thumbing through history books, reading about those famous 51 Scientists of the Circle who were doing experimental work on Pluto back in the year 2100. I memorized their uniforms, and this bronze badge. I couldn't mistake it. There was a rumor that they were experimenting with some new universal power weapon."

"A myth," said Logan.

"Who knows? Maybe. Maybe not. But before that super weapon was completed, Earth fell beneath Mar's assault. The 51 Scientists destroyed themselves and their Base when the Martians came. The—myth—says that if the Martians had been only a month later—the weapon would have been out of blueprint and into metal."

Brandon stopped talking and looked at the long-boned, easily slumbering Scientist.

"And now he shows up. One of the original 51. I wonder what happened? Maybe he tried to reach Earth and had to leap into space to escape the Martians. Logan, we've got history with us, pulled in out of space, cold and stark under our hands."

Logan laughed uneasily. "Yeah. Now, if we only had that weapon. Baby, that'd be something to sing about, by God."

Brandon jerked.

Logan looked at him. "What's eating you?"

Brandon laid his fingers on the dead Scientist's skull.

"Maybe—just maybe—we *have* got the weapon," he said.

His hand trembled.

*****

The coroner pumps throbbed warmly under the table, while manipulating tendrils darted swiftly, effectively over the dead Scientist's body. Brandon moved, too, like a machine. In a regular fury he had forced Logan to hurry the body down into the preparations room, inject adrenalin, thermal units, apply the blood pump and accomplish a thousand other demanding and instantaneous tasks.

"Now, out of the way, Logan. You're more trouble than help!"

Logan stumbled back. "Okay, okay. Don't get snotty. It won't work. I keep telling you. All these years."

Brandon could see nothing. Logan's voice was muffled, far away. There was only the surge of pumps, the sweating heat of the little cubicle, and niche number 12 waiting to receive this body if he failed. Brandon swallowed, tightly. Niche number 12 waiting, cold, ready, waiting for a body to fill it. He'd have to fight to keep it empty.

He began to sing-song words over and over as he injected stimulants into the body. He didn't know where the words came from, from childhood, maybe, from his old religious memories:

"Lazarus come forth," Brandon said softly, bending close, adjusting the manipulatory tendrils. "Lazarus, come forth."

Logan snorted. "Lazarus! Will you can that!"

Brandon had to talk to himself. "Inside his brain he's got that energy weapon that Earth can use to end the war. It's been frozen in there three hundred years. If we can thaw it out—"

"Who ever heard of reviving a body after that long?"

"He's perfectly preserved. Perfectly frozen. Oh, God, this is Fate. I know it. I feel it. Came to find Richard and I found something bigger! Lazarus! Lazarus, come forth from the tomb!"

The machines thrummed louder, beating into his ears. Brandon listened, watched for just one pulse, just one beat, one word, one moment of life.

"Air for the lungs," and Brandon attached oxygen cones over the fine nose and relaxed lips. "Pressure on the ribs." Metal plates pressuring the rib case slowly out and in. "Circulation." Brandon touched the control at the foot of the table and the whole table tilted back and forth in a whining teeter-tauter.

A report clipped through on the audio:

"Morgue Ship. Battle Unit 766 calling Morgue Ship. Off orbit of Pluto 234CC, point zero-two, off 32, one by seven, follow up. Battle just terminated. Six Martian ships destroyed. One Earth ship blasted apart and bodies thrown into space. Please recover. 79 men. Bodies in orbit heading toward sun at 23456 an hour. Check."

Logan flipped his cigarette away. "That's us. We got work to do. Come on. Let that stiff cool. He'll be here when we come back."

"No!" Brandon fairly shouted it, eyes wild. "He's more important than all those men out there. We can help them later. He can help us now!"

The table came to a halt, bringing absolute silence.

Brandon bent forward to press his ear against the warmed rib-casing.

"Wait."

There it was. Unbelievably, there it was. A tiny pulse stirring like a termite down under, softly and sluggishly moving through the body, jabbing the heart and—NOW! Brandon cried out. He was shaking all over. He was setting the machine in operation again, and talking and laughing and going crazy with it.

"He's alive! He's alive! Lazarus has come from the tomb! Lazarus reborn again! Notify Earth immediately!"

*****

At the end of an hour, the pulse was timing normal, the temperature was lowering down from a fever, and Brandon moved about the preparations' room watching every quiver of the body's internal organs through the tubular-fluoroscope.

He exulted. This was having Richard alive again. It was compensation. You roared into space looking somewhere for your lost self-respect, your pride, looking for your son who is shooting on some soundless orbit into nothing, and now the biggest child of Fate is deposited in your arms to warm and bring to life. It was impossible. It was good. Brandon almost laughed. He almost forgot he had ever known fear of death. This was conquering it. This was like bringing Richard back to life, but even more. It meant things to earth and humanity; things about weapons and power and peace.

Logan interrupted Brandon's exultant thinking by blowing smoke in his face. "You know something, Brandy? This is damn good! You done something, Mister. Yeah."

"I thought I told you to notify Earth."

"Ah, I been watching you. Like a mama hen and her chick. I been thinking, too. Yeah." Logan shook ashes off his smoke. "Ever since you pulled in this prize fish, I been turning it over in my mind."

"Go up to the radio room and call Earth. We've got to rush the Scientist to Moon Base immediately. We can talk later."

There was that hard green shine to Logan's narrow eyes again. He poked a finger at Brandon. "Here's the way I get it. Do we get rewarded for finding this guy? Hell, no. It's our routine work. We're *supposed* to pick up bodies. Here we got a guy who's the key to the whole damn war."

Brandon's lips hardly moved. "Call Earth."

"Now, hold on a moment, Brandy. Let me finish this. I been thinking, maybe the Martians'd like to own him, too. Maybe they'd like to be around when he starts talking."

Brandon made a fist. "You heard what I said."

Logan put his hand behind him. "I just want to talk peaceable with you, Brandy. I don't want trouble. But all we'll get for finding this stiff is a kiss on the cheek and a medal on the chest. Hell!"

Brandon was going to hit him hard, before he saw the gun in Logan's fingers, whipped out and pointing.

"Take a look at this, Brandy, and don't lose your supper."

In spite of himself, Brandon quailed. It was almost an involuntary action. His whole body plunged back, aching, pulling with it.

"Now, let's march up to the radio room. I got a little calling to do. Get on with you. Hup!"

In the radio-room, Logan touched studs, raised a mike to his lips and said:

"Beam to Mars. Beam to Mars. Morgue Ship of Earth calling. Mars Beam answer."

After an interval, Mars gave answer. Logan said:

"I've just picked up the body of a 51 Circle Scientist. He's been resuscitated. Give me your fleet commander. I got things to talk over with him." Logan smiled. "Oh, *hello*, commander!"

*****

Half an hour later, the discussions were over, the plans made. Logan hung up, satisfied. Brandon looked at him as if he couldn't believe he was serious.

Back down in the control room, Logan set a course, and then forced Brandon to get the body ready. He bragged about the deal. "A half ton of radium, Brandy. Not bad, eh? Good pay. More than Earth'd ever give me for my routine duty."

Brandon shuddered. "You fool. The Martians will kill us."

"Uh-uh." Logan pantomimed him into moving the body onto a rollered table and taking it to the emergency life-craft air-lock. "I'm not that dumb. I'm having you wire this emergency life-boat with explosive. We collect the minerals first. We blow up the body if the Martians act funny. We make them wait until we've collected our half and gotten five hours' start toward Earth before we allow them to pick up the body. Nice, huh?"

Brandon swayed over the task of wiring the life-boat with explosive. "You're cutting your own throat. Handing over a weapon like that to the Martian enemy."

It was no again from Logan. "After the Martians pick up the body and we're safely on our way home to Earth, I press a button and the whole damn thing blows up. They call it double-crossing."

"Destroy the body?"

"Hell, yes. Think I want a weapon like that turned over to the enemy? Guh!"

"The war'll go on for years."

"So Earth'll wind up winning, anyhow. We're getting along, slow but sure. And when the war's over, I got a load of radium to set myself up in business and a big future in front of me."

"So you kill millions of men, for that."

"What'd they do for me? Ruined my guts in the last war!"

There had to be some argument, something to say, quick, something to do to a man like Logan. Brandon thought, quickly. "Look, Logan, we can work this, but save the body."

"Don't be funny."

"Put one of the *other* bodies in the ship we send out. Save Lazarus' body and run back to Earth with it!" insisted Brandon.

The little assistant shook his head. "The Martians'll have an intra-material beam focused on the emergency ship when they get within one hundred thousand miles of her. They'll be able to tell then if the body's dead or alive. No dice, Brandy."

It was hardly like leaping himself, thought Brandon. It was just frustration and rage and unthinking action. Brandon jumped. Logan hardly flicked an eyelid as he pressed the trigger of his paragun. It paralyzed the legs from under Brandon and he collapsed. The gun sprayed over his groin and chest and face, too, in a withering shower of red-hot needles. The lights went out.

*****

There was a loose sensation of empty space, and acceleration minus power. Pure soundless momentum. Brandon forced his eyes open painfully, and found himself alone in the preparations' room, lying stretched upon one of the coroner tables, bound with metal fibre.

"Logan!" he bellowed it up through the ship. He waited. He did it again. "Logan!"

He fought the metal fibre, knotting his fists, twisting his arms. He yanked himself back and forth. It pretty well held, except for a looseness in the right hand binding. He worked on that. Upstairs, a queer, detached Martian bass voice intoned itself.

"500,000 miles. Prepare your emergency craft with the body of the Scientist inside of it, Morgue Ship. At 300,000 miles, release the emergency craft. We'll release *our* mineral payment ship now, giving you a half hour leeway to pick it up. It contains the exact amount you asked for."

Logan's voice next:

"Good. The Scientist is alive, still, and doing well. You're getting a bargain."

Brandon's face whitened, bringing out all the hard, scared bones of it, the cheeks and brow and chin bones. He jerked against the binding and it only jumped the air from his lungs so he sobbed. Breathing deeply, he lay back. They were taking his child back out into space. Lazarus, his second son, whom he had birthed out of space with a metal retriever, they were taking back out and away from him. You can't have your real son; so you take the second best and you slap him into breathing life, into breathing consciousness, and before he is a day old they try to tear him away from you again. Brandon fairly yelled against his manacles of wire. Sweat came down his face, and the stuff from his eyes wasn't all sweat.

Logan tiptoed down the hard rungs, grinning.

"Awake, Sleeping Beauty?"

Brandon said nothing. His right hand was loosened. It was wet and loosened, working like a small white animal at his side, slipping from its wire trap.

"You can't go ahead with it, Logan."

"Why not?"

"The Earth Tribunal will find out."

"You won't tell them." Logan was doing something across the room. He was the only moving thing in front of a hundred cold shelves of sleeping warriors.

Brandon gasped, tried to get up, fell back. "How'll you fake my death?"

"With an injection of sulfacardium. Heart failure. Too much pulse on a too old heart. Simple." Logan turned and there was a hypodermic in his hand.

Brandon lay there. The ship went on and on. The body was upstairs, lying breathing in its metal cradle, mothered by him and jerked to life by him, and now going away. Brandon managed to say:

"Do me a favor?"

"What?"

"Give me the drug now. I don't want to be awake when you send Lazarus out. I don't want that."

"Sure." Logan came walking across the deck, raising the hypodermic. It glittered hard and silver fine, and sharp.

"One more thing, Logan."

"Hurry it up!"

Only one arm free, one leg able to move slightly. Logan was pressing against the table, now. The hypodermic hesitated in his fingers.

"This!" said Brandon.

*****

With one foot, Brandon kicked the teeter-tauter control at the base of the board. The board, whining, began to elevate swiftly. With his free arm, instantly pulling the last way free from the wire, Brandon clutched Logan's screaming head and jammed it down under the table, under the descending board. Board and metal base ground together and kept on going three inches. Logan screamed only once. The sounds after that were so horrible that Brandon retched. Logan's body slumped and hung, arms slack, hypo dropped and shattered on the deck.

The whole table kept going up and down, up and down.

It made Brandon sicker with each movement. The whole room revolved, tipped, spun sickishly. The corpses in all their niches seemed to shiver with it.

He managed to kick the control to neutral and the table poised, elevated at the heels, so blood pounded hotly into Brandon's pale face, lighting, coloring it. His heart was pounding furiously and the chronometer upon the hull-wall clicked out time passing, time passing and miles with it, and Martians coming so much the closer....

He fought the remaining wires continuously, cursing, bringing threads and beads of blood from raw wrist, ankle and hips. Red lights buzzed like insects on the ceiling, spelling out:

"ROCKET COMING ... UNKNOWN CRAFT ... ROCKET APPROACHING...."

Hold on, Lazarus. Don't let them wake you all the way up. Don't let them take you. Better for you to go on slumbering forever.

The wire on his left wrist sprang open. It took another five minutes to bleed himself out of the ankle wires. The ship spun on, all too quickly.

Not looking at Logan's body, Brandon sprang from the table and with an infinite weariness tried to speed himself up the rungs. His mind raced ahead, but his body could only sludge rung after rung upward into the radio room. The door to the emergency rocket boat was wide and inside, living quietly, cheeks pink, pulse beating softly in throat, Lazarus lay unthinking, unknowing that his new father had come into his presence.

Brandon glanced at his wrist chronometer. Almost time to slam that door, shoving Lazarus out into space to meet the Martians. Five minutes.

He stood there, sweating. Then, decided, he put a tight audio beam straight on through to green Earth. Earth.

"*Morgue Ship coming home. Morgue Ship coming home! Important cargo. Important cargo. Please meet us off the Moon!*"

Setting the ship controls into an automatic mesh, he felt the thundering jets explode to life under him. It was not alone their shaking that pulsed through his body. It was something of himself, too. He was sick. He wanted to get back to Earth so badly he was violently ill with the desire. To forget all of war and death.

He could give Lazarus to the enemy and then turn homeward. Yes, he supposed he could do that. But, give up a second son where you already have given up one? No. No. Or, destroy the body now? Brandon fingered a ray-gun momentarily. Then he threw it away from him, eyes closed, swaying. No.

And if he should try to run away to Earth now? The Martians would pursue and capture him. There was no speed in a Morgue Ship to outdistance superior craft.

Brandon walked unsteadily to the side of the sleeping Scientist. He watched him a moment, touching him, looking at him with a lost light in his eyes.

Then, he began the final preparations, lifting the Scientist, going toward the life rocket.

*****

The Martians intercepted the emergency life-rocket at 5199CVZ. The Morgue Ship itself was nowhere visible. It had already completed its arc and was driving back toward Earth.

The body of Lazarus was hurried into the hospital cubicle of the Martian rocket. The body was laid upon a table, and immediate efforts were made to bring it out of its centuries of rest.

Lazarus reclined, silver uniform belted across the middle with soft mouse-grey leather, bronze symbol 51 over the heart.

Breathlessly, the Martians crowded in about the body, probing, examining, trying, waiting. The room got very warm. The little purple eyes blinked hot and tensed.

Lazarus was breathing deeply now, sighing into full aware life, Lazarus coming from the tomb. After three hundred years of avoid death.

Armed guards stood on both sides of the medical table, weapons poised, torture mechanisms ready to make Lazarus speak if he refused to tell.

The eyes of Lazarus fluttered open. Lazarus out of the tomb. Lazarus seeing his companions, iris widening upon itself, forcing shape out of mist. Seeing the curious blue skulls of anxious Martians collected in a watching crowd about him. Lazarus living, breathing, ready to speak.

Lazarus lifted his head, curiously, parted his lips, wetted them with his tongue, and then spoke. His first words were:

"What time is it?"

It was a simple sentence, and all of the Martians bent forward to catch its significance as one of the Martians replied:

"23:45."

Lazarus nodded and closed his eyes and lay back. "Good. He's safe then, by now. He's safe."

The Martians closed in, waiting for the next important words of the waking dead.

Lazarus kept his eyes closed, and he trembled a little, as if, in spite of himself, he couldn't help it.

He said:

"*My name is Brandon.*"

Then, Lazarus laughed....

Morgue Ship

This was Burnett's last trip. Three more shelves to fill with space-slain warriors—and he would be among the living again.

*****

He heard the star-port grind open, and the movement of the metal claws groping into space, and then the star-port closed.

There was another dead man aboard the *Constellation*.

Sam Burnett shook his long head, trying to think clearly. Pallid and quiet, three bodies lay on the cold transparent tables around him; machines stirred, revolved, hummed. He didn't see them. He didn't see anything but a red haze over his mind. It blotted out the far wall of the laboratory where the shelves went up and down, numbered in scarlet, keeping the bodies of soldiers from all further harm.

Burnett didn't move. He stood there in his rumpled white surgical gown, staring at his fingers gloved in bone-white rubber; feeling all tight and wild inside himself. It went on for days. Moving the ship. Opening the star-port. Extending the retriever claw. Plucking some poor warrior's body out of the void.

He didn't like it any more. Ten years is too long to go back and forth from Earth to nowhere. You came out empty and you went back full-cargoed with a lot of warriors who didn't laugh or talk or smoke, who just lay on their shelves, all one hundred of them, waiting for a decent burial.

"Number ninety-eight." Coming matter of fact and slow, Rice's voice from the ceiling radio hit Burnett.

"Number ninety-eight," Burnett repeated. "Working on ninety-five, ninety-six and ninety-seven now. Blood-pumps, preservative, slight surgery." Off a million miles away his voice was talking. It sounded deep. It didn't belong to him anymore.

Rice said:

"Boyohbody! Two more pick-ups and back to New York. Me for a ten-day drunk!"

Burnett peeled the gloves off his huge, red, soft hands, slapped them into a floor incinerator mouth. Back to Earth. Then spin around and shoot right out again in the trail of the war-rockets that blasted one another in galactic fury, to sidle up behind gutted wrecks of ships, salvaging any bodies still intact after the conflict.

Two men. Rice and himself. Sharing a cozy morgue ship with a hundred other men who had forgotten, quite suddenly, however, to talk again.

Ten years of it. Every hour of those ten years eating like maggots inside, working out to the surface of Burnett's face, working under the husk of his starved eyes and starved limbs. Starved for life. Starved for action.

This would be his last trip, or he'd know the reason why!

"Sam!"

Burnett jerked. Rice's voice clipped through the drainage-preservative lab, bounded against glassite retorts, echoed from the refrigerator shelves. Burnett stared at the tabled bodies as if they would leap to life, even while preservative was being pumped into their veins.

"Sam! On the double! Up the rungs!"

Burnett closed his eyes and said a couple of words, firmly. Nothing was worth running for any more. Another body. There had been one hundred thousand bodies preceding it. Nothing unusual about a body with blood cooling in it.

*****

Shaking his head, he walked unsteadily toward the rungs that gleamed up into the air-lock, control-room sector of the rocket. He climbed without making any noise on the rungs.

He kept thinking the one thing he couldn't forget.

You never catch up with the war.

All the color is ahead of you. The drive of orange rocket traces across stars, the whamming of steel-nosed bombs into elusive targets, the titanic explosions and breathless pursuits, the flags and the excited glory are always a million miles ahead.

He bit his teeth together.

You never catch up with the war.

You come along when space has settled back, when the vacuum has stopped trembling from unleashed forces between worlds. You come along in the dark quiet of death to find the wreckage plunging with all the fury of its original acceleration in no particular direction. You can only see it; you don't hear anything in space but your own heart kicking your ribs.

You see bodies, each in its own terrific orbit, given impetus by grinding collisions, tossed from mother ships and dancing head over feet forever and forever with no goal. Bits of flesh in ruptured space suits, mouths open for air that had never been there in a hundred billion centuries. And they kept dancing without music until you extended the retriever-claw and culled them into the air-lock.

That was all the war-glory he got. Nothing but the stunned, shivering silence, the memory of rockets long gone, and the shelves filling up all too quickly with men who had once loved laughing.

You wondered who all the men were; and who the next ones would be. After ten years you made yourself blind to them. You went around doing your job with mechanical hands.

But even a machine breaks down....

*****

"Sam!" Rice turned swiftly as Burnett dragged himself up the ladder. Red and warm, Rice's face hovered over the body of a sprawled enemy official. "Take a look at this!"

Burnett caught his breath. His eyes narrowed. There was something wrong with the body; his experienced glance knew that. He didn't know what it was.

Maybe it was because the body looked a little *too* dead.

Burnett didn't say anything, but he climbed the rest of the way, stood quietly in the grey-metal air-lock. The enemy official was as delicately made as a fine white spider. Eyelids, closed, were faintly blue. The hair was thin silken strands of pale gold, waved and pressed close to a veined skull. Where the thin-lipped mouth fell open a cluster of needle-tipped teeth glittered. The fragile body was enclosed completely in milk-pale syntha-silk, a holstered gun at the middle.

Burnett rubbed his jaw. "Well?"

Rice exploded. His eyes were hot in his young, sharp-cut face, hot and black. "Good Lord, Sam, do you know who this is?"

Burnett scowled uneasily and said no.

"It's Lethla!" Rice retorted.

Burnett said, "Lethla?" And then: "Oh, yes! Kriere's majordomo. That right?"

"Don't say it calm, Sam. Say it big. Say it big! If Lethla is here in space, then Kriere's not far away from him!"

Burnett shrugged. More bodies, more people, more war. What the hell. What the hell. He was tired. Talk about bodies and rulers to someone else.

Rice grabbed him by the shoulders. "Snap out of it, Sam. Think! Kriere—The All-Mighty—in our territory. His right hand man dead. That means Kriere was in an accident, too!"

Sam opened his thin lips and the words fell out all by themselves. "Look, Rice, you're new at this game. I've been at it ever since the Venus-Earth mess started. It's been see-sawing back and forth since the day you played hookey in the tenth grade, and I've been in the thick of it. When there's nothing left but seared memories, I'll be prowling through the void picking up warriors and taking them back to the good green Earth. Grisly, yes, but it's routine.

"As for Kriere—if he's anywhere around, he's smart. Every precaution is taken to protect that one."

"But Lethla! His body must mean something!"

"And if it does? Have we got guns aboard this morgue-ship? Are we a battle-cuiser to go against him?"

"We'll radio for help?"

"Yeah? If there's a warship within our radio range, seven hundred thousand miles, we'll get it. Unfortunately, the tide of battle has swept out past Earth in a new war concerning Io. That's out, Rice."

Rice stood about three inches below Sam Burnett's six-foot-one. Jaw hard and determined, he stared at Sam, a funny light in his eyes. His fingers twitched all by themselves at his sides. His mouth twisted, "You're one hell of a patriot, Sam Burnett!"

Burnett reached out with one long finger, tapped it quietly on Rice's barrel-chest. "Haul a cargo of corpses for three thousand nights and days and see how patriotic you feel. All those fine muscled lads bloated and crushed by space pressures and heat-blasts. Fine lads who start out smiling and get the smile burned off down to the bone—"

Burnett swallowed and didn't say anything more, but he closed his eyes. He stood there, smelling the death-odor in the hot air of the ship, hearing the chug-chug-chug of the blood pumps down below, and his own heart waiting warm and heavy at the base of his throat.

"This is my last cargo, Rice. I can't take it any longer. And I don't care much how I go back to earth. This Venusian here—what's his name? Lethla. He's number ninety-eight. Shove me into shelf ninety-nine beside him and get the hell home. That's how I feel!"

Rice was going to say something, but he didn't have time.

Lethla was alive.

He rose from the floor with slow, easy movements, almost like a dream. He didn't say anything. The heat-blast in his white fingers did all the necessary talking. It didn't say anything either, but Burnett knew what language it would use if it had to.

Burnett swallowed hard. The body had looked funny. Too dead. Now he knew why. Involuntarily, Burnett moved forward. Lethla moved like a pale spider, flicking his fragile arm to cover Burnett, the gun in it like a dead cold star.

Rice sucked in his breath. Burnett forced himself to take it easy. From the corners of his eyes he saw Rice's expression go deep and tight, biting lines into his sharp face.

Rice got it out, finally. "How'd you do it?" he demanded, bitterly. "How'd you live in the void? It's impossible!"

A crazy thought came ramming down and exploded in Burnett's head. *You never catch up with the war!*

But what if the war catches up with you?

What in hell would Lethla be wanting aboard a morgue ship?

*****

Lethla half-crouched in the midst of the smell of death and the chugging of blood-pumps below. In the silence he reached up with quick fingers, tapped a tiny crystal stud upon the back of his head, and the halves of a microscopically thin chrysalis parted transparently off of his face. He shucked it off, trailing air-tendrils that had been inserted, hidden in the uniform, ending in thin globules of oxygen.

He spoke. Triumph warmed his crystal-thin voice. "That's how I did it, Earthman."

"Glassite!" said Rice. "A face-moulded mask of glassite!"

Lethla nodded. His milk-blue eyes dilated. "Very marvelously pared to an unbreakable thickness of one-thirtieth of an inch; worn only on the head. You have to look quickly to notice it, and, unfortunately, viewed as you saw it, outside the ship, floating in the void, not discernible at all."

Prickles of sweat appeared on Rice's face. He swore at the Venusian and the Venusian laughed like some sort of stringed instrument, high and quick.

Burnett laughed, too. Ironically. "First time in years a man ever came aboard the Constellation alive. It's a welcome change."

Lethla showed his needle-like teeth. "I thought it might be. Where's your radio?"

"Go find it!" snapped Rice, hotly.

"I will." One hand, blue-veined, on the ladder-rungs, Lethla paused. "I know you're weaponless; Purple Cross regulations. And this air-lock is safe. Don't move." Whispering, his naked feet padded white up the ladder. Two long breaths later something crashed; metal and glass and coils. The radio.

Burnett put his shoulder blades against the wall-metal, looking at his feet. When he glanced up, Rice's fresh, animated face was spoiled by the new bitterness in it.

Lethla came down. Like a breath of air on the rungs.

He smiled. "That's better. Now. We can talk—"

Rice said it, slow:

"Interplanetary law declares it straight, Lethla! Get out! Only dead men belong here."

Lethla's gun grip tightened. "More talk of that nature, and only dead men there will be." He blinked. "But first—we must rescue Kriere...."

"Kriere!" Rice acted as if he had been hit in the jaw.

Burnett moved his tongue back and forth on his lips silently, his eyes lidded, listening to the two of them as if they were a radio drama. Lethla's voice came next:

"Rather unfortunately, yes. He's still alive, heading toward Venus at an orbital velocity of two thousand m.p.h., wearing one of these air-chrysali. Enough air for two more hours. Our flag ship was attacked unexpectedly yesterday near Mars. We were forced to take to the life-boats, scattering, Kriere and I in one, the others sacrificing their lives to cover our escape. We were lucky. We got through the Earth cordon unseen. But luck can't last forever.

"We saw your morgue ship an hour ago. It's a long, long way to Venus. We were running out of fuel, food, water. Radio was broken. Capture was certain. You were coming our way; we took the chance. We set a small time-bomb to destroy the life-rocket, and cast off, wearing our chrysali-helmets. It was the first time we had ever tried using them to trick anyone. We knew you wouldn't know we were alive until it was too late and we controlled your ship. We knew you picked up all bodies for brief exams, returning alien corpses to space later."

Rice's voice was sullen. "A set-up for you, huh? Traveling under the protection of the Purple Cross you can get your damned All-Mighty safe to Venus."

Lethla bowed slightly. "Who would suspect a Morgue Rocket of providing safe hiding for precious Venusian cargo?"

"Precious is the word for you, brother!" said Rice.

"Enough!" Lethla moved his gun several inches.

"Accelerate toward Venus, mote-detectors wide open. Kriere must be picked up—*now!*"

*****

Rice didn't move. Burnett moved first, feeling alive for the first time in years. "Sure," said Sam, smiling. "We'll pick him up."

"No tricks," said Lethla.

Burnett scowled and smiled together. "No tricks. You'll have Kriere on board the *Constellation* in half an hour or I'm no coroner."

"Follow me up the ladder."

Lethla danced up, turned, waved his gun. "Come on."

Burnett went up, quick. Almost as if he enjoyed doing Lethla a favor. Rice grumbled and cursed after him.

On the way up, Burnett thought about it. About Lethla poised like a white feather at the top, holding death in his hand. You never knew whose body would come in through the star-port next. Number ninety-eight was Lethla. Number ninety-nine would be Kriere.

There were two shelves numbered and empty. They should be filled. And what more proper than that Kriere and Lethla should fill them? But, he chewed his lip, that would need a bit of doing. And even then the cargo wouldn't be full. Still one more body to get; one hundred. And you never knew who it would be.

He came out of the quick thoughts when he looped his long leg over the hole-rim, stepped up, faced Lethla in a cramped control room that was one glittering swirl of silver levers, audio-plates and visuals. Chronometers, clicking, told of the steady dropping toward the sun at a slow pace.

Burnett set his teeth together, bone against bone. Help Kriere escape? See him safely to Venus, and then be freed? Sounded easy, wouldn't be hard. Venusians weren't blind with malice. Rice and he could come out alive; if they cooperated.

But there were a lot of warriors sleeping on a lot of numbered shelves in the dim corridors of the long years. And their dead lips were stirring to life in Burnett's ears. Not so easily could they be ignored.

You may never catch up with the war again.

The last trip!

Yes, this could be it. Capture Kriere and end the war. But what ridiculous fantasy was it made him believe he could actually do it?

Two muscles moved on Burnett, one in each long cheek. The sag in his body vanished as he tautened his spine, flexed his lean-sinewed arms, wet thin lips.

"Now, where do you want this crate?" he asked Lethla easily.

Lethla exhaled softly. "Cooperation. I like it. You're wise, Earthman."

"Very," said Burnett.

He was thinking about three thousand eternal nights of young bodies being ripped, slaughtered, flung to the vacuum tides. Ten years of hating a job and hoping that some day there would be a last trip and it would all be over.

Burnett laughed through his nose. Controls moved under his fingers like fluid; loved, caressed, tended by his familiar touching. Looking ahead, he squinted.

"There's your Ruler now, Lethla. Doing somersaults. Looks dead. A good trick."

"Cut power! We don't want to burn him!"

*****

Burnett cut. Kriere's milky face floated dreamily into a visual-screen, eyes sealed, lips gaping, hands sagging, clutching emptily at the stars.

"We're about fifty miles from him, catching up." Burnett turned to Lethla with an intent scowl. Funny. This was the first and the last time anybody would ever board the *Constellation* alive. His stomach went flat, tautened with sudden weakening fear.

If Kriere could be captured, that meant the end of the war, the end of shelves stacked with sleeping warriors, the end of this blind searching. Kriere, then, had to be taken aboard. After that—

Kriere, the All-Mighty. At whose behest all space had quivered like a smitten gong for part of a century. Kriere, revolving in his neat, water-blue uniform, emblems shining gold, heat-gun tucked in glossy jet holster. With Kriere aboard, chances of overcoming him would be eliminated. Now: Rice and Burnett against Lethla. Lethla favored because of his gun.

Kriere would make odds impossible.

Something had to be done before Kriere came in.

Lethla had to be yanked off guard. Shocked, bewildered, fooled—somehow. But—how?

Burnett's jaw froze tight. He could feel a spot on his shoulder-blade where Lethla would send a bullet crashing into rib, sinew, artery—heart.

There was a way. And there was a weapon. And the war would be over and this would be the last trip.

Sweat covered his palms in a nervous smear.

"Steady, Rice," he said, matter of factly. With the rockets cut, there was too much silence, and his voice sounded guilty standing up alone in the center of that silence. "Take controls, Rice. I'll manipulate the star-port."

Burnett slipped from the control console. Rice replaced him grimly. Burnett strode to the next console of levers. That spot on his back kept aching like it was sear-branded X. For the place where the bullet sings and rips. And if you turn quick, catching it in the arm first, why—

Kriere loomed bigger, a white spider delicately dancing on a web of stars. His eyes flicked open behind the glassite sheath, and saw the *Constellation*. Kriere smiled. His hands came up. He knew he was about to be rescued.

Burnett smiled right back at him. What Kriere didn't know was that he was about to end a ten-years' war.

There was only *one* way of drawing Lethla off guard, and it had to be fast.

Burnett jabbed a purple-topped stud. The star-port clashed open as it had done a thousand times before; but for the first time it was a good sound. And out of the star-port, at Sam Burnett's easily fingered directions, slid the long claw-like mechanism that picked up bodies from space.

Lethla watched, intent and cold and quiet. The gun was cold and quiet, too.

The claw glided toward Kriere without a sound, now, dream-like in its slowness.

It reached Kriere.

Burnett inhaled a deep breath.

The metal claw cuddled Kriere in its shiny palm.

Lethla watched.

He watched while Burnett exhaled, touched another lever and said: "You know, Lethla, there's an old saying that only dead men come aboard the *Constellation*. I believe it."

*****

And the claw closed as Burnett spoke, closed slowly and certainly, all around Kriere, crushing him into a ridiculous posture of silence. There was blood running on the claw, and the only recognizable part was the head, which was carefully preserved for identification.

That was the only way to draw Lethla off guard.

Burnett spun about and leaped.

The horror on Lethla's face didn't go away as he fired his gun.

Rice came in fighting, too, but not before something like a red-hot ramrod stabbed Sam Burnett, catching him in the ribs, spinning him back like a drunken idiot to fall in a corner.

Fists made blunt flesh noises. Lethla went down, weaponless and screaming. Rice kicked. After awhile Lethla quit screaming, and the room swam around in Burnett's eyes, and he closed them tight and started laughing.

He didn't finish laughing for maybe ten minutes. He heard the retriever claws come inside, and the star-port grind shut.

Out of the red darkness, Rice's voice came and then he could see Rice's young face over him. Burnett groaned.

Rice said, "Sam, you shouldn't have done it. You shouldn't have, Sam."

"To hell with it." Burnett winced, and fought to keep his eyes open. Something wet and sticky covered his chest. "I said this was my last trip and I meant it. One way or the other, I'd have quit!"

"This is the hard way—"

"Maybe. I dunno. Kind of nice to think of all those kids who'll never have to come aboard the *Constellation*, though, Rice." His voice trailed off. "You watch the shelves fill up and you never know who'll be next. Who'd have thought, four days ago—"

Something happened to his tongue so it felt like hard ice blocking his mouth. He had a lot more words to say, but only time to get a few of them out:

"Rice?"

"Yeah, Sam?"

"We haven't got a full cargo, boy."

"Full enough for me, sir."

"But still not full. If we went back to Center Base without filling the shelves, it wouldn't be right. Look there—number ninety-eight is Lethla—number ninety-nine is Kriere. Three thousand days of rolling this rocket, and not once come back without a bunch of the kids who want to sleep easy on the good green earth. Not right to be going back any way—but—the way—we used to—"

His voice got all full of fog. As thick as the fists of a dozen warriors. Rice was going away from him. Rice was standing still, and Burnett was lying down, not moving, but somehow Rice was going away a million miles.

"Ain't I one hell of a patriot, Rice?"

Then everything got dark except Rice's face. And that was starting to dissolve.

Ninety-eight: Lethla. Ninety-nine: Kriere.

He could still see Rice standing over him for a long time, breathing out and in. Down under the tables the blood-pumps pulsed and pulsed, thick and slow. Rice looked down at Burnett and then at the empty shelf at the far end of the room, and then back at Burnett again.

And then he said softly:

"*One hundred.*"

The Monster Maker

"Get Gunther," the official orders read. It was to laugh! For Click and Irish were marooned on the pirate's asteroid—their only weapons a single gun and a news-reel camera.

*****

Suddenly, it was there. There wasn't time to blink or speak or get scared. Click Hathaway's camera was loaded and he stood there listening to it rack-spin film between his fingers, and he knew he was getting a damned sweet picture of everything that was happening.

The picture of Marnagan hunched huge over the control-console, wrenching levers, jamming studs with freckled fists. And out in the dark of the fore-part there was space and a star-sprinkling and this meteor coming like blazing fury.

Click Hathaway felt the ship move under him like a sensitive animal's skin. And then the meteor hit. It made a spiked fist and knocked the rear-jets flat, and the ship spun like a cosmic merry-go-round.

There was plenty of noise. Too damned much. Hathaway only knew he was picked up and hurled against a lever-bank, and that Marnagan wasn't long in following, swearing loud words. Click remembered hanging on to his camera and gritting to keep holding it. What a sweet shot that had been of the meteor! A sweeter one still of Marnagan beating hell out of the controls and keeping his words to himself until just now.

It got quiet. It got so quiet you could almost hear the asteroids rushing up, cold, blue and hard. You could hear your heart kicking a tom-tom between your sick stomach and your empty lungs.

Stars, asteroids revolved. Click grabbed Marnagan because he was the nearest thing, and held on. You came hunting for a space-raider and you ended up cradled in a slab-sized Irishman's arms, diving at a hunk of metal death. What a fade-out!

"Irish!" he heard himself say. "Is this IT?"

"Is this *what*?" yelled Marnagan inside his helmet.

"Is this where the Big Producer yells CUT!?"

Marnagan fumed. "I'll die when I'm damned good and ready. And when I'm ready I'll inform you and you can picture me profile for Cosmic Films!"

They both waited, thrust against the shipside and held by a hand of gravity; listening to each other's breathing hard in the earphones.

The ship struck, once. Bouncing, it struck again. It turned end over and stopped. Hathaway felt himself grabbed; he and Marnagan rattled around—human dice in a croupier's cup. The shell of the ship burst, air and energy flung out.

Hathaway screamed the air out of his lungs, but his brain was thinking quick crazy, unimportant things. The best scenes in life never reach film, or an audience. Like this one, dammit! Like *this* one! His brain spun, racketing like the instantaneous, flicking motions of his camera.

*****

Silence came and engulfed all the noise, ate it up and swallowed it. Hathaway shook his head, instinctively grabbed at the camera locked to his mid-belt. There was nothing but stars, twisted wreckage, cold that pierced through his vac-suit, and silence. He wriggled out of the wreckage into that silence.

He didn't know what he was doing until he found the camera in his fingers as if it had grown there when he was born. He stood there, thinking "Well, I'll at least have a few good scenes on film. I'll—"

A hunk of metal teetered, fell with a crash. Marnagan elevated seven feet of bellowing manhood from the wreck.

"Hold it!" cracked Hathaway's high voice. Marnagan froze. The camera whirred. "Low angle shot; Interplanetary Patrolman emerges unscathed from asteroid crackup. Swell stuff. I'll get a raise for this!"

"From the toe of me boot!" snarled Marnagan brusquely. Oxen shoulders flexed inside his vac-suit. "I might've died in there, and you nursin' that film-contraption!"

Hathaway felt funny inside, suddenly. "I never thought of that. Marnagan die? I just took it for granted you'd come through. You always have. Funny, but you don't think about dying. You try not to." Hathaway stared at his gloved hand, but the gloving was so thick and heavy he couldn't tell if it was shaking. Muscles in his bony face went down, pale. "Where are we?"

"A million miles from nobody."

They stood in the middle of a pocked, time-eroded meteor plain that stretched off, dipping down into silent indigo and a rash of stars. Overhead, the sun poised; black and stars all around it, making it look sick.

"If we walk in opposite directions, Click Hathaway, we'd be shaking hands the other side of this rock in two hours." Marnagan shook his mop of dusty red hair. "And I promised the boys at Luna Base this time I'd capture that Gunther lad!"

His voice stopped and the silence spoke.

Hathaway felt his heart pumping slow, hot pumps of blood. "I checked my oxygen, Irish. Sixty minutes of breathing left."

The silence punctuated that sentence, too. Upon the sharp meteoric rocks Hathaway saw the tangled insides of the radio, the food supply mashed and scattered. They were lucky to have escaped. Or *was* suffocation a better death...? *Sixty minutes.*

They stood and looked at one another.

"Damn that meteor!" said Marnagan, hotly.

Hathaway got hold of an idea; remembering something. He said it out: "Somebody tossed that meteor, Irish. I took a picture of it, looked it right in the eye when it rolled at us, and it was poker-hot. Space-meteors are never hot and glowing. If it's proof you want, I've got it here, on film."

Marnagan winced his freckled square of face. "It's not proof we need now, Click. Oxygen. And then *food*. And then some way back to Earth."

Hathaway went on saying his thoughts: "This is Gunther's work. He's here somewhere, probably laughing his guts out at the job he did us. Oh, God, this would make great news-release stuff if we ever get back to Earth. I.P.'s Irish Marnagan, temporarily indisposed by a pirate whose dirty face has never been seen, Gunther by name, finally wins through to a triumphant finish. Photographed on the spot, in color, by yours truly, Click Hathaway. Cosmic Films, please notice."

*****

They started walking, fast, over the pocked, rubbled plain toward a bony ridge of metal. They kept their eyes wide and awake. There wasn't much to see, but it was better than standing still, waiting.

Marnagan said, "We're working on margin, and we got nothin' to sweat with except your suspicions about this not being an accident. We got fifty minutes to prove you're right. After that—right or wrong—you'll be Cosmic Films prettiest unmoving, unbreathin' genius. But talk all you like, Click. It's times like this when we all need words, any words, on our tongues. You got your camera and your scoop. Talk about it. As for me—" he twisted his glossy red face. "Keeping alive is me hobby. And this sort of two-bit death I did not order."

Click nodded. "Gunther knows how you'd hate dying this way, Irish. It's irony clean through. That's probably why he planned the meteor and the crash this way."

Marnagan said nothing, but his thick lips went down at the corners, far down, and the green eyes blazed.

They stopped, together.

"Oops!" Click said.

"Hey!" Marnagan blinked. "Did you feel *that*?"

Hathaway's body felt feathery, light as a whisper, boneless and limbless, suddenly. "Irish! We lost weight, coming over that ridge!"

They ran back. "Let's try it again."

They tried it. They scowled at each other. The same thing happened. "Gravity should not act this way, Click."

"Are you telling me? It's man-made. Better than that—it's Gunther! No wonder we fell so fast—we were dragged down by a super-gravity set-up! Gunther'd do anything to—did I say *anything*?"

Hathaway leaped backward in reaction. His eyes widened and his hand came up, jabbing. Over a hill-ridge swarmed a brew of unbelievable horrors. Progeny from Frankenstein's ARK. Immense crimson beasts with numerous legs and gnashing mandibles, brown-black creatures, some tubular and fat, others like thin white poisonous whips slashing along in the air. Fangs caught starlight white on them.

Hathaway yelled and ran, Marnagan at his heels, lumbering. Sweat broke cold on his body. The immense things rolled, slithered and squirmed after him. A blast of light. Marnagan, firing his proton-gun. Then, in Click's ears, the Irishman's incredulous bellow. The gun didn't hurt the creatures at all.

"Irish!" Hathaway flung himself over the ridge, slid down an incline toward the mouth a small cave. "This way, fella!"

Hathaway made it first, Marnagan bellowing just behind him. "They're too big; they can't get us in here!" Click's voice gasped it out, as Marnagan squeezed his two-hundred-fifty pounds beside him. Instinctively, Hathaway added, "Asteroid monsters! My camera! What a scene!"

"Damn your damn camera!" yelled Marnagan. "They might come in!"

"Use your gun."

"They got impervious hides. No use. Gahh! And that was a pretty chase, eh, Click?"

"Yeah. Sure. *You* enjoyed it, every moment of it."

"I did that." Irish grinned, showing white uneven teeth. "Now, what will we be doing with these uninvited guests at our door?"

"Let me think—"

"Lots of time, little man. Forty more minutes of air, to be exact."

*****

They sat, staring at the monsters for about a minute. Hathaway felt funny about something; didn't know what. Something about these monsters and Gunther and—

"Which one will you be having?" asked Irish, casually. "A red one or a blue one?"

Hathaway laughed nervously. "A pink one with yellow ruffles—Good God, now you've got *me* doing it. Joking in the face of death."

"Me father taught me; keep laughing and you'll have Irish luck."

That didn't please the photographer. "I'm an Anglo-Swede," he pointed out.

Marnagan shifted uneasily. "Here, now. You're doing nothing but sitting, looking like a little boy locked in a bedroom closet, so take me a profile shot of the beasties and myself."

Hathaway petted his camera reluctantly. "What in hell's the use? All this swell film shot. Nobody'll ever see it."

"Then," retorted Marnagan, "we'll develop it for our own benefit; while waitin' for the U.S. Cavalry to come riding over the hill to our rescue!"

Hathaway snorted. "U.S. Cavalry."

Marnagan raised his proton-gun dramatically. "Snap me this pose," he said. "I paid your salary to trot along, photographing, we hoped, my capture of Gunther, now the least you can do is record peace negotiations betwixt me and these pixies."

Marnagan wasn't fooling anybody. Hathaway knew the superficial palaver for nothing but a covering over the fast, furious thinking running around in that red-cropped skull. Hathaway played the palaver, too, but his mind was whirring faster than his camera as he spun a picture of Marnagan standing there with a useless gun pointed at the animals.

Montage. Marnagan sitting, chatting at the monsters. Marnagan smiling for the camera. Marnagan in profile. Marnagan looking grim, without much effort, for the camera. And then, a closeup of the thrashing death wall that holed them in. Click took them all, those shots, not saying anything. Nobody fooled nobody with this act. Death was near and they had sweaty faces, dry mouths and frozen guts.

When Click finished filming, Irish sat down to save oxygen, and used it up arguing about Gunther. Click came back at him:

"Gunther drew us down here, sure as Ceres! That gravity change we felt back on that ridge, Irish; that proves it. Gunther's short on men. So, what's he do; he builds an asteroid-base, and drags ships down. Space war isn't perfect yet, guns don't prime true in space, trajectory is lousy over long distances. So what's the best weapon, which dispenses with losing valuable, rare ships and a small bunch of men? Super-gravity and a couple of well-tossed meteors. Saves all around. It's a good front, this damned iron pebble. From it, Gunther strikes unseen; ships simply crash, that's all. A subtle hand, with all aces."

Marnagan rumbled. "Where is the dirty son, then!"

"He didn't have to appear, Irish. He sent—them." Hathaway nodded at the beasts. "People crashing here die from air-lack, no food, or from wounds caused at the crackup. If they survive all that—the animals tend to them. It all looks like Nature was responsible. See how subtle his attack is? Looks like accidental death instead of murder, if the Patrol happens to land and finds us. No reason for undue investigation, then."

"I don't see no Base around."

*****

Click shrugged. "Still doubt it? Okay. Look." He tapped his camera and a spool popped out onto his gloved palm. Holding it up, he stripped it out to its full twenty inch length, held it to the light while it developed, smiling. It was one of his best inventions. Self-developing film. The first light struck film-surface, destroyed one chemical, leaving imprints; the second exposure simply hardened, secured the impressions. Quick stuff.

Inserting the film-tongue into a micro-viewer in the camera's base, Click handed the whole thing over. "Look."

Marnagan put the viewer up against the helmet glass, squinted. "Ah, Click. Now, now. This is one lousy film you invented."

"Huh?"

"It's a strange process'll develop my picture and ignore the asteroid monsters complete."

"What!"

Hathaway grabbed the camera, gasped, squinted, and gasped again: Pictures in montage; Marnagan sitting down, chatting conversationally with *nothing*; Marnagan shooting his gun at *nothing*; Marnagan pretending to be happy in front of *nothing*.

Then, closeup—of—NOTHING!

The monsters had failed to image the film. Marnagan was there, his hair like a red banner, his freckled face with the blue eyes bright in it. Maybe—

Hathaway said it, loud: "Irish! Irish! I think I see a way out of this mess! Here—"

He elucidated it over and over again to the Patrolman. About the film, the beasts, and how the film couldn't be wrong. If the film said the monsters weren't there, they weren't there.

"Yeah," said Marnagan. "But step outside this cave—"

"If my theory is correct I'll do it, unafraid," said Click.

Marnagan scowled. "You sure them beasts don't radiate ultra-violet or infra-red or something that won't come out on film?"

"Nuts! Any color *we* see, the camera sees. We've been fooled."

"Hey, where *you* going?" Marnagan blocked Hathaway as the smaller man tried pushing past him.

"Get out of the way," said Hathaway.

Marnagan put his big fists on his hips. "If anyone is going anywhere, it'll be me does the going."

"I can't let you do that, Irish."

"Why not?"

"You'd be going on my say-so."

"Ain't your say-so good enough for me?"

"Yes. Sure. Of course. I guess—"

"If you say them animals ain't there, that's all I need. Now, stand aside, you film-developing flea, and let an Irishman settle their bones." He took an unnecessary hitch in trousers that didn't exist except under an inch of porous metal plate. "Your express purpose on this voyage, Hathaway, is taking films to be used by the Patrol later for teaching Junior Patrolmen how to act in tough spots. First-hand education. Poke another spool of film in that contraption and give me profile a scan. This is lesson number seven: Daniel Walks Into The Lion's Den."

"Irish, I—"

"Shut up and load up."

Hathaway nervously loaded the film-slot, raised it.

"Ready, Click?"

"I—I guess so," said Hathaway. "And remember, think it hard, Irish. Think it hard. There aren't any animals—"

"Keep me in focus, lad."

"All the way, Irish."

"What do they say...? Oh, yeah. Action. Lights. Camera!"

Marnagan held his gun out in front of him and still smiling took one, two, three, four steps out into the outside world. The monsters were waiting for him at the fifth step. Marnagan kept walking.

Right out into the middle of them....

*****

That was the sweetest shot Hathaway ever took. Marnagan and the monsters!

Only now it was only Marnagan.

No more monsters.

Marnagan smiled a smile broader than his shoulders. "Hey, Click, look at me! I'm in one piece. Why, hell, the damned things turned tail and ran away!"

"Ran, hell!" cried Hathaway, rushing out, his face flushed and animated. "They just plain vanished. They were only imaginative figments!"

"And to think we let them hole us in that way, Click Hathaway, you coward!"

"Smile when you say that, Irish."

"Sure, and ain't I always smilin'? Ah, Click boy, are them tears in your sweet grey eyes?"

"Damn," swore the photographer, embarrassedly. "Why don't they put window-wipers in these helmets?"

"I'll take it up with the Board, lad."

"Forget it. I was so blamed glad to see your homely carcass in one hunk, I couldn't help—Look, now, about Gunther. Those animals are part of his set-up. Explorers who land here inadvertently, are chased back into their ships, forced to take off. Tourists and the like. Nothing suspicious about animals. And if the tourists don't leave, the animals kill them."

"Shaw, now. Those animals can't kill."

"Think not, Mr. Marnagan? As long as we believed in them they could have frightened us to death, forced us, maybe, to commit suicide. If that isn't being dangerous—"

The Irishman whistled.

"But, we've got to *move*, Irish. We've got twenty minutes of oxygen. In that time we've got to trace those monsters to their source, Gunther's Base, fight our way in, and get fresh oxy-cannisters." Click attached his camera to his mid-belt. "Gunther probably thinks we're dead by now. Everyone else's been fooled by his playmates; they never had a chance to disbelieve them."

"If it hadn't been for you taking them pictures, Click—"

"Coupled with your damned stubborn attitude about the accident—" Click stopped and felt his insides turning to water. He shook his head and felt a film slip down over his eyes. He spread his legs out to steady himself, and swayed. "I—I don't think my oxygen is as full as yours. This excitement had me double-breathing and I feel sick."

Marnagan's homely face grimaced in sympathy. "Hold tight, Click. The guy that invented these fish-bowls didn't provide for a sick stomach."

"Hold tight, hell, let's move. We've got to find where those animals came from! And the only way to do that is to get the animals to come back!"

"Come back? How?"

"They're waiting, just outside the aura of our thoughts, and if we believe in them again, they'll return."

Marnagan didn't like it. "Won't—won't they kill us—if they come—if we believe in 'em?"

Hathaway shook a head that was tons heavy and weary. "Not if we believe in them to a *certain point*.

Psychologically they can both be seen and felt. We only want to *see* them coming at us again."

"*Do* we, now?"

"With twenty minutes left, maybe less—"

"All right, Click, let's bring 'em back. How do we do it?"

Hathaway fought against the mist in his eyes. "Just think—I will see the monsters again. I will see them again and I will not feel them. Think it over and over."

Marnagan's hulk stirred uneasily. "And—what if I forget to remember all that? What if I get excited...?"

Hathaway didn't answer. But his eyes told the story by just looking at Irish.

Marnagan cursed. "All right, lad. Let's have at it!"

The monsters returned.

*****

A soundless deluge of them, pouring over the rubbled horizon, swarming in malevolent anticipation about the two men.

"This way, Irish. They come from this way! There's a focal point, a sending station for these telepathic brutes. Come on!"

Hathaway sludged into the pressing tide of color, mouths, contorted faces, silvery fat bodies misting as he plowed through them.

Marnagan was making good progress ahead of Hathaway. But he stopped and raised his gun and made quick moves with it. "Click! This one here! It's real!" He fell back and something struck him down. His immense frame slammed against rock, noiselessly.

Hathaway darted forward, flung his body over Marnagan's, covered the helmet glass with his hands, shouting:

"Marnagan! Get a grip, dammit! It's not real—don't let it force into your mind! It's not real, I tell you!"

"Click—" Marnagan's face was a bitter, tortured movement behind glass. "Click—" He was fighting hard. "I—I—sure now. Sure—" He smiled. "It—it's only a shanty fake!"

"Keep saying it, Irish. Keep it up."

Marnagan's thick lips opened. "It's only a fake," he said. And then, irritated, "Get the hell off me, Hathaway. Let me up to my feet!"

Hathaway got up, shakily. The air in his helmet smelled stale, and little bubbles danced in his eyes. "Irish, *you* forget the monsters. Let me handle them, I know how. They might fool you again, you might forget."

Marnagan showed his teeth. "Gah! Let a flea have all the fun? And besides, Click, I like to look at them. They're pretty."

The outpour of animals came from a low lying mound a mile farther on. Evidently the telepathic source lay there. They approached it warily.

"We'll be taking our chances on guard," hissed Irish. "I'll go ahead, draw their attention, maybe get captured. Then, *you* show up with *your* gun...."

"I haven't got one."

"We'll chance it, then. You stick here until I see what's ahead. They probably got scanners out. Let them see me—"

And before Hathaway could object, Marnagan walked off. He walked about five hundred yards, bent down, applied his fingers to something, heaved up, and there was a door opening in the rock.

His voice came back across the distance, into Click's earphones. "A door, an air-lock, Click. A tunnel leading down inside!"

Then, Marnagan dropped into the tunnel, disappearing. Click heard the thud of his feet hitting the metal flooring.

Click sucked in his breath, hard and fast.

"All right, put 'em up!" a new harsh voice cried over a different radio. One of Gunther's guards.

Three shots sizzled out, and Marnagan bellowed.

The strange harsh voice said, "That's better. Don't try and pick that gun up now. Oh, so it's you. I thought Gunther had finished you off. How'd you get past the animals?"

Click started running. He switched off his *sending* audio, kept his *receiving* on. Marnagan, weaponless. *One* guard. Click gasped. Things were getting dark. Had to have air. Air. Air. He ran and kept running and listening to Marnagan's lying voice:

"I tied them pink elephants of Gunther's in neat alphabetical bundles and stacked them up to dry, ya louse!" Marnagan said. "But, damn you, they killed my partner before he had a chance!"

The guard laughed.

*****

The air-lock door was still wide open when Click reached it, his head swimming darkly, his lungs crammed with pain-fire and hell-rockets. He let himself down in, quiet and soft. He didn't have a weapon. He didn't have a weapon. Oh, damn, damn!

A tunnel curved, ending in light, and two men silhouetted in that yellow glare. Marnagan, backed against a wall, his helmet cracked, air hissing slowly out of it, his face turning blue. And the guard, a proton gun extended stiffly before him, also in a vac-suit. The guard had his profile toward Hathaway, his lips twisting: "I think I'll let you stand right there and die," he said quietly. "That what Gunther wanted, anway. A nice sordid death."

Hathaway took three strides, his hands out in front of him.

"Don't move!" he snapped. "I've got a weapon stronger than yours. One twitch and I'll blast you and the whole damned wall out from behind you! Freeze!"

The guard whirled. He widened his sharp eyes, and reluctantly, dropped his gun to the floor.

"Get his gun, Irish."

Marnagan made as if to move, crumpled clumsily forward.

Hathaway ran in, snatched up the gun, smirked at the guard. "Thanks for posing," he said. "That shot will go down in film history for candid acting."

"What!"

"Ah: ah! Keep your place. I've got a real gun now. Where's the door leading into the Base?"

The guard moved his head sullenly over his left shoulder.

Click was afraid he would show his weak dizziness. He needed air. "Okay. Drag Marnagan with you, open the door and we'll have air. Double time! Double!"

Ten minutes later, Marnagan and Hathaway, fresh tanks of oxygen on their backs, Marnagan in a fresh bulger and helmet, trussed the guard, hid him in a huge trash receptacle. "Where he belongs," observed Irish tersely.

They found themselves in a complete inner world; an asteroid nothing more than a honey-comb fortress sliding through the void unchallenged. Perfect front for a raider who had little equipment and was short-handed of men. Gunther simply waited for specific cargo ships to rocket by, pulled them or knocked them down and swarmed over them for cargo. The animals served simply to insure against suspicion and the swarms of tourists that filled the void these days. Small fry weren't wanted. They were scared off.

The telepathic sending station for the animals was a great bank of intricate, glittering machine, through which strips of colored film with images slid into slots and machine mouths that translated them into thought-emanations. A damned neat piece of genius.

"So here we are, still not much better off than we were," growled Irish. "We haven't a ship or a space-radio, and more guards'll turn up any moment. You think we could refocus this doohingey, project the monsters inside the asteroid to fool the pirates themselves?"

"What good would that do?" Hathaway gnawed his lip. "They wouldn't fool the engineers who created them, you nut."

Marnagan exhaled disgustedly. "Ah, if only the U.S. Cavalry would come riding over the hill—"

*****

"Irish!" Hathaway snapped that, his face lighting up. "Irish. The U.S. Cavalry it is!" His eyes darted over the machines. "Here. Help me. We'll stage everything on the most colossal raid of the century."

Marnagan winced. "You breathing oxygen or whiskey?"

"There's only one stipulation I make, Irish. I want a complete picture of Marnagan capturing Raider's Base. I want a picture of Gunther's face when you do it. Snap it, now, we've got rush work to do. How good an actor are you?"

"That's a silly question."

"You only have to do three things. Walk with your gun out in front of you, firing. That's number one. Number two is to clutch at your heart and fall down dead. Number three is to clutch at your side, fall down and twitch on the ground. Is that clear?"

"Clear as the Coal Sack Nebula...."

An hour later Hathaway trudged down a passageway that led out into a sort of city street inside the asteroid. There were about six streets, lined with cube houses in yellow metal, ending near Hathaway in a wide, green-lawned Plaza.

Hathaway, weaponless, idly carrying his camera in one hand, walked across the Plaza as if he owned it. He was heading for a building that was pretentious enough to be Gunther's quarters.

He got halfway there when he felt a gun in his back.

He didn't resist. They took him straight ahead to his destination and pushed him into a room where Gunther sat.

Hathaway looked at him. "So you're Gunther?" he said, calmly. The pirate was incredibly old, his bulging forehead stood out over sunken, questioningly dark eyes, and his scrawny body was lost in folds of metal-link cloth. He glanced up from a paper-file, surprised. Before he could speak, Hathaway said:

"Everything's over with, Mr. Gunther. The Patrol is in the city now and we're capturing your Base. Don't try to fight. We've a thousand men against your eighty-five."

Gunther sat there, blinking at Hathaway, not moving. His thin hands twitched in his lap. "You are bluffing," he said, finally, with a firm directness. "A ship hasn't landed here for an hour. Your ship was the last. Two people were on it. The last I saw of them they were being pursued to the death by the Beasts. One of you escaped, it seemed."

"Both. The other guy went after the Patrol."

"Impossible!"

"I can't respect your opinion, Mr. Gunther."

A shouting rose from the Plaza. About fifty of Gunther's men, lounging on carved benches during their time-off, stirred to their feet and started yelling. Gunther turned slowly to the huge window in one side of his office. He stared, hard.

The Patrol was coming!

Across the Plaza, marching quietly and decisively, came the Patrol. Five hundred Patrolmen in one long, incredible line, carrying paralysis guns with them in their tight hands.

Gunther babbled like a child, his voice a shrill dagger in the air. "Get out there, you men! Throw them back! We're outnumbered!"

Guns flared. But the Patrol came on. Gunther's men didn't run, Hathaway had to credit them on that. They took it, standing.

Hathaway chuckled inside, deep. What a sweet, sweet shot this was. His camera whirred, clicked and whirred again. Nobody stopped him from filming it. Everything was too wild, hot and angry. Gunther was throwing a fit, still seated at his desk, unable to move because of his fragile, bony legs and their atrophied state.

Some of the Patrol were killed. Hathaway chuckled again as he saw three of the Patrolmen clutch at their hearts, crumple, lie on the ground and twitch. God, what photography!

Gunther raged, and swept a small pistol from his linked corselet. He fired wildly until Hathaway hit him over the head with a paper-weight. Then Hathaway took a picture of Gunther slumped at his desk, the chaos taking place immediately outside his window.

The pirates broke and fled, those that were left. A mere handful. And out of the chaos came Marnagan's voice, "Here!"

*****

One of the Patrolmen stopped firing, and ran toward Click and the Building. He got inside. "Did you see them run, Click boy? What an idea. How did we do?"

"Fine, Irish. Fine!"

"So here's Gunther, the spalpeen! Gunther, the little dried up pirate, eh?" Marnagan whacked Hathaway on the back. "I'll have to hand it to you, this is the best plan o' battle ever laid out. And proud I was to fight with such splendid men as these—" He gestured toward the Plaza.

Click laughed with him. "You should be proud. Five hundred Patrolmen with hair like red banners flying, with thick Irish brogues and broad shoulders and freckles and blue eyes and a body as tall as your stories!"

Marnagan roared. "I always said, I said—if ever there could be an army of Marnagans, we could lick the whole damn uneeverse! Did you photograph it, Click?"

"I did." Hathaway tapped his camera happily.

"Ah, then, won't that be a scoop for you, boy? Money from the Patrol so they can use the film as instruction in Classes and money from Cosmic Films for the news-reel headlines! And what a scene, and what acting! Five hundred duplicates of Steve Marnagan, broadcast telepathically into the minds of the pirates, walking across a Plaza, capturing the whole she-bang! How did you like my death-scenes?"

"You're a ham. And anyway—five hundred duplicates, nothing!" said Click. He ripped the film-spool from the camera, spread it in the air to develop, inserted it in the micro-viewer. "Have a look—"

Marnagan looked. "Ah, now. Ah, now," he said over and over. "There's the Plaza, and there's Gunther's men fighting and then they're turning and running. And what are they running from? One man! Me. Irish Marnagan! Walking all by myself across the lawn, paralyzing them. One against a hundred, and the cowards running from me!

"Sure, Click, this is better than I thought. I forgot that the film wouldn't register telepathic emanations, them other Marnagans. It makes it look like I'm a mighty brave man, does it not? It does. Ah, look—look at me, Hathaway, I'm enjoying every minute of it, I am."

*****

Hathaway swatted him on his back-side. "Look here, you egocentric son of Erin, there's more work to be done. More pirates to be captured. The Patrol is still marching around and someone might be suspicious if they looked too close and saw all that red hair."

"All right, Click, we'll clean up the rest of them now. We're a combination, we two, we are. I take it all back about your pictures, Click, if you hadn't thought of taking pictures of me and inserting it into those telepath machines we'd be dead ducks now. Well—here I go...."

Hathaway stopped him. "Hold it. Until I load my camera again."

Irish grinned. "Hurry it up. Here come three guards. They're unarmed. I think I'll handle them with me fists for a change. The gentle art of uppercuts. Are you ready, Hathaway?"

"Ready."

Marnagan lifted his big ham-fists.

The camera whirred. Hathaway chuckled, to himself.

What a sweet fade-out this was!

Ray Bradbury was an American fantasy and horror author who rejected being categorized as a science fiction author, claiming that his work was based on the fantastical and unreal. His best known novel is *Fahrenheit 451*, a dystopian study of future American society in which critical thought is outlawed. He is also remembered for several other popular works, including *The Martian Chronicles* and *Something Wicked This Way Comes*. Bradbury won the Pulitzer in 2007, and is one of the most celebrated authors of the 21st century.

The *Planet Stories* Collection is part of the:

More books in the series are

COMING SOON!

More books you can expect in the

Collection:

Books by authors such as

Leigh Brackett

Nelson S. Bond

Henry Hasse

Bryce Walton

Poul Anderson

Alfred Coppel

Basil Wells

Raymond Z. Gallun

Wilbur S. Peacock

Ray Cummings

Robert Emmett McDowell

Gardner F. Fox

and MANY MORE!

www.ingramcontent.com/pod-product-compliance
Lightning Source LLC
Chambersburg PA
CBHW030421310726
48979CB00009B/1552/J

* 9 7 8 1 9 5 4 9 2 9 0 0 5 *